Before You Judge: The Sean Carter Story

The Underworld Collection

Nako

To fully understand this story, it is advised that you first read *Please Catch My Soul, Pointe of No Return, From His Rib, The Christ Family, Stranger In My Eyes, The Arraignment, Resentment, The Arraignment II, Redemption and Orange Moon.*

The Underworld is an eleven-book street-crime collection.

This particular story features characters from *The Connect* series written by National Best Selling author, Nako.

It is suggested that you read *The Connect* before reading *Before You Judge: The Sean Carter Story.*

Nako

Underdog is defined as a competitor thought to have little chance of winning a fight or contest. **Underdog** is defined as one who is expected to lose a contest or struggle. **Underdog** is defined as a person who is expected to lose in a contest or conflict.

Sean Carter, **The Underdog** of **The Underworld**.

Enjoy.

Prologue

Before The Arraignment...

Jackie lay atop her husband with one thick thigh over his long hairy leg, and the other resting on the gold duvet that covered their California King bed. Her only prayer was that God kept her husband because this was her favorite part of the day. Those few hours before they dozed off into la-la land is where she believed they bonded. That part of the night was more important than sex. Sometimes, Jackie wouldn't have to share how her day was, it was as if he already knew. They vibed off each other's energy. They were more than husband and wife, they were friends.

The lights were dim, and a Mahogany Teakwood candle burned slowly on the nightstand. Sean was full, high and had a lot on his mind. He was expecting the worst, and that was unfortunate, but he never got his hopes up for anything to go his way. He didn't look forward to the best only because he didn't enjoy disappointing himself. Sean was prepared for whatever life threw at him because he had to reap what he had sown. And sadly, he had done more wrong than right in his years on earth.

"What would you be doing right now if we weren't going through this?" Jackie asked her husband. She desperately wanted to know what life would be like if there was no Underworld.

He chewed slightly on his bottom lip and pondered over her question. Once upon a time, a long very fucking time ago, Sean had dreams, goals and aspirations. He had a lot he wanted to do with his time, but of course, things never seemed to go as planned. He took a deep breath being that it had been so long since he went down memory lane.

"Baby, if I told you my childhood dreams, I swear you wouldn't even believe me." He was sure of that.

Because he was such a quiet man, he never corrected people when they assumed they knew him or predicted how he lived his life. But nine times out of ten, they were always wrong. Yeah, he was a product of his environment, born and raised in the hood and still fucked around in the hood, but he had real goals. Sean had a promising future. It wasn't his intentions to sling dope for a living, but shit happens.

Jackie nudged him, knowing how easily he could deflect.

"Yeah, baby?" he said.

She looked up at him, giving him a Cheshire smile. Her hair was wrapped tightly in a Versace scarf, and she had on the pajamas to match.

"Where are you tonight, baby? You been spaced out all week," she finally shared with him her concerns. "I know you're worried about the case..." her voice trailed.

One thing for sure was that his wife was solid. While he questioned the loyalty of the other wives, he knew without a doubt his wife wouldn't fold under pressure. Jackie knew the game and had played the game for many years before she even thought about being with Sean.They could call her to the stand, and she would know what and what not to say. She was a soldier, and that was one of the reasons he was so eager to marry her all those years ago._No one wanted to be with someone who couldn't hold them down if shit got rough. That was the question he wanted to pose for his fellow comrades; could they trust their spouses?

"Nah, I'm not worried, my lawyers know what they doing. Shit, I'm paying them enough," he mumbled under his breath. He needed to tell Jackie about the gun...and the murder, but he couldn't. Sean didn't want to risk losing his wife. His cousin, Boo, told him that everything would work out. He always added that word for safety measures. It was nothing like telling a nigga you're coming home and walking away from this scot-free and that not be true.

"So, back to our conversation then."

He reached down and kissed her forehead and then groped her behind. "I thought I was going to be a boxer, like the next Holyfield or some shit."

Sean had always been infatuated with the sport. That was why he invested into the casino in Vegas because he knew that fights brought in a lot of revenue for hotels in Vegas. He was also a private donor in a gym in the heart of Atlanta, Georgia where kids went to train.

Jackie was shocked to hear that. "For real, bae?"

He nodded his head. "Yeah, ask my mama. I was good too. Scholarship to college and everything."

"College?" She was in disbelief.

He closed his eyes, thinking about how in the blink of an eye he had fucked everything up. "Yeah."

Jackie wanted to probe, but she knew how her man was. "Well, maybe when all this is over you can somehow revisit those goals."

Wishful thinking. "Baby, if I get through this, all I wanna do is get the fuck out of the states and go retire on somebody's island," he told her truthfully.

"So, y'all are done?" she asked him.

"I am for sure, can't speak on another man." Sean wouldn't break another piece of bread with them niggas. The Arraignment had brought out the worst in them all, including himself. Sean wouldn't place the blame on everyone else because his thinking pattern had changed once he heard words such as *life sentence, death penalty* and all kinds of other horrifying terms. It was as if they were never one big family to begin with, and that had hurt him more than anything.

The Arraignment was less than a blink away, and he could only imagine what the FEDS had on him. He closed his eyes, not wanting to think about that shit.

"Let's get some sleep," Jackie sighed.

He was thankful she didn't press him for more. Sean rolled over with his wife still glued to him. "I love you."

Jackie loved him so much more. "Til infinity, baby, no matter what."

Whenever she said that, it made him feel like the grimiest nigga in the world. Sean knew he needed to tell her the truth because it would damn sure set him free, literally. But he couldn't be without Jackie, and the truth would have her packing her shit up quick, fast and in a hurry.

"To infinity, baby."

Before You Judge: The Sean Carter Story starts now.
Turn The Page...

Many Years ago...

Eyes rolling, toes curling, sweat dripping, pussy clenching, balls slapping, ass twerking, heart beating rapidly...no let me start over. Biting the lip, eyebrow scrunched up, nipples hard, dick jumping, pussy so wet he's slipping, room silent, atmosphere set....okay no, one more time, let me start over. Back arched, hips tightening with every stroke, tongues intertwined, pussy wide open, mind focused, lips being put to work....

"Jack, come on now, man. Bend over, we ain't got all day," Sean complained. He had to make his flight but wanted to sex her before he headed to New York.

Jackie was trying to get into poetry, but he never wanted to hear it. Rolling her eyes, she still obeyed him as she only did when they were nestled away in the silence of her home. Jacqueline bent over and arched her back perfectly, her mouth forming a large "O" as he slid in slowly.

Their lovemaking was always intense, and throughout the years, Jackie assumed it would get easier to handle, but every time he entered her it always felt like the first time.

Sean bit his bottom lip trying to hold in his satisfaction. If he even let a moan slip out Jackie would stop and tell him to get the fuck out. He so desperately wanted to tell her that her children already knew he was in the back room beating down their mother's guts, but didn't want her to freak out. Before anything she was a mother, and a damn good one at that. But they were boys, smart boys, they knew what was going on.

Sean closed his eyes and threw his head back. He felt like magic was happening from the base of his dick to his left ball. Jackie had that fire between her legs and not the run to the clinic kind. He wanted her in more ways than one, but she wouldn't dare give him the chance. And then, Sean wasn't ready for no damn relationship. He didn't have the energy or the free time in his schedule. Jackie was mean, but he figured that was a cover-up, well he hoped it was. Their time was spent in the bedroom, and on occasion he might get a home cooked meal on his way *out* the door.

Jackie would never admit to caring about him in any way. In fact, she didn't even have his number saved. Their only conversation was, "Pick up some rubbers" or "I'm outside, open the door."

Sean stopped pursuing anything serious with her, but let Jackie tell it, he never tried. However, he always showed her respect and left money on the night stand, but Jackie never touched it. She didn't need him and if she did, he wouldn't know. She was independent like that. Sean fucked with her because she had her own and wasn't looking for someone to play superman and rescue her and her two kids from the hood. Jackie's crib was nice and clean. Although she stayed in a bad neighborhood and Sean had begged her to move, it was her shit, and she was proud of it.

Minutes later, their quickie on her lunch break had come to an end, and Sean eased up out of her dripping vagina and walked backwards to the wall to catch his breath.

Jackie was moaning furiously into the pillow. Even when Sean pulled away, her pussy was still doing the happy dance. Seconds after she came down from her sexual high, she matched Sean's smirk with a middle finger. He shook his head and went to take a quick shower, hoping she would follow him.

Jackie slipped on her silk robe and went to check on her children. They were busy playing video games and talking shit to each other. Jackie closed her bedroom door when she returned and joined Sean in the shower.

"You working out?" he asked, inspecting her washboard abs and toned thighs.

Jackie ignored him while taking a washcloth and washing his back. She was ready for him to leave. Sean turned around and slipped the bar of soap in between her legs, and Jackie jumped, she was still incredibly sore.

"I got you, boo," Sean said and smiled.

Jackie rolled her eyes. "You need to stop it."

"Why? Give me three reasons," he countered.

She took a deep breath and stepped out of the shower. He was getting on her nerves, and she knew it was time for this "relationship" to come to an end. She figured she was clean enough and got out so she could get ready for work. Sean stayed in a little longer being that he was going straight to the airport once he left her house.

She leaned into the mirror closer and saw that there was a passion mark on her neck. She shook her head in irritation. Sean was doing a little too much for her liking. He came from behind her and tried to kiss her, but she wasn't in the mood. Plus, he could never kiss her. The funny thing was, she was the only person he ever wanted to put his lips on.

"Stop pushing me away, Jack," he said, annoyed. Jackie moved out of his way and went to get dressed for overtime. She wanted her boys to have a nice Christmas, so until December she would work as many hours as possible. "Jack!" Sean followed her into her closet, which was so small he wondered how it held all her clothes, but she was organized and always made do with what was given to her. "Answer my question, man," he asked again.

"Sean, what the fuck do you want me to say? Oh yes, baby, let's be together, move me and my bad ass kids into your mansion in Brookhaven. I would love to be with you baby, you're my everything!" she yelled.

Sean was surprised by her use of profanity and that she raised her voice, but he was happy to get some sort of emotion out of her. And he had forgotten all about his crib in Brookhaven. He was happy she mentioned that property because he either needed to rent it out or sell it.

"And why would that be a problem if you know I really like you?" he questioned. Sean needed to stop talking to her about a possible future being that he wasn't even sure what he wanted. On the low, he enjoyed watching Jackie get mad at him. She was a cold individual and rarely showed emotion, even when they were having sex. Jackie treated him as if he was a mandatory appointment. She used Sean for a sexual release.

"Okay, you want your three fucking reasons? Here is number one: I don't date drug dealers, two, you are my supposed to be dead husband's best friend, oh and number three, my all-time favorite, until somebody can bring me his head on a platter, I'm not moving on," she said to him with dark eyes and a trembling lip. There weren't too many things that got her worked up, but her husband was one. Sean had ruffled her feathers today.

Sean nodded his head and got dressed just as quickly as he came. Jackie meant everything she said and wouldn't apologize. She was relieved he was leaving. Sean was cool and all and was extremely supportive during some dark times in her life, but her heart and soul would not rest until her husband's death was proven to be true. Years had passed since he was supposedly shot, but Jackie didn't believe the story when the police told it to her. So until then, she stayed out the way, put herself through nursing school by scraping pennies and stripping at a few clubs on the outskirts of the city and overcame the bullshit. Jackie would be damned if she gave her heart to another, even though she felt butterflies every time Sean entered her. He would never know that. Her emotions didn't make decisions for her.

Sean pulled a knot of money out of his back pocket and as always without counting, tossed the wad on the nightstand and left the bedroom.

Jackie twirled the wedding ring on her finger and placed her thoughts on the back burner. Time was money, and she had to get to work.

Chapter 1

It was about ten minutes to four...in the morning. But these were his hours. This was when he made his moves being that he slept all day. Sean yawned loudly and then turned the tunes of some old school rap down. It was too much going on at once; the music, the blunt that wouldn't spark because his lighter was fucking up and then he wasn't sure if his mind was playing tricks on him or not, but a black Crown Vic had been behind him since he left his shawty's house. He now regretted coming out of the house because he sure was comfortable. The plate she cooked put him to sleep as soon as he finished, and it wasn't until he heard her baby crying did he wake up and peel out.

It was on his agenda to check on a few traps and then head out to his secret place and drop some money in a safe, but this damn car following him had him off schedule.

Sean would be a fool if he led him to any of the places he was headed, so for the past ten minutes he had been driving to nowhere in particular. The nigga was definitely following him, and he wished he wasn't. Sean pulled his gun from under the seat and sat it on his lap. It was already off safety for situations like this. He cracked his neck and said aloud although he was in the car alone, "I swear I ain't feeling like doing this shit tonight." As if having to kill a mother fucker was normal.

A red light was upon him, and this was the opportunity he needed to see if they were trailing him or not because sometimes it was a pure coincidence. He wasn't one of those dudes that kept his hands on the steering wheel and bobbed his head to act as if he wasn't being nosey. Nope, that wasn't Sean. Plus, he had shit to do, and this was holding him up, so he had no pleasantries tonight. Sean was ready to get straight to the point. The nigga was either out this late doing the same shit he was, or he was following him.

When he was younger, his auntie used to warn him about hanging so close with his cousin, Boo. Years later, Sean owed it all to his cousin. He was the cold-hearted nigga he was because of Boo's heartless demeanor. Sean didn't trust easily, and his trigger finger was forever ready for those who deserved to die. He didn't kill just because or pop shit because he could, everything he did hada purpose.

He slowed his whip down once the red light was shining brightly at him and winded his window down. The person didn't do the same, so Sean honked the horn, ready for whatever.

"You got some nerve, nigga?" he said once the man rolled his window down. The man had a mouth full of gold teeth but because it was dark outside, Sean couldn't recognize him. "Where you headed?" Sean asked out of curiosity.

The guy chuckled and went for his gun. "Homie, you better-"

Sean assumed he was attempting to kill him, so he shot him quickly; twice, but not in places he could kill him. That wasn't the plan...yet. Sean needed some information out of his ass first.

He placed his car in park and made sure the coast was clear, but in case it wasn't, he reached over and slid a red fitted cap over his head and got out of the car. He left the keys in the ignition of the nigga's car and the gun.

"Man, who is this nigga?" he asked himself.

The dude was groaning loudly at being shot and wondering how Sean aimed so perfectly sitting down, but Sean was a perfect shooter. He had been trained effectively by having hands-on experience. It took him about four minutes to throw his ass in the trunk and get his phone and shit.

Sean pulled off from the street and hit a few back roads.The one person he trusted with his life was most likely sleeping right now,so Sean went back home and did the same, deciding to deal with the nigga in the morning. In case he had super powers and knew how to chew his way out of a trunk, Sean placed a black box on top of the trunk. He wasn't a hard sleeper nor was he worried about the nigga escaping, but to be sure, he locked his bedroom door and left his gun on the nightstand.

Sean needed more sleep anyway being that he had been road-running for the past few nights. He laid down and took a deep breath, wondering why the nigga was following him and most importantly, who sent him?

The next morning, his own snoring woke him up. Sean used his back hand to wipe the corners of his mouth as he sat up and remembered where he was. He didn't spend that much time at his own place, so it took him a few seconds for everything to register.

Sean fished for his trap phone in the pocket of his Levi jeans and called his cousin. He wasn't sure of the time but knew his cousin was up by now.

"What it do," Boo's voice was low and raspy.

"You still sleep, nigga?"

"Nah, with my lady, early morning session," Boo laughed.

Sean heard his wife going off in the background. "Tell Sammy I said hey."

Boo asked what was up knowing that Sean didn't call to sit on the phone like two bitches.

"I got a situation, call me when you come out the house."

"I'll meet you at the spot," Boo told him, and they ended the call.

Sean went to check on the nigga in the trunk. He had either bled out or was sleeping. Either way, everything was in place. He didn't hear any noises from the garage, so he locked the door, set the alarm and went to wash his ass. His plan was to deal with this shit and then do everything he was supposed to do last night before he headed to New York for a meeting.

Sean walked through his ranch-styled home in Riverdale, Georgia. All the money he had, he could have lived anywhere in Atlanta. In fact, his mama's house was bigger than his, almost three times bigger, but she was his Queen, why would he not do what's right and bless her with a beautiful home?

Sean had a lil condo in the city for when he entertained guests, mainly females that came in town and wanted to see him. His home was in Riverdale, Georgia, on a quiet street where his neighbors were in their early and late fifties and all retired.

He loved how nosey they were because that let him know that if anything was out of the norm, they wouldn't hesitate to call him. Every time he went out of town to a nice island, he bought Mrs. Rodgers a souvenir and her husband a bottle of White Hennessy.

Sean Carter was born and raised in Atlanta, Georgia, straight out of the hood, and he wore his hood on his back. He grew up watching the hustlers pouring poison in the streets and doing nothing for the kids or the community. Sean promised himself that once he made enough money to be able to give back, he would.

For the past six years, every summer he threw a big pool party before school went back and gave away bikes and book bags and often was an Angel in disguise for many of the single mothers in the hood.

He didn't believe in blocking any blessings, and as long as he could help another person in need, that's he what he would do. Sean was never too good to post up and have a good time, but the higher he climbed up the pole in relations to wealth and connections, the less he needed to be seen. So, you wouldn't catch him around often, but when you did, he made sure to show love.

Sean was a quiet man. He never had a lot to say because he was too busy listening and observing. Sean had one sister, and they were close mostly, considering he was always on the move. He kept in constant contact with her by phone. His other phone rang, and he sighed before answering.

"I'll be there tonight," was the first thing he said instead of hello.

"All right, we meeting at Papa's house," informed Chi, a member of The Underworld.

"Bet." Sean looked at the time on the cable box in his room and saw that it was ten in the morning. He needed to get a move on today so he could be in New York on time for that meeting.

"Be safe, homie." Malachi was a passionate man, and Sean respected that about him.

"I will, talk to you tonight," he told him, and they ended their call.

He threw on a pair of jeans and a fresh white t-shirt along with a pair of crisp Air Force Ones. Sean didn't take clothes with him to New York because he had a place up there, and the closet was stocked with attire. Plus, he didn't plan on being in New York longer than he had to, he hated up North.

Thankfully, he was able to balance his role in The Underworld and everything else he had going on.

Sean's hands were in a few other cookie jars, and one thing no one could ever take from him was that he was about his money. He was always doing research on stocks and what was happening in technology. If the streets hadn't captured him at such a young age, he would have gone to school for Engineering.

Sean had an eye for certain things and loved working on different projects. He had invested in a group of students at Georgia Tech who were putting together some kind of app. Sean took a bet on their smart asses, knowing they had a good idea and only needed the resources, which included money, to make it happen.

He surrounded himself with people he could learn from. They were extremely smart, and any questions he had they were always eager to answer. Sean even let them crash at his condo sometimes to get a break from the dorms and supplied them with hella weed and food. As long they kept the wheels in their brains turning, he would keep them around.

He pulled out of his garage and bobbed his head to the tunes playing on 107.9, the local radio station in Atlanta. As he expected, his neighbors were outside cutting the grass and talking. He honked the horn, waved and kept it moving. Sean had a body in the trunk and didn't need this nigga waking up and acting a fool while he was being cordial with his neighbors.

Once he got to the end of the street, he told Boo he was en route to the spot. His cousin could probably place a name to his face or advise him on what to do next, and then he would suggest that he kill him. Boo didn't believe in letting niggas go after they confessed. They always came back seeking revenge, whether it was a year from now or five. He had to learn that shit the hard way.

Boo pulled up a few minutes after Sean to the place they used for situations such as these. The landfill was full of dead bodies and money. It was an hour outside of Atlanta, and he had never seen anyone on the street other than them.

Last year, he had a dream that the FEDS found the property, so he now had cameras on the land and a gate that could be opened with a handprint; not even a fucking four digit code. Sean prided himself on privacy. He had to in the business he was in. There were only a handful of people who knew what he dibbed and dabbed in, everyone else assumed he sold weed, and that was cool with him. He didn't think it was worth a conversation, and he didn't need to tell bitches he was the plug just to score some pussy. He was a handsome man and got them on his looks and charm alone.

Sean wasn't the tallest nigga. He stood at about 5'7, however, he had a lot of heart and personality. His vocabulary was extensive and whenever he had an intellectual conversation whether with his niggas or with a room full of billionaires, they were often impressed and left speechless because of his heavy Southern drawl.

His eyes were little and chinky, his nose long and pointy and his lips...now those were his greatest feature, and he had a bad habit of licking them before he spoke or smiled. His lips were full and pink, and that bottom lip was every girl's dream, to bite on that bottom lip while they rode him.

Sean was a hidden gem. He was handsome and easy on the eyes, but it was his internal parts that had the greater effect on people. He was a great friend, amazing person to be around and he brought shit to the table.

But to be clear, no one was perfect. And for all of those good qualities came negative ones. He was never available, physically or emotionally, and he had trust issues. He wasn't looking for anything serious and tended to not call or text back after fucking. It wasn't personal, but it was business, and that always came first.

Sean didn't try to make things work with people. When they left, he told them goodbye and moved on with life. He loved to have a good time and lived in the moment. His only long-term goal consisted of making more money and saving it all. He didn't want to die or end up in jail, and his cousin was proof that being in the streets didn't always come with a death certificate.

Sean was optimistic about his future, and that's why the nigga in the trunk had to tell him why he was following him. He left his phones in the cup holder and got out of the car to chop it up with his cousin and best friend. Himand Boo grew up together and were only a few years apart. His mother raised them together, and they always protected each other.

Boo wasn't a fan of The Underworld, but Sean told him to trust him. He was a member of The Underworld for a reason and although it had been years since he joined and had formed a partnership, a brotherhood and a bond with the team, he still had his mind on that one reason.

And no, don't get it twisted, it wasn't no trifling shit. He was just a business man trying to handle his business. Things with Sean didn't get personal often because he was forever focused and had his eyes on the prize.

"I promised my wife I wasn't leaving the house today, so what I'm out here for?" Boo asked.

What people failed to realize was that there was a big difference between rude and direct. Rude was being nice-nasty, short with people and offensive. Direct was straight-forward, to the point and not beating around the bush. Many people thought Boo was rude and arrogant, but to Sean the nigga just didn't want to waste his time and so for that, he was direct.

Sean didn't bother with a greeting or a dap, he simply popped the trunk and stepped back.

Boo took his Cartier shades off. "Who the fuck is this ugly ass nigga? Damn, he look like a gorilla," he laughed. Bloody bodies didn't make him bat an eyelash. Money piled to the ceiling, pure cocaine, heroin and some good weed, now that made his eyes buck. Clear-cut diamonds, private flights, his wife in designer shoes butt-booty naked, that's what made his dick hard. But this ugly nigga holding on to his last breath wasn't surprising.

"I don't know, he was following me last night-"

Boo cut him off. "And you shot him and put him in your trunk?"

"Nigga, what would you have done?" he questioned his cousin.

"He stayed in your trunk all night?"

Sean nodded his head. "Yeah, I knew you wasn't'tcoming out last night, it was about four in the morning."

Boo was a husband and a father now, so his time was limited, and he rarely got his hands dirty these days. He and his wife were filthy rich, so there was no need to parlay with his freedom when they were set for life.

Boo walked up to the man and pulled him out of the trunk and then kicked him.

"Wake yo' ass up!" he barked.

The man stirred, he had lost a lot of blood. "I need a doctor," he stumbled over his words.

Boo crouched down in front of the guy. "Who sent you?" It was a simple question, and he only needed a name.

"My nigga, fuck you!"

He had heart, that was cute. "Do you want to die or you want a doctor?" Sean asked him.

"Again, *fuck-*"

Boo punched him in the face. "Don't be disrespecting my cousin, nigga. He's a nice guy. Now tell us who sent you? Why was you following him?"

Sean then remembered that he had his phone and ID. He went to his trunk and looked around for those items. A torn Gucci wallet had a few loose bills in it.

"No ID? You driving with no license?"

"I'm not gon' tell you shit." He wasn't giving up a name.

Boo nodded his head. "Okay. Well, we about to kill you and then drop your ass in one of them holes behind me." His tone was convincing.

"You're a dead man," the man said.

"And you are too!" Sean laughed at the nigga while he went through the man's phone. It was filled with calls to unknown numbers and text messages to hoes. Sean called the last number in the log. One particular number had called four times this morning.

The voice on the phone said, "What did you find?"

Sean smoked a lot of weed, so he wasn't the sharpest tack in the drawer, but there were some voices you never forgot. That voice sounded way too fucking familiar, but he couldn't be sure. He hung the phone up and then turned it off.

"Kill him," he told Boo.

His cousin looked at him. "I ain't got nothing out of him yet."

Sean shook his head. "Shoot him, I got shit to do." He planned to leave the car and when the niggas came to dump his body, have them detail his car.

Boo got up and took a deep breath. "Nigga, what's going on?" He still hadn't shot the man.

Sean was irritated and pulled his gun and gave him one aim to the dome. "I think somebody from The Underworld following me," he told his cousin.

"For what?" Boo didn't understand. If he had a Rolls Royce for every time his cousin shared with him the shit going on with The Underworld, he could open a car dealership. He joked with him all the time that he had never seen so many drug dealers with drama. Boo warned Sean to leave The Underworld and do his own thing or he could retire, it wasn't like he didn't have the money to do so.

"It could either be because of this or that." He was in deep thought. That's what Sean had to figure out. Why was he following him, and what was the motive?

The Underworld was a great opportunity, and it took his pockets from *Just getting by* to *Nigga, I made it*. He was in a great position and considered it a blessing to have been able to travel around the world making money and memories at the same time.

But, if Sean could do a few things differently, he would. For starters, he would have never agreed to the percentage he received every month. He would have asked for an exit package if he ever decided to leave, and lastly, but this was the most important, he would have done way more research on every member of the organization, including the "leader" Nasir King.

Over the years the organization had hit many road blocks, stumbled over some sticky situations and endured trials and tribulations, and they still stood. On top of all that, there was always some "dark" secret appearing, scandals happening and all kinds of shit. Sean was never caught up in that mess because he lived in Atlanta and only appeared when he was summoned for a meeting. He had no desire to be closer to them any more than he already was.

Things with Nasir had been sort of sticky ever since he found out that Sean had fucked Lo, his supposed to be ride-or-die down bitch for life, or something of that nature. It was just a fuck for them both. After it happened, neither contacted the other or tried to make it more than what it was. Nasir was so hurt behind the action and had yet to let it go.

Sean wasn't sweating no pussy that wasn't his and according to Lauren, she was over him and wouldn't dare fuck with him again. Sean highly doubted the latter, but she wasn't his concern. They kept in touch now and then, and Sean would admit that he did like her and was attracted to her, but it didn't go further than that.

Things had been shaky, and that was another reason Sean kept his distance from everyone. He didn't have time for drama. As long as shipments and re-ups were done on time, he was good to go. Sean didn't hang with them like he used to, but to shake things up he planned to stay a few days in New York instead of flying back first thing in the morning like he had planned on doing. Sean knew how to play the game to get the toy he wanted, and Nasir had the wrong one.

He didn't take it lightly that he had to kill someone because he was being followed. To make him feel better about the dead body before him, he told himself that it was Nas or someone else in The Underworld who left him no choice but to shoot the nigga.

Boo asked his cousin again, "So he got an issue with you, that's nothing new, but what's it about this time?" Boo knew about the Lauren thing, but if he was married now, why did it bother him so much, something that happened years ago?

"He mad about some pussy that ain't mine or his." He shook his head in disbelief.

η

Sean ran his errands and then had time to stop and see a very special lady. A cold-hearted, rude, delusional, paranoid, crazy ass woman, but she was his...kinda. Well, he wanted her to be if she stopped playing so many games with him. Sean was ready to give her the world, but Jackie wasn't stunting him. He never knew what side of her he would get, but today he needed the sweet version of her.

He rang the doorbell and then knocked on the door, and she answered the door with a smug expression.

"Damn, why you gotta look at me like that?" he said as he crossed over into her home.

She tried to keep walking, but he grabbed her arm and pulled her close. Jackie was the only person who got the sweetheart version of him, but she didn't want it. Jackie couldn't care less about all of his homes, cars and how his passport had tons of stamps in it. She didn't bat an eyelash at any of that shit. He was able to whisk her to a few places, but it was always on her terms. Jackie ran him, and she knew that. Sean still fucked with different bitches but would gladly cut them all off if Jackie was nicer to him.

She told him she enjoyed the distance between them being that he was always on the go. Sean would do anything to hear her say, "I miss you" just once in a lifetime.

"I ain't in the mood today, let me go," she snapped.

He ignored her and squeezed her ass. "You ain't never in the mood, so shut up. And you smell good." He got a good whiff of her neck. Jackie took a deep breath, knowing he wouldn't let her go until she at least met eye contact with him or hugged him back.

"What be wrong with you, girl?"

She was always mad about something. Jackie was a dime, and she had no clue on how bad she was. Her chocolate skin had a natural glow to it, and her smile and light voice brought him to his knees sometimes. Jackie lived in the gym and although she was knocking on forty and had pushed out two big-headed boys naturally, her body bore no evidence. Her perky double-D's and abs were solid. The beautiful thing was, even though she lived in the gym, she had the fattest, softest ass and juiciest thighs a woman could have. Her personality was snappy and jazzy, and she rocked her hair in short cuts with the back shaven. Jackie always smelled good and dressed nice and when she wasn't at work as a nurse, she was in the kitchen cooking and baking.

Sean was in his early thirties, and she was in her late thirties knocking on her forties, but he couldn't care less about their age difference. She was always referring to herself as a cougar, and he ignored her every time. What they had going on was their business.

It took Sean many years to make progress with her and for a long time she wouldn't allow him to do anything for her, but now she accepted all gifts. Even the Lexus outside was a recent gift from him. Sean would do whatever to see her smile. Jackie held a special place in his heart, even if she thought they were nothing more than a good time on the late night tip.

"Nothing, why you ain't call first?"

He looked at her as if she were crazy. "Call for what?"

Jackie finally pulled away from him. "My man may have been over here," she teased before going back in the kitchen.

Sean didn't find that shit funny. "Don't play with me." He didn't want her talking or entertaining another nigga, even if he was just at a chick's house less than twenty-four hours ago. Sean was very protective of her and her kids.

"What you gon' do? Sean, I ain't yours." She laughed after she made that statement.

He came into the kitchen with a scowl on her face as she iced a chocolate cake. "Damn let me get a slice." He went for the cabinet where the plates were.

"Hmm-hmm, this is for my boss," she shook her head as she licked her finger.

"Make me one, I get back in town in a few days."

Sean was always out of town. "New York?" she questioned.

He nodded his head. Jackie had come up there a few times to visit him or accompany him to a dinner or whatever The Underworld had going on. He didn't trust many people, but he trusted her. In case of emergency, Jackie had his cousin's information, his lawyer's contact and some other shit that was imperative for her to know in case he was no longer around to see about her.

She was as real as they came, which was one reason he kept trying to lock her down. Sean enjoyed his freedom, but Jackie was worth retiring his player card. She was everything he would want in a wife when that time came plus, she didn't want anymore kids, and that was perfect because he didn't want any either.

"You gon' miss me?" Sean asked her.

He knew she would tell him hell the fuck no, but surprisingly, she nodded her head and told him, "Maybe, Sean, I don't know."

η

Thankfully, his flight to New York was smooth, but his mind wouldn't shift from the conversation he had with Jackie. Sean liked her, that he knew for a fact, but was it because he wanted to protect her and her kids out of loyalty, or did he really enjoy being around her? She wasn't even his type, so is that why he was so attracted to her? It was a few things he needed to figure out concerning Jackie.

She texted him and told him to have a safe trip and thanked him for the money. Jackie never counted the money either, she would drop it in a bag in the back of her closet knowing that rainy days came out of nowhere and when they appeared, she would be prepared. He wanted to text her back spilling his guts and asking her to trust him, but he wouldn't go there with her tonight, he had business to handle.

Sean pushed her to the back of his head as he sat in the back of a cab headed to his crib. He didn't have much time to shower and change, but it wouldn't kill him if he was a few minutes late, although he prided himself on always being on time.

His stomach was growling, but since the meeting was at Papa's house, that meant dinner was included because his wife was a homemaker and could cook her ass off.

Sean changed into all-black and then grabbed his 9mm before heading to the parking garage where one of his three cars was parked. There was a time where shit was slow and he was in New York a lot because he had met a cool ass chick up here, but now if it didn't pertain to business, you wouldn't catch him in the city.

Sean headed to Papa's house wondering if he would bring up that he had to kill a nigga for following him. If he did, it would be a ploy to see who would react. Sean would study facial expressions and their reactions, mainly Nasir. He didn't think they were plotting against him, at least he prayed they weren't.

He loved them niggas, but no one was ever to be trusted. Money and power paired with a bunch of niggas was never a good combination, however they made it work over the years.

Sean raked his mind trying to think of any other beef or problems big enough for someone to follow him, and he came up with nothing. And it couldn't have been the FEDS because that nigga wasn't an undercover. This was some street shit. Sean's phone rang, it was his cousin, Boo.

"You made it?" Boo asked. Sean told him that he did. "Did you meet up with them niggas yet?"

"Headed there now, hungry as shit." His stomach was growling, and he hadn't smoked all day.

"Shit, so I told Sammy about the issue from earlier, and she asked did you get the plates so she could run 'em?"

Sean banged his hand on the steering wheel. "Man, hell nah, I wish I would have. I wonder is the car still out there."

"Get somebody on that and get back to me," Boo told him. That's exactly what he was about to do before he went in Papa's house. "Aye!" Boo called out before Sean hung up the phone. "Be careful, man. I don't trust them niggas." He was always telling him that.

Sean wasn't worried....yet. "Everything good, they family," he said slowly, praying he never regretted those words.

Chapter 2
"I done slept with rats and roaches, that's why I don't smoke no roaches."
– 21 Savage

You ever woke up one day and said, "Thank ya, Lord?" Sean did it every morning, even when he woke up in deep thought wondering why he kept having the same nightmare over and over again. Last night's meeting went well, and he decided to hold on to his last murder knowing that eventually it would come to light. Sean had planned to stick around the city for a few days but decided to head back to Atlanta. It was nothing like the South. New York could hardly compare.

He made sure his place was locked up and the alarm set before heading downstairs where he planned on catching a cab to the airport. When he turned around, Nasir was standing right behind him.

"What the fuck is you on?" was the first thing he said. Nasir appeared relaxed, but Sean couldn't care less. He stuck his hand out for a shake, and Sean didn't even want to shake the nigga's hand, but he did. "What's good?" he asked Nas.

Nasir asked him, "You heading back already?"

They all knew he went back and forth, so why did he ask him that? "Yeah, business to handle," he kept his answer short.

"Oh okay, I'll walk with you downstairs. I was lost for a second, you know I've only been here once," his voice trailed as he thought about the time he found Lauren at Sean's house. Boy was he pissed. "So, how is the new pack doing?" Nas asked him. Sean told him that everything was rolling as it always did. "Cool, cool, we may double that next time. Can you handle three hundred?"

Nasir was challenging him. "Yep, send it on," he said, nodding his head. He looked over his shoulder as they walked down the hallway and then got on the elevator. He stayed in upper Tribeca in a modern area that was mainly eat, play and live, but Sean rarely did anything other than play with bitches when he was in the city.

On the elevator, Sean remained silent, and Nasir did the same...until the doors were about to open, and Nasir pressed another floor.

"You forgot something?"

"Nah, I'm getting off on another floor, don't want to be seen together. I been feeling like somebody been following me lately...shit been creeping me out."

"And you just came to this conclusion?" Sean asked him. His phone rang, but he didn't answer, too busy studying this nigga.

"Yeah, catch you next time," he said and then got off the elevator.

Sean smiled as the doors closed. He was ready for whatever, anytime and anywhere. He had a lot of heart and would never hesitate to do what he had to do to stay alive.

Sean ended up being late to the airport due to the congested traffic on the street that led to JFK airport. He texted Jackie right before the plane took off, telling her that his cake better be ready and something good to eat. He planned on kicking it over her crib for the next two days. Sean needed to sit back and think some shit through, and her house was full of peace, especially when her kids weren't home.

He had to get the bottom of this "following" situation. Sean didn't believe a word Nasir said about being followed. He had a team of security, so if the nigga was really being trailed, his people would have handled it immediately. Sean would respect him so much more if he learned to keep it real, but he never did.

As soon as he touched down in Atlanta, he let his cousin know he was back and then caught another cab to his house.Sean was spending too much money on thesedamn cabs and was eager to hop back in one of his whips.

He showered and threw some clothes in an overnight bag before heading to Jackie's house.He never told her he was on the way, she wouldn't know he wanted to see her until he rang the doorbell and knocked on the door.

"I want to know how you can use them long ass fingers of yours to demand plates and pussy but can't text me when you on the way?" she grumbled as she unlocked the door.

"That takes the spontaneity out of what we got going on," he teased.

Jackie wasn't stunting that shit. "Hmm-hmm, let me fix you a plate. You staying?" She saw the bag in his hand.

"I might, depending on how you act tonight."

She bypassed him and went to make him a plate of what she had made last night. "You know I have to work," she reminded him.

"Trust me, I'm aware of the rules, don't come out of the room until you get here."

He respected the way she raised her sons, but Sean wasn't a stranger to them. At one time he was over their house every day...when her husband, their father and his best friend, was alive.

To the kids he was Uncle Sean, and now he was bagging their mother. Shit happens. Sean made sure her kids didn't miss a beat. Birthdays and Christmas were the same, even after their father *passed*. He would never see them without and kept them out of trouble.

Jackie had never told him that she appreciated his presence in their life, but she really did. It wasn't easy raising two boys alone, and she was thankful her kids didn't turn to the streets for solace nor were they too out of control. A few times she had to put her foot in their asses, but that was normal, they were growing up.

Sean took a seat at her dining room table and texted a few people while Jackie handled her business in the kitchen.

"What you cooked last night?"

"Honey, you about to eat in two seconds, so you will see."

Her sassiness turned him on, and he normally let her talk to him however she wanted. Jackie had him wrapped around her finger. She placed a hot plate of food in front of him and then sat down with a newspaper and a pair of scissors in her apron.

"What you about to do?" he asked her after he said his grace.

"Clip some coupons." Jackie was old school and was always looking for a good sale.

"You good? The boys need anything?"

She shook her head. "You do enough."

She had been a hustler even before her husband's disappearance. Jackie never said out loud that he was dead. Her heart never gave her that closure. He looked down at her wedding ring and secretly cringed.

"Do you think you'll ever get married again?"

She cut her eyes at him. "Don't start."

They had never had a serious conversation. Ever. Jackie kept things very simple between the two. She was cool with him coming over on the late night or him stopping by in the middle of the day. She was even okay with fixing him a plate, but dinner dates, movies, kissing and laying up? None of that had ever happened. And it wouldn't.

"Nah, I'm saying, like, you're a beautiful woman-"

"Who is married, Sean," she reminded him. Sometimes Jackie wondered how close he and her husband were because he never brought him up or acted like he was affected. She figured because he was a man and men didn't really express their emotions, but they were close. Tight. Extremely tight. They kicked shit together and got money together, so now and then she wanted to ask him if his death had affected him at all.

"You deserve happiness," he told her, making sure they made direct eye contact when he spoke.

Jackie had shared with him once that she hated a nigga that couldn't look at her because they were too busy ogling her large breasts.

"I'm good, and my kids are happy, that's whose happiness matters to me." She could go all day with him but wouldn't. "How is your food?"

Sean was playing around with the plate because he needed to smoke. It wasn't that he wasn't hungry because he definitely was.

"Can I smoke on the back porch?" he asked her. He rarely had an appetite when he wasn't high.

"Yeah, the boys aren't here."

He wanted to tell her them lil' niggas been smoking since they were twelve but didn't want to break her heart. Sean got up and grabbed his phone. He had already rolled a few blunts before he came over and had one behind his ear, so he was good to go.

"You want something to drink?"

He shook his head. "No, but thanks for being the perfect hostess, sexy." Sean was always dry flirting with her. He wouldn't stop until she told him to.

"I'm about to finish this up and then take me a nap before I have to go to work." She looked at the time on her watch and mentally mapped out the rest of her day.

He hated that she worked so hard. Jackie punched that clock faithfully and sometimes worked twenty-four hours straight. He never heard her complain about being tired, feet hurting or nothing.

"All right."

Sean smoked and watched videos on his phone until he was done with the blunt. His stomach was now grumbling even louder than it was on the plane, so he heated the plate up and demolished it. Jackie's sons came in with a few of their friends just as he was cutting a slice of cake.

"I knew that was your car," Kevin, Jackie's oldest son dapped him up and said.

"Yeah, I came to get something to eat." It wasn't his place to sit them down and tell them anything. And if he did, Jackie would cut his ass off real quick.

Kevin and Jonathan both looked at each other with a goofy look on their face.

"What?" Sean was acting as if he was confused.

"Nothing, you got something to smoke?"

Their friends were surprised to hear them ask a grown man for weed being they were teenagers and not supposed to be smoking. They knew nothing of Sean's relationship with them. He had taken them to a strip club, and their first blunt was smoked with Sean. He kept money in their pockets and promised them that as long as they stayed out of trouble, kept good grades and minded their mother, he would make sure they were straight.

When Kevin turned seventeen, Sean copped him an Escalade truck. Jackie was pissed off but knew her baby boy deserved it, so she cursed Sean out and then put Kevin on a strict curfew.

About a year ago, some lil ratchet bitch Jonathan was fucking with ended up pregnant, and Sean had his cousin take the girl to get an abortion so her parents wouldn't find out. He was the dad they needed, and they loved him, but like their mother, they never told him that shit.

Sean wasn't one of those niggas who needed to be pacified or told thank you every single time he made shit happen. He didn't do things for a pat on the back or recognition. He genuinely loved and cared about their family and would do anything to see them smile. Sean didn't fuck with any other woman on the level he did with Jackie, but he did fuck off, a lot. No one was on the same pedestal as Jackie or her children, and no one ever would be.

"About to go check on your mom, it's a blunt on the table I ain't smoke," he told them before going down the hallway with a paper plate in his hand.

Before he opened Jackie's door, he heard one of their friends ask, "Is that your step-dad?"

Jonathan quickly said, "Hell nah, that's our uncle."

Sean's shoulders dropped. They would never see him as more than their dad's best friend, even if he secretly wanted to marry their mother and move them into one of his many homes.

Jackie was knocked out under the covers, and one of her legs dangled over the mattress. Sean decided to leave, especially since she had to work tonight anyway. He told the boys to come lock the front door, and then he headed to the hood to kick shit with his family.

η

His mother, who was known as Neet, had a beautiful home. She also had a gambling problem out of this world. Instead of being home all day, she'd rather sit at the gas station and gamble. Neet had not a care in the world and did what she wanted to do every day, courtesy of her baby boy. Sean spoiled her rotten, and she was so proud of his hard work and success; even if he was a drug dealer. Luckily, she hadn't been in too much trouble with her gambling and when they were younger, that's how she kept her family afloat. Neet would be two or three days away from getting evicted and would use her last to play Dominoes or another gambling game, and she would hit big. People used to call her lucky back in the day because she came up out of nowhere all the time. She would win up to twenty-thousand dollars playing the lotteries and then go fuck it up in the casino.

When Sean pulled up to the Texaco in Mechanicsville, a hood in Atlanta, all he had to do was honk the horn, and his mother looked up and out of the window of the gas station.

Sean was one hood ass nigga, and his mother was too. He had tried to get her to switch up her style and wear some new shit, but she loved her Michael Kors purses and sandals.

Neet had been going to the hair stylist since she was seventeen-years-old, the lady did hair out of her basement and had no plans on moving into a salon since her clientele was solid.

She gave Sean a big happy smile, exposing her pretty teeth with one of her front tooth dipped in gold and a cursive "N" on it.

"Ma, I been calling you," he complained.

Neet fished her pockets for a phone. "It's probably in the car." She pointed behind her to the Mercedes Benz truck she was currently pushing.

"What you in there doing besides blowing money, big baller?" He was always teasing about her being richer than him.

Neet mushed him in the head playfully. "Shit, nigga, I ain't got nothing, you need to give me some money. Boo told me you was in New York, when you get back?" she asked.

His mama needed nothing. He faithfully deposited stacks into an account for her. Neet was doing better than everybody around her, and they all knew to not fuck with her.

She checked her six-inch finger nails that were covered in rhinestones along with rings on each finger. His mother still had one foot in the nineties, seriously. He told her that he had just touched down.

"Oh, everything good ain't it, baby?" Neet never got into her son's business, but the streets talked enough for her to know what he had going on. Her only concern was his safety. Although he could handle his own, it was natural to worry being that he was her only boy.

Sean nodded his head. "Always. Ride with me. I'm about to go check on grama house," he told her.

Neet rolled her eyes. She really wasn't done gambling, but it wasn't often her son asked her to kick it with him, nor did he spend as much time with the family as she wanted him to do.

"My truck up here, I'll meet you down there," she reminded him, thinking that would be her way to stay at the gas station a bit longer.

"I'll wait on you," he told her. His mother thought she was slick.

Neet had a smirk on her face. "Hmm-hmm, honey, all right." She went to cash out and then hopped in her truck, honking her horn at the stragglers around the gas station. Sean shook his head wishing his mama found something else to do with her time.

They pulled up in Gammy's parking lot and headed inside. Boo was already in there.

"What it do, nigga?" He was always elated to see his family.

"How my sister been doing?" Neet asked about Honey Gal.

Boo's face tightened, she was such a sensitive topic for him. "Good, stop by and see her sometimes," he shot back.

Sean eyed him but said nothing, knowing how sensitive his cousin could be. That was the one thing they didn't have in common.

Jackie texted Sean asking why he left, and he didn't respond to her. He wanted more from her and realized that he would never get it. Sean wondered if he was wasting his time or not being upfront enough for her. He didn't know what she wanted or expected from him.

Jackie was hot and cold with her feelings, and the up and down confused him, so he decided that once he left her house to fall back. If she wanted him, she would show him.

"I will do just that as long as your bad ass-"

Sean cut her off, "What your folks back there doing? Go check on them."

Boo was two seconds from saying something to Neet's ass. Their grandmother had been dead for many years, but no one could bring themselves to clear her house out, so it served as the meet-up place and gathering spot for holidays and just about any other day.

At any time you could pull up and one of the cousins would be in there making a sandwich on their lunch break or cooling, as Boo was doing. The basement served as a storehouse, but that was no one's business but Boo and Sean.

Gammy's presence was still very much felt in the house, and that was one reason the family kept it up. She was the matriarch and still was in a sense.

Neet told Sean, "Don't leave here without giving me no money," she reminded him before walking off.

Boo shook his head. "Your mama ain't nothing to play with." He dealt with Neet from a distance because her mouth was too fresh for him. On several occasions they had gotten into it, and Boo had to remind himself that she was family and not some hoe on the street.

"How long you been over here?" Sean asked Boo.

Boo sat back down and went back to rolling a blunt. He told Sean that he hadn't been there long. "I'm killing some time, and then I had to come make sure the refrigerator wasn't still running. The other day shit was all over the kitchen." Boo had actually lived in this house, so he was more attached than Sean was.

"I was over Jackie house, but she fell asleep so I went to pull up on my mama."

Boo shook his head. "That shit not weird to you?" he had to ask.

Sean knew that on the outside looking in shit looked fucked up, but he really rocked with Jackie. "Nah, have you seen her?" he smirked.

Boo couldn't care less about her being thick in all the right places, he believed in karma and a lot of other shit. "I wish a nigga would fuck my wife, I'll come back and haunt that nigga in his sleep every night." Just the thought of someone touching Samira angered him.

"He was cheating on her," he reminded his cousin.

That still didn't make it right. "Nigga, so what nigga ain't cheated? It's still not right, cuz."

Sean didn't want to hear that. "Well, she grown and can make her own conscious decisions. I ain't got a gun to her head."

He saw that his cousin was taking offense to what he was saying, so Boo dropped the subject. "Aye, man, get out your feelings!" he laughed, exposing all the golds in his mouth.

"I fuck with her for real, like on some I wanna be with her forever type shit," he kept it one hundred with him.

"Why her? She got kids, and she older than you on top of all the other shit. It's others out here, cuz." He wanted him to keep an open mind, that's all.

"I connect with her."

Boo had been there before, but sometimes niggas thought with their dick and not their mind. "Or are you attached to the pussy?" he posed the question.

Sean sat back and stared at him. "What?" he wasn't sure what the fuck that meant.

"Are you connected to her on a deeper level, or are you attached to her pussy? Cus it's a big difference." Boo was far from a therapist, but he knew love, had experienced it firsthand with his wife, but it was after he had been with a few bitches. It took him awhile to understand who he had as a woman. Boo didn't appreciate Samira when they first started talking. Even after she stayed down with him after he had got locked up, he still was on some bullshit. Boo loved her, but he wasn't in love with her for a long time. Their relationship was intact now, and that was because relationships weren't easy. Married for years, kids and a big house meant nothing if the trust wasn't there. Every day, he prided himself on doing whatever to reassure her they were good. Boo had to learn about his wife and what she expected from him, and the more time they spent together and the more years that passed, it seemed as if she wanted more from him.

"I fucks with her, and it's not all about sex," he told Boo.

"Yeah, all right, nigga."

They shared a blunt and just like that, the conversation was over, but not for Sean. He revisited the words *attached* and *connected* and wondered how she felt. Was she attached? Did she sense a possible connection? That was hard for him to figure out because shawty was so nonchalant and didn't do a good job at expressing her feelings. In fact, she never did. Sean was the one doing everything, and that was why he decided to fall back because there were plenty in line wanting more from him and willing to do whatever it took to lock him down. But...his eyes were on Jackie. His heart wanted her only.

"Don't be over there contemplating life and shit. It's a good day, you alive and not in jail," Boo told him.

"Nah, I'm good, for real. It's a lot on my mind, not just her." And that was the truth. Nas had challenged him with that heavy ass load, but he would get it handled as he always did. No one worked harder than Sean in The Underworld.

From the very beginning, Sean felt like he had been proving himself to that nigga, but it was funny because at the end of the day, the underdog always came out on top.

η

The next morning, he was up bright and early for an appointment that would have slipped his mind but thankfully, a courtesy call was given.

Sean left his car with valet and took the elevator up to the third floor of the building and signed in. Every two weeks like clockwork he found himself meeting with a therapist. And no, he wasn't pyscho. He wasn't tripping out of his mind or anything of that nature. He simply had no one he could fully trust with his thoughts and being that his therapist charged him almost six-hundred dollars an hour, he had no choice but to trust her.

Their sessions sometimes were light and easygoing, and at other times they became intense and would leave Sean in a doozy for the remainder of the day.

He waited on her to come to the lobby to get him and while doing so, he sent out several messages to his soldiers in Atlanta. If Nasir was about to drop off more loads on him then that meant his peoples needed to cop more. Sean had put a plan in motion while he waited on Dr. Robinson.

"Can't believe you're early today. Come on, I'm ready for you," she told him as she walked in front of him.

Sean gave her a light smile. "I'm never late." He was normally on time, but to Dr. Robinson that was considered late.

She stopped at the receptionist desk and grabbed a file before they went into her office and closed the door. "So, how have you been?" She checked her cell phone and then sat down, giving her patient her full attention.

Dr. Robinson was a beautiful woman in her early forties. She was of West Indian descent, and her caramel macchiato complexion bounced off the walls when paired with her emerald eyes and the nicest pair of lips a woman could probably have. If Sean mixed business with personal, he would have taken a swim in her pool, but opted out.

Dr. Robinson was newly divorced and the mother to twin girls. She had shared little with Sean over the years, but enough for him to know that she was a good person in and outside of the office. He never missed her birthday and gave her a nice hefty Christmas gift every year.

Dr. Robinson once told him that he didn't "really" need a therapist, but Sean quickly told her that he did....he fought demons every day as he lived an undercover life as a drug lord; a life Dr. Robinson knew nothing about. He was sure she probably had an idea, but she never asked about it, and he didn't bother disclosing that tidbit of information.

"I'm good, just got back in town, actually." He scratched his head and stretched his legs before him. Sean peered over to the chaise and asked, "Do people really lay on that and tell you all their business?"

Dr. Robinson chuckled and removed her lime green glasses that complimented her oval face very well. "Sometimes. Do you want to lay down today?" She had been meeting with him for quite some time, so she could easily detect what kind of mood he was in.

Sean was quiet, but his expressions and emotions is what gave everything away when his mouth wouldn't move. "Nah, I'm good, everything is Gucci my way," he said and shook his head.

She wouldn't press him. "How are things going with the women?" Often, Dr. Robinson dug deep into Sean's lack of commitment for the opposite sex and would even add the word disregard. Only because it seemed as if he had no desire to settle down, but lately Sean's disposition had changed.

"Well, I'm still fucking all of them if that's what you're asking." He was blunt and direct with his answer.

"And how is Jackie?"

Jack. That was his weak spot. "I want her, Doc...bad." His voice trailed as he thought of the last time he entered her and how good she felt.

"What steps are you taking to make that happen?" she asked, pulling out her notepad, ready to record whatever he said she deemed beneficial in writing down.

Sean hadn't thought of any steps. His actions over the past years should have been enough, but instead he said, "Going over there earlier in the day to show her that I want more than a late night fuck."

"And are y'all having sex still? Even though you're going over there early?"

He pursed his lips together as he thought about what his cousin Boo said to him yesterday about being attached and disconnected.

"You know what... I ain't fuckin' her no more." He had decided right then and there.

Dr. Robinson was amused with his outburst. "And why is that?"

Sean wanted more out of her and saw a future with her, so for that to take place he had to start showing her that he could be her man and not just a piece of meat.

"I don't think she takes me serious."

Jackie worked, and that was it. She didn't go out with friends, and the few trips she had taken were with him or her sons. She didn't give a fuck about a relationship. Her heart was still throbbing from the sudden loss of her husband.

"And do you take yourself serious in relations to her?"

He nodded his head. "She's the only one for me."

"And the other women are what to you?" Dr. Robinson never shied away from her utter disgust at the way Sean had careless sex and disposed of women when he felt like it. She told him that he did that for a deeper reason that she was still trying to figure out. Dr. Robison wanted to blame it on how he was raised, but because Sean had a great relationship with his mother, she didn't think that was the main reason.

"Nothing, I told you that already," he mumbled.

She didn't get it, and it wasn't just Sean, but many men felt this way, including her ex-husband. "So... why lead them on?"

"What that gotta do with me being with Jackie?"

She closed the notepad. "She probably doesn't take you serious because she knows you're doing your own thing. You said she's older than you, correct? How do you expect her to believe you're ready tosettle down?"

"It's a lot...she got some issues too," he added. Jackie had a lot she needed to deal with instead of working to keep her tears at bay.

"As in what?" Dr. Robinson opened the notepad again, she was all ears.

"Her husband died, remember I told you?"

She nodded her head. "Yes, and you knew him. How well did you know him?" Getting a patient to open up was better than an orgasm, and Dr. Robinson was itching towards an explosion as she finally got Sean to talk more and not beat around the bush.

"Real good."

She needed more. "Good as in neighbors? Or good as in y'all were-"

"Best friend, he was my best friend."

That changed the game. Dr. Robinson suddenly had flashbacks of the day she came home early and caught her husband in bed with her best friend of almost fifteen years. Her skin rapidly went from bronze to crimson red as his revelation hit her hard. She crunched the piece of paper up and gave him her full attention. Why did men do the shit they did? She would never know.

Sean saw the disgruntled look on her face. "I know it's fucked up," he sighed.

It wasn't her place to tell him what was wrong or right, but from her own personal experiences she spoke, "Sean, you can't do that to him."

"He's dead!" he argued. The nigga was dead, and he desperately wanted Jackie to accept her husband's death and move on with him.

She rolled her eyes. "It doesn't matter. How can you live a happy life knowing you're in love with your best friend's wife? Oh gosh, were y'all messing around while-"

He shook his head and told her quickly, "Hell no, Jack is as loyal as they come." That was one thing he knew for sure.

"So why now? Was it an emotional night, and you were there to comfort her?"

That wasn't important. "Look, I want her to get some counseling. Can you talk to her?" he asked.

She nodded her head. "You do know I won't be able to discuss what she shares with me?"

He looked at her in disbelief. "Even if I pay you?" He knew those dollar bills could easily change any conversation. Sean often spoke with money.

Dr. Robinson figured he was rich, but she couldn't care less about the money. Her career would be on the line. "Totally confidential." She wouldn't budge.

"All right, well give me some advice so I can go, I got shit to do today." Sometimes he stayed for the whole hour, and other times he would literally ask her one question and then leave. However, he was still charged for a sixty minute session.

Dr. Robinson had no advice for him today. "Pray," was all she had.

He was shocked. "No write this down or none of that?" She was always giving him an assignment.

"I don't agree with you pursuing her after what you told me, and something tells me that it's more to the story."

Sean asked out of curiosity, "Like what?" He held his chin in his hand and waited on her to answer.

She stood and smoothed out her linen skirt. "Not sure yet." She wouldn't tell him what she had expected just yet.

"You're lying." Such as she was learning him, he had been studying her as well.

She smiled. "Good seeing you, Sean. Before you leave, make sure I'll be here for our next appointment. I'm supposed to be testifying in court for a client."

"You do that?"

She was unsure of what, *You do that?* meant. Dr. Robinson sometimes struggled with keeping up with Sean and his slang. "Beg your pardon?"

He asked his question again, "In court, you can testify against a person?"

His therapist shook her head. "Not technically, so basically if my patient is in some sort of trouble they'll call me in to testify that he may or may not was in his right mind."

"And they can plead insanity?" The wheels in his head were turning.

Dr. Robinson said slowly, "Depends..."

He saw her looking at him so he smiled. "Learn something new every day, see you next time, Doc." He winked his eye and exited her office.

Sean went home to change his clothes, grab his gun, roll a few blunts and then he was back out the door. He honked at his neighbors as he drove out of his driveway.

"Another day to trap," he told himself as he turned the music up in his ride and headed to the hood.

Chapter 3

"Niggas puttin' niggas in the graveyard." – Meek Mill

The Underworld was a batch of hustlers and hard-working niggas that came from many backgrounds, but there was one common denominator; that green dollar bill. They were all grinding for their kids' kids and those kids' kids. Sean was interested in generational wealth but had no children, so everything he did was for a purpose. He wasn't selling his soul for nothing. He had his family on his back, and their future depended on him. It was nothing for him to send one of the young girls in the hood to college. As long as they had a dream, he would help turn it into a reality.

Sean was counting a few hundred-thousand dollars with a blunt dangling in the corner of his mouth. He had a bad redbone with nothing on but a La Perla lingerie set on helping him count the money. They were ducked off in New Orleans, and she would drive the money to New York to Nasir in a few days.

"You not tired?" she asked him as she stifled a yawn. They had been up for a few hours, and she could have sworn Sean had counted that money ten times. Her eyes were bloodshot red, and her stomach grumbled. "Are you hungry?" she asked, knowing that if she was starving he had to be too. He ignored her, not wanting to mess up the count. "I'm ordering room service. What you want?" She pushed the heavy stacks of cash away so she could get up.

Being that he was a man that loved ass, he got a good glance of her cheeks in the lavender thong she had on. Ten minutes later, he was done counting the money and told her to order him a burger and fries with honey mustard.

Sean placed the stacks into four duffel bags and then sat them in the closet. "You remember what to do right?" he asked her again.

She rolled her eyes. "This is not my first time going up there," she reminded him.

"I know, but you smoke and shit, I need you to be in your right mind on the road," he scolded and shook his head while he stared at her.

She crossed her arms and pouted her lips. "What I gotta do for you to know I won't let you down, daddy?"

Sunshine had been making runs for Sean since she was seventeen and now that she was twenty-one, he hadn't been able to stop fucking her and sending her lil young ass on the road. In return, she was living well, courtesy of The Underworld and would do whatever for Sean.

"Nothing, I'm making sure. A nigga be paranoid," he admitted.

She didn't know why. In her years of taking cash up the road, she had been pulled over once and called Sean as soon as she placed the car in park. Her eyes lit up when she mentioned The Underworld, and the only thing the police man did was tip his hat and back away from the car. It was as if she said the magic word, and he got the fuck on. Sunshine wasn't even scared no more. She could make a trip with her eyes closed.

"How about you take a shower? That may help you relax?" she suggested.

Sean didn't need her telling him what the fuck to do, he didn't like that shit. "Nah, how about you go take one, and I'll listen out for the food?"

Sunshine had no problem with that. The room they copped at the Double Tree came with a rainfall shower head, and she had fallen in love with it.

As soon as he heard her humming, he took the bags from the closet and left in a hurry. He had another room on the 8th floor, and that's where he would leave the cash until it was time for her to ride out.

Sean had known her for a while, but that didn't mean a mother fucking thing, he would never let his guard down for no bitch.

Jackie had texted him with the word *Stranger.* He was in the middle of rolling a blunt but stopped to hit her back. Sean kept things short when he was out of town, but he let her know she was on his mind and so were her kids. She would be his first stop when he touched back down in the city.

Sunshine came out of the shower soaking wet. She wrapped a towel around her body and asked about the food.

"Not yet," he told her. He was licking the blunt to conceal it before he showered.

"I'll roll the rest," she offered.

Sean shook his head. "This it for me tonight." He would never let her roll his blunts if he wasn't watching her do it. He had heard horror stories of some of the trifling things bitches did to niggas to set them up.

Sunshine would be fucked if she did something to him because he had already moved the money and if he was dead or even if he wasn't, he would never tell her where the money was. The only person who knew the room number was Miko, and that was because she was the head of finances with The Underworld and had booked the room.

Sean read Jackie's text message, which was a dry "okay" and rolled his eyes. He wanted her to be mushy and carefree with him, but it wasn't her style. And maybe that was why he dug her so much because she didn't cater to him. She didn't chase him, hell, she barely showed any interest.

He looked over at Sunshine as he stood on his feet. She was such a beautifulgirl, but he would never take her serious. This was a business set up that occasionally came with pussy, good pussy at that.

"When you gon' fuck me? Damn, Sean, we been here for two days," she whined.

He smiled at her. "I got you, shawty. Let me wash my dick, a nigga been grinding all day."

Sean grabbed his gun and went to take a shit and a shower. He reentered the suite with nothing on other than his shorts and a pair of white Polo socks. Sunshine was already munching down on her food.

"Why don't you have any tattoos?" she asked.

He looked down at his arms. "Why, do I need any tattoos?"

"You'll be finer with them," she said and shrugged her shoulders, apparently not having a better reason.

He shook his head. "I'm good without them, youngin'."

"So you never wanted one? Not a cross or a rest in peace tattoo?" she asked him.

Sean laughed. "Man, hell nah." He wasn't caught up in the other shit that people thought was cool. If tattoos made him sexier then he didn't want them. Sunshine saying that stupid ass shit told him how shallow she really was, and he always made it connect to why he should be with Jackie. She was older and mature and wasn't caught up in the hype of what was "in" or what was cool.Jackie didn't care about tattoos, designer clothes, nice whips and all that other shit that girls used to replace the important qualities a man should have, such as consistency, respect and loyalty.

Sunshine saw what Sean had instead of what he had going on mentally. He sat beside her and lit the blunt. "What are your goals, Sunshine?"

She wiped her mouth and took a sip of her Sprite. "Go to school for sure."

He was surprised to hear that. "Oh yeah? For what?"

"I wanna do facials and body waxing, it's a lot of money in that right now."

"Well, you done made enough money working for me, so what's your hold up?"

She bit on her bottom lip. "I got bad money habits," she admitted.

"What does that mean?" He had been dirt poor before, so he valued a dollar.

She used her hands to show how much money she had made over the years. "I don't even have $100 right now," she said and shook her head.

Seanhad nothing to say anything; Sunshine was disappointed in her gotdamn self. "Girl, I just gave you ten racks three weeks ago. I thought you stayed with your sister?"

"I ended up moving out into a condo. I'm paying $2400 a month and then my car note is $621."

"Six-hundred dollars a month? How much you put down?" he shouted.

"Three thousand, but my interest rate is high as hell, Sean, almost 14%."

His head was hurting at all the foolish things that left her mouth. "You have got to be kidding me! They raped your young ass at the dealership."

She rolled her eyes. "Money burns a hole in my pocket." Sunshine fucked up any money she got as soon as she got it. She had more designer clothes and purses than her little closet could hold.

"You gotta start saving your money, baby girl. This shit ain't promised," he told her the truth.

She knew that. "And I told you I want to go to school so I can start my own business."

"Yeah, but wanting and doing are two different things."

Sunshine knew that Sean was a smart guy, she trusted him wholeheartedly. "Can I ask you something?"

He nodded his head and then passed her the blunt. "Shoot."

"Is there a way you can hold my money, like put me on payroll and save the rest for me? Sean, I don't wanna be scrounging for pennies. I make too much money to be so damn broke all the time." She had tears welling in her eyes, but she was right. She had easily made a hundred-thousand with him, and for her to say she had nothing to her name was horrible.

"Yeah, I can do that for you." He would help her out. "Don't be blowing me up begging for your money cus I ain't gon' give it to you. Matter fact, write down all your bills, gas and all that, and add it up. What we gon' do is give you that amount with a hundred dollars extra every two weeks. The rest of it will be your savings and for emergencies only," he told her. The idea of finally saving her money sounded good. "Sunshine, you gotta do better. All them designer bags don't mean shit if you can't put no money in 'em," he let her know.

She wiped her damp face. "I'm about to get on it, Sean, for real."

He finished up his food and then dragged the cart outside of the door. "Tomorrow we gon' do some ripping and running, and then you'll get on the road around eight," he told her. He needed sleep. Sean had been ripping and running with hardly any rest. His body was shutting down on him.

"You sleepy?" she asked.

He nodded his head. "Hell yeah," he yawned.

Sunshine really wanted to have sex tonight, but his bloodshot eyes and slumped shoulders told her it wasn't happening this time around.

Sean still wanted to dick her down, but he needed a few hours of shut-eye to regain some of his lost energy. He laid down and as soon as his head hit the pillow, he was knocked out.

The next morning, Sean woke up to something wet and warm on his penis. Sunshine knew how to wake a nigga up. He slowly opened his eyes, and a wide smile crept across his face.

She pulled his boxers way past his knees. "Goooood morning, Mr. Carter," she said sexily. Sunshine handed him a rolled blunt, but he shook his head. "I'm good." He used his hand to push her head back to where it belonged.She used her tongue and her lips to bring him to life. His butter pecan penis sprang from a shy three-inches to almost nine and a half.

"Shit," he groaned and moaned as she licked from the base of his dick to the tip. Sunshine's tongue was abnormally fat and long, and that's probably why she talked funny. Her head bobbed all over his lap, and red and blonde extensions were everywhere as she did her best to please him. Sean was satisfied with her advances.

He was brought as close to an orgasm as possible, but rarely did he release via fellatio. He preferred to be balls deep before nutting. Sean pulled her up while bending over to get a condom out of his jeans.

"I'm on the pill," she told him.

He gave her a look before saying, "Come on, mama, we gotta practice safe sex." He would never run up in her ass raw.

Sunshine remained quiet as he slid the rubber on his dick and then picked her up and sat her right down on his hardness.

"Fuck!" Every time she fucked Sean she felt like she was losing her virginity all over again. He was big. And fat.

He moved his hips slowly right along with hers, and she rode him with intensity. Gratification and satisfaction was all over her face, and she smiled down at him. "Does it feel good?" She wanted to know if she was making progress with him being that he was so silent while she gave him sloppy toppy.

He nodded his head. "Make that ass move." He wanted to feel her cheeks vibrating.

Sunshine knew how to work her pussy muscles and twerk that ass at the same damn time and when she began the combination, his eyes rolled to the back of his head as he held onto his bottom lip to keep from screaming out her name.

Sunshine loved that tiny scar under his lip that ran alongside his chin. She was turned on even more when he pushed his nails into the side of her hips.

"Right...there." He didn't want her to stop whatever the fuck she was doing.He had sex a lot, all the time. It was a sort of hobby for him. Sean enjoyed getting rode more than anything, and Sunshine always excelled in that position. But now he wanted her from the back.

"Get up," he said roughly.

She wondered how he treated his bitch. Although she had never seen him with a woman or asked him if he had one, the way he moved she was sure he had a lady in his bed waiting on him to get there. Sean kept things business with her, but he never passed on fucking her. And as soon as they were done, he went back to being her boss and her, the employee.

Sean never called or texted if it had nothing to do with business. He never hugged or kissed her. Things never went there, and Sunshine knew to not even try. She would take whatever dick he gave her. Sean was fine, but this was her only source of income. She would be an idiot to cut her money off for catching feelings for him.

"Damn, baby," she moaned as he slid in her from behind.

Sean fucked her with no remorse. He had caught a glimpse of the time on a clock on the wall, and he had shit to do. Sean only took his time with women he cared about, and Sunshine's name was not on that list.

"Yeah, hell yeah," she panted as yet another nut rolled out of her. Sean closed his eyes and put his all into her once more before busting in the condom. He fell back on his legs, breathing loudly while she finished herself off.

"Shit, nigga." She was out of breath.

Sean got up to pee and shower again. The smell of sex was in the room, and it was giving him a headache. When he took the condom off, it was covered in blood, and he was fucking disgusted.

He waited until he was out of the shower, face washed and teeth brushed before he came back into the room to dress and ask Sunshine, "Aye, are you on your cycle?"

She shrugged her shoulders. "I'm spotting, why?" she answered as if her bleeding on him was perfectly fine. It was not. Sunshine had him fucked up, and he would never in his life touch her again.

"My dick was covered in blood."

"You wore a condom," she reminded him.

He was turned off completely. "Sunshine, you not my bitch. Don't let me fuck you like that again."

She smirked, "Oh, so you do have a girlfriend?" She had always wanted to know.

He shook his head and grabbed his suitcase so he could get dressed. It was time for him to make better decisions about who he dipped in and out of. Sunshine was cute but lost and broke, he had no business even crossing the line with her. In all actuality, that was probably his tenth or maybe twelfth time fucking her, so it was about time for him to dispose of that pussy anyway. She was bound to catch feelings, and that was a headache he did not want to deal with.

He was relieved when he waved her goodbye way before schedule and headed to the airport. Sean couldn't wait to tell Dr. Robinson about this turning point in life, she would be well pleased with his maturity.

After he made it back to the peach state, the first thing he did was take a good hot bath. Sean low-key suffered from obsessive compulsive disorder, and he could barely relax on the plane because he felt as if her grimy blood was still speckled on his penis.

Sean scrubbed his dick for a good thirty minutes before being satisfied that he was squeaky clean again. He placed a call to the Chinese joint up the street and ordered delivery and then checked on his traps while rolling a few blunts to last him through the night.

After a successful run, he remained low-key and off the map, not leaving the house unless it was for more blunts and food. He was sort of superstitious when it came to his routine; a routine he had in motion for a very long time. Sean hadn't successfully stayed out of jail all these years by being some flashy ass nigga. He did things in order.

A knock at the door took him from the magazine he was flipping through full of old-school cars, white chicks and silver engines. He assumed it was his food being that he was not expecting any company. However, it wasn't Chung Yi with his chicken and shrimp fried rice, it was Jackie.

"Oh, you know where I stay?" he asked sarcastically. She rolled her eyes and showed him the white grocery bag of what was most likely food she had cooked. "How you know I was in town?" was his second question to the lady standing before him.

She huffed and made her way in. "I'll heat this up for you, your Chinese food is here as well," she let him know and went into the kitchen.

Sean smirked as he watched that fat ass walked away from him. He hurriedly took the food from the man and told him he could keep the change. An almost twenty-dollar tip was more than enough for their service.

Jackie was heating the food up when he joined her in the kitchen. "How you know I want your cooking?"

She gave him a look that told him today wasn't a good day for her, so he pushed the jokes aside and seriously asked her, "What's wrong, Jack?"

Those weren't tears falling down her face, were they? He hadn't seen her cry too many times. She was such a hard ass. He didn't cower over her knowing she would most likely push him away.

She used her left hand, showing her wedding ring without trying to, and Sean cringed at the three-carat diamonds and band.

"You know what I want?"

If I did you would have it, he thought to himself.

"I want a fairytale." She took a deep breath and then crossed her arms across her chest ."Every day I want it to be peaches and cream. I've already had one shitty relationship and will never have another one. And you know what else, Sean? I don't care if love isn't perfect because I want a perfect love. I want that shit to be like the movies," she cried. Her body shook as she finally told him how she truly felt. "You look at me like I'm all you want. Even though I know you out here fucking bitches, you still hold me on this invisible pedestal that makes me feel like I'm worthy of that fairytale."

He remained silent, knowing she had more to say. He could feel it with every word she spoke.

"I pray for you, Sean, every single morning when I wake up I ask God to keep you. Cus ain't nobody cared about me and my kids the way you have, not even *him...*" she spoke of her husband.

He never deserved you Jackie.

"You gotta cut em' all off. Every one of them hoes gotta go." She made a scissor-like motion with her fingers to show her seriousness.

He nodded his head. "All right." He would give her the world if she asked for it.

"And as a man, you need to tell my sons because...I can't do that." She would never be able to mumble those words to them. How could she explain how mama fell in love with daddy's best friend? It was fucked up, but Jackie didn't care. She wanted love, and Sean had been damn near begging her for permission to love her. So here she was, laying it all on the line. She had faith that this time around things would be right...and if they weren't, she was cutting him off and tucking her heart far away.

"I will." He had no problem telling Kevin and Jonathan what was going on, although he was sure they already knew.

"And I'm not quitting my job," she argued.

He smiled, loving that feisty, "I got my own money don't need a nigga for nothing" sass she had about herself.

"Okay, Jackie, that's fine."

She took a deep breath. "Do you love me? Can you love me?" She knew she wasn't the youngest or the nicest. Jackie had a lot to work on, and she was willing to do so.

The funny thing was, she was perfect in his eyes. God clearly had taken His time with her, she was molded in His image. Jackie was an angel in Sean's eyes. She moved gracefully and that sharp attitude, he wouldn't change a thing about it. She wasn't easily impressed which would keep him on his toes forever. Sean appreciated the challenge that Jackie presented. She wasn't with the shits, and he didn't plan on slacking up either.

"Yeah I do, but I think you know that already." He stroked the side of his face.

Sean's phone rang, but he didn't go back into the living room to catch the call. This moment right here...was something he had been waiting on for a very long time. He couldn't miss this.

"Well, I don't love you yet," she let him know. Jackie wasn't a liar.

He laughed, "Ain't worried about that, I know what to do." He was confident that in due time everything would be right between the two.

"And another thing, all of that late-"

He walked over to her, and she stopped talking. Sean told her that he was all ears and there was no need for her to pause the conversation. "I'm listening."

She tried to back up, but there was no space available to do so, so she backed into the counter.

"I don't want you coming in late at-"

He was confused. "You moving in?"

She shook her head. "Hell no."

"I'll cop you a new crib, *us* a new crib."

Jackie pursed her lips together. She definitely wanted something new, but wouldn't just come out and say that.

"What else you need me to do?" he asked as he pulled her close and wrapped his arm around her waist. *Your wish is my command.*

"Nothing, Sean. I don't need nothing from you but consistency, attention and respect."

"What about some dick?" He pushed his penis into the center of her body.

"Who's here?" she questioned.

He looked at her. "Come on, you know ain't nobody in my shit." His home was his haven, everyone couldn't know where he laid his head.

She didn't know shit. Sean wasn't a saint. "When was the last time you had sex?" she asked.

He blew a breath of frustration. "Why is that important to you?" He never understood why women asked questions they really weren't prepared to know the answer to. Did Jackie really want to know how good Sunshine's pussy felt on his dick? Or how she rode him until the sun came up? Or about how she could gag on his dick? Nah, Jackie couldn't handle that.

"It's very important, cus I'm not about to let you up in me-"

"I use a rubber every time."

Jackie didn't have a valuable argument. She was defeated.

"What's next on your list of topics to handle?" he asked her. Sean stepped backward and leaned against the island in the kitchen.

"I want you to promise that you won't be in the streets forever."

That was the one thing he didn't want to lie about. "Jacquelyn..." He used her real name, and that told her some bullshit was about to fall from his lips.

"Sean..."

"As a real nigga, I can tell you that no man wants to hustle forever. I have a number in my head and once I hit the ballpark of that number, I'm wrapping it up."

That was somewhat acceptable. "And how far off are you from that number?"

She was smart, Sean had to remember that. "It depends on what these next few runs look like," he gave her a somewhat closed answer.

"I don't want to visit you in jail or at a cemetery." And that's really all she had to say about it. Jackie couldn't stay any longer, she had to get to work. That was when he noticed she was in scrubs. "Don't forget to talk to the boys, then we can begin our fairytale," she told him with a hopeful look in her eyes.

Sean smiled at her. "I will stop by there tonight. I know them lil niggas already know though," he went on and told her.

She shook her head. "I don't care what they think they know, tell it to them straight."

Sean walked her to the door and gave her a tight hug. "Let me know when you make it to work."

She held on to the hug a little longer, maybe because that was something they never did. "Are you really touchy?"

He shook his head. "Let me do me, don't start that shit." Jackie would be brought out of her comfort zone completely. Whatever she did with that nigga would be erased; how he broke her confidence, betrayed her trust and made her this cold-hearted woman. Sean was prepared to put in overtime to take those tainted thoughts away. Jackie deserved a love she never had to question, and he would give it to her wholeheartedly.

About thirty minutes after she left, he was on the couch smoking and had a question, so he called her.

"Pulling up at work," she said as soon as she answered her phone.

Yeah, he would have to get that mouth together too with her lil mean ass. "What made you change your mind?"

Curiosity killed the cat.Plus, he was a street nigga. Sean had been pursuing her for a while, and she never budged. He wanted to know why now.

Jackie took her seatbelt off and placed her car in park. "I went to church," she started off. He waited on her to continue. "It's been years since I been to church and this pastor...he didn't even know, but he called on me and told me that God keeps trying to push me forward but I'm like a rubber band...I keep bouncing back into my past." Jackie took a deep breath before telling him what the man of God said next. "And then he told me that God has already sent what I've been secretly praying for, but my past has a blinder over my eyes, and that's why I can't see the blessing. And I knew it was you, Sean, you are my blessing."

She didn't plan on sharing that with him ever. Jackie had a chip on her shoulder from losing her husband, so maybe it was because she blamed God. Or maybe it was because they weren't doing well, and the horrid things that came to light after she lost him brought her to her knees.

Jackie wasn't sure, but that church service had blessed her in a million different ways. From the praise and worship to the sermon, she knew that everything was working together for her good. The Pastor was right on time with his prophecy.

"From day one, you've never left our side. Even when I was being a bitch, you made sure my kids was straight, and I'm thankful for that. I want to grow to love you, I know you're it for me. All I ask is that you be patient."

That was touching, it really was, but he had to let her know that if she really didn't want to be with him, she didn't have to. It was never any pressure on a relationship. Sean was a mover and a shaker anyway, and the words Jackie had used didn't move him in the way he thought they would.

"I don't want you to think you gotta make yourself like me or even love me. I'm still going to do for y'all."

She figured he would take that the wrong way. "Sean, I like you. What are you talking about?"

He begged to think otherwise right about now. "Cus the Pastor told you to like me or what?"

She shook her head. "The one time I open up to you, and this is what you do? You question every single word?" She was shocked.

"I'm saying, don't be with me cus you fell out at church, be with me cus you want to." It was plain and simple.

"Fuck you!"

The call ended, and that was cool with him because he had another call coming in.

"Wassup," he said to his cousin.

Boo was coughing profusely into the phone, most likely smoking on something potent.

"Not shit, you back?"

Sean's mind was on Jackie, and he really wanted to pull up at her job. "Yeah." He wasn't in the mood to be around nobody or to be sitting on the phone.

"You coming out the house?"

Sean decided to wrap this conversation up. "Nah, I'll hit you later," he told him and hung the phone up.

Boo looked at the phone and mumbled, "Sensitive ass nigga." He and his cousin were too close for their own good.

Sean sat back and lit the blunt again. He needed to get high right away. Jackie had fucked his mind up with her revelation.

He woke up with a glob of slob on his hand and someone beating on the door. Instantly, he grabbed the nine sitting on top of the coffee table. He yawned as he got up and went to the door, barefoot and shirtless. That weed had him gone for a few hours, Sean didn'teven know he fell asleep. He saw who was at the door and unlocked it to let her in.

"You ain't see me call you?"

He yawned again. "Do it look like I been up?" He wasn't in the mood for her nasty ass attitude.

"Listen, Sean, it took a lot out of me to come over here and keep it real with you. I don't cry, I don't do all of that-"

"I don't care about what you don't do. I'm not that nigga, so you ain't gotta keep being mean to me. I did nothing to deserve that," he spat. Here he was speaking out on how he felt....shawty was changing him already. She was stuck. "Oh now you ain't got nothing to say?" Sean wasn't with the shits.

She made a move that he wasn't expecting her to do, maybe because she never let him kiss her. There were nights he would silently beg to kiss her face, and she would tell him no.

Jackie planted her lips on top of his and moaned loudly, "I'm yours."

She submitted. Sean kissed her back, not caring that his breath was probably funky as hell. He slid his tongue into the tiny slit she made available for him and danced across her teeth and then smooched her lips over and over again.

"Don't hurt me," she whispered.

He could have told her the same thing, but he didn't. They shared that one kiss for quite some time.

Jackie really needed to get back to work, but she needed a fix. She used her hand to let him know what she had a taste for.

"What you doing?" His voice was low and husky as he watched her drop on her knees. Sean would never let her do that. "Get up, baby." He held her up and walked her back toward the wall and slid her scrubs down.

Jackie pulled his dick out of his boxers. "Do it how I like it," she asked him kindly.

"Don't tell me what to do." Sean was about to start putting his foot down. Jackie was bossy as fuck.

He grabbed her neck and moved it to the left, and then he planted his lips in a place where he knew she'd go weak.Jackie's eyes rolled back as he turned her into jello. It always felt like the first time when he entered her. Jackie held on to her bottom lip as he pushed inside of her without protection. She could have stopped and reminded him, but she knew she wasn't having any more damn kids. Sean groaned as he made it home.

"This been my pussy, ain't it?" He knew the answer, but her saying yes would shift him into turbo gear. She was on the clock, so they didn't have time to hit the bed, but this quickie would be on her mind all day. Sean was sure of that.

"Yes, it has!" she shrieked as he fucked her hard against the wall. The paintings he had on the wall shook as they threatened to fall, but Sean could give two fucks about those million-dollar paintings. He had to let her know what she had committed to.

"It's mine, so I'ma fuck you whenever I want to, and you gon' let me kiss you wherever, ain't you?" He needed to know that they were on the same page. He wasn't holding back with her any longer. Sean pulled his dick out and smiled at the sight of her creamy juices covering his penis. "This ma'fucka is soaking, baby!" He was pleased, well-pleased.

"It's for you, Sean, it's for you."

Her face had a lil sweat on it, and he eagerly licked it off, loving the salty taste paired with lavender and vanilla from whatever oil she used this morning while getting dressed.

He went back in and hit for a home run. Explosions and fireworks were heard behind him, but he knew it was only him cumming and her squirting. The feeling was bliss. The temperature was hot, yet she was warm. He pulled out of her, spilling the leftover semen on his hardwood floors.

Jackie wanted more, she wasn't done with him just yet. She dropped to her knees again, not caring that he didn't want her down there and placed his wet and seeping penis into her mouth and sucked him until he swelled like a balloon.

"Jack..." He tried to warn her that head, good head, especially....amazing head, made him do things in return that she didn't have time for. "*Work*, baby, you gotta get back to work. Don't start something you can't finish."

Jackie ignored him and moved his hands back so she could take all of him while looking directly into his orbs as she did so.

"What you mother fucking doing with that tongue?" He eyed her as she stroked his dick while taking her lips and tongue elsewhere. Oh, she was a lil' nasty something.

Jackie had never done the shit she was doing right now, but this was the perks of commitment. He didn't even know he had a *spot* under his balls. It was unknown and forbidden, but she had found it with her tongue.

Sean wasn't no bitch, but he did shout out louder than expected. "Shit!" He pulled away, knowing he had to give her double what she had just given him. "Lay down, nah...take all that shit off first," he said as he went to get something from the living room.

Jackie did as he asked. When he returned, she was butt naked in the hallway of his house. She was glistening too. He lit his blunt and puffed on it twice before going back into the living room.

"How long we got?"

"Like nine minutes," she said after checking her watch.

Sean licked his lips. "I can do so much in that time." He was confident that she could bust two more nuts before then. He didn't wait on her for a response, he raised her Amazon legs to the top of the ceiling and went looking for the honey pot as if he were a bee that hadn't eaten. Jackie's body melted as soon as he placed his lips at her clitoris, and then he had the nerve to blow.

"What cha' doing?" Her southern twang turned him on even more than he already was.

Sean licked, bit, nibbled, pulled and did everything under the sun to her pussy before he went in for the kill and literally feasted on her like she was Sunday dinner. A four-course meal was presented before him the way the nut poured out of that one little hole.

Sean hungrily licked and lapped it all, wanting more if he could have it.Jackie was his favorite meal, his favorite candy, his favorite flavor and so much more. Jackie humped her pussy into his face as he used his tongue to dig deeper into her.

"I can't take no more," she exhaled and dropped her head onto the floor, but tapping out in the last two minutes was unacceptable.

Sean inserted himself into her and gave her long and deep strokes until she begged him to fuck her harder for that last nut. That last nut would be sure to send her over the edge.

"It's coming out right now!" she wept. Jackie had let her guard down and had turned into a kitten as she purred while tears fell down her face. He was making her feel so fucking good.

Sean stroked and stroked and stroked until he too came. "God damn it!" he panted loudly.

Jackie got up and quickly went to wash up in the half bathroom at the end of the hallway. When she was put back together, she walked slowly into the hallway, looking for her clothes.

"Here," he said and handed her the bottoms to her scrubs first and then her panties.

"I sweated my hair out," she complained.

"I'll get it fixed, ain't no thing," he said while chewing on a piece of baked chicken.

"I gotta go, will you be here all night?"

Sean shook his head. "Nah, I'm actually about to shower and head to your crib." He looked at her directly so she could see he was serious about doing the right thing and taking the next steps.

She smiled sheepishly, and sort of unsure but confident at the same time...if that made any kind of sense. "Good, well I guess I'll see you when I get off. It's food in the fridge," she added.

Sean walked her to the door for the second time today. "What I want ain't in there." He winked his eye at his older and very jazzy lady. Shit still seemed unreal, she was finally his.

"Hopefully you had enough to last you until then," she shot back and licked her lips, thinking of how good he tasted. Jackie wanted him just as much as he wanted her.

It felt good when everyone was on the same page, when shit was flowing just right. That's what life is about, making your money and kicking it with the one you wanna spend the rest of your days with.

"I did." He kissed her forehead and pushed her gently over the threshold. "If you don't gon' and leave, I'ma have your ass bent over this couch."

Jackie really had to get back to work, so she left, honking once she hit the end of the driveway. Sean closed the door and locked it behind him.

"Finally." He got the woman of his dreams. *Finally.*

Chapter 4

"That money mix up with that greed, it happens all the time." – Meek Mill

Jackie's mother was confused and had a lot of questions, a bunch of them as she sat across from Sean and her daughter at some fancy ass restaurant she'd rather not be at.

"So, Jackie say you in the streets. Is that true? She has sons, do you want them in the streets too?" she asked right out.

Sean damn near choked on the water he was sipping.

Jackie took a long deep breath and patted her new boyfriend's back. She tried to warn him that she was as real as it gets, but he swore he could handle meeting the parents. However, this little woman was more than he bargained for.

"Uh, well I have businesses as well. I'm a part owner of a casino in Las Vegas, actually it's the seventh largest one-"

She didn't want to hear that shit. "When are you retiring? Do you have some money put up for them if your ass get snatched up?" She had a lot of concerns.

Sean looked at Jackie, wondering what the fuck she had told her mother. He planned on having a long ass talk with her as soon as they got in the car. She couldn't be pillow talking. Sean was more than a local weed man; he was the plug.

"Ma'am, with all due respect-"

She was waiting on him to continue. "I'm listening, *Sean,*" she said his name with so much filth.

He hated that he was being judged by how he made his money. "I come from a good family-"

"Your mother Neet, ain't it?"

Sean's face scrunched up, praying he didn't have to cuss this woman out for disrespecting his mother. He nodded his head. "Yeah, that's her."

"Yes, the gambler. That's your mother, and you say you come from a good family?"

"Well, y'all ain't the Kennedy's either," he shot back. Jackie gave him a shocked look, but he didn't care. He was a grown ass man, and she was grown too. "Look, what I'm trying to say is that I'm a good person. I'm aware of what your daughter has been through, and I'm not here to hurt her or put her in danger, and I love those boys like they're my own. I'll never do the wrong thing around them. What I do outside of her house stays there. I'm working towards going as legit as I can and have been doing so for many years," he told her with sincerity.

By now their food had arrived, so her mother said, "Let us pray."

He was relieved that the conversation was changing because she had been grilling into him since they sat down almost forty minutes ago.

"Father God, we thank you for this meal. We thank you for life, and we thank you for your grace and your mercy. God, I don't know this fellow my daughter claims she loves, but you do.God, you know him inside and out and upside down. If he is *not* the one you, show Jackie in her sleep. You send her a dream tonight, oh God. You let her know clear as day to run far away. And God, we thank you for my precious grandbabies, keep your loving arms around them and bless this overpriced food. In Jesus name I pray, amen." She ended the prayer with a smile and then rolled her eyes at Sean.

"I'm going to give you a chance. One, not two. You better not put your hands on her or stick your lil pecker nowhere else other than her-"

Jackie exclaimed, "All right now, mama. He got it, eat your food," she finally chimed in.

Sean smiled at her. She was a tough cookie, but now he knew where his baby got it from. "You gon' love me, ma," he told her with confidence.

He had never met a chick he was messing with family before, and he was honored that although Jackie was older and not in need of her mother's approval, she was really serious about them meeting each other.

She pointed her steak knife in his direction before she used it to cut her prime rib and told him, "You don't get to call me that yet."

The word, "Yet" gave him hope, and he was cool with that. After they declined dessert and the check was paid, they made sure Jackie's mother got into her Buick safe and sound before waving her goodbye.

"If she like me by Christmas, we gotta get moms a new car," he told his girl.

She patted his back. "You did real good, baby." She was relieved they didn't get into it. "She hated *him*..." her voice trailed as she thought about her ex-husband.

Sean thought to himself, *Yeah, me too.* He opened the door to let her slide her thick ass into the front seat and then he walked over to the driver's seat and got in.

"You wanna go get a few drinks or head home?" He was down with whatever she was, especially since he would be in New York for the rest of the week.

Sean kept his home and copped Jackie a new one. She loved it and was still in the process of decorating. He had tried over and over again to throw her his American Express card with no limit, but homegirl told him she had her own money.With each check, Jackie did little by little when she could have had the entire house decked out in no time.

He saw that it was very important that she held her own. She paid the light, water and cable bill and still gave her boys allowance every two weeks. Sean didn't trip on her because he would be contradicting himself. He finally had an independent chick that didn't have her hand out every other day for some pennies, so he considered that a blessing.

They rode through the city of Atlanta looking for a bar that also served Mexican food since Jackie swore her stomach was still growling. The one thing he was sure to teach her once they made it official was how to roll his blunts.

Now, every morning when he stayed at her house there was a fresh one on the nightstand. Jackie kept a smile on his face, his stomach full and his balls empty, what more could a man ask for? His money was right, family happy and his team was progressing and becoming their own bosses. Life was grand in his eyes.

He used his spare hand to massage her neck while he drove. At the sight of her pearling his blunt, his dick got hard.

"You sure you don't wanna drink at home?" he asked, ready to bend her over right fucking now.

She could tell by the tone of his voice what he wanted to do. She had known him for many years, but with them spending real time together lately, actual quality time, she was picking up on everything.

Jackie's eyes became hooded as she looked at him with matched lust. "I'm following your lead."

"Say less." Sean did an illegal U-turn in the street, hit Interstate 85 and headed to Jackie's new crib. He bobbed his head to the beat of some song that Jackie's son was working on. They had turned one of the rooms in the basement into a studio for the boys. Jackie was against it, thinking they would neglect their studies to sit in the studio all night, but he convinced her to let them go ahead with the studio, knowing it would keep them in the house safe.

Jackie quickly agreed with that. Black boys in their new nice neighborhood were eye sores, and she didn't want any trouble.

Sean put the boys in private school but promised them they could see their friends whenever they wanted to once the weekend came. He ensured them that a quality education would be more appreciated in the long run, although they couldn't see it now.

Jackie bit her tongue and almost had a heart attack when Sean gave her a check for forty-thousand to pay Woodward Academy to enroll them in the middle of the school year. She told him it wasn't necessary and that they could stay at their old school, but Clayton County's school system was failing tremendously, and Sean wanted better for the kids.

Once they made it home, music was blasting loudly, and Sean let Jackie curse them out on her own. He now had the blunt she had already rolled in the car lit and went to the patio to smoke before taking a shower and joining her in bed.

He phoned his mother to check on her since he was heading out bright and early in the morning, but she didn't answer. Neet would hit him back as soon as she saw the call. It was very rare that her only son's calls went unanswered, so he wasn't tripping.

He finished his blunt in less than fifteen minutes and tossed the roach out to the wind.

"I want a dog," was the first thing Jackie told him once he made it to the bedroom.

"Did you cut the alarm on?" he asked as he pulled his sneakers and jeans off.

She crossed her arms. "You ain't hear me?" she asked, knowing he did.

"Yeah, but you already know the world is yours. Jackie, get the dog if you really want it."

"I want you to get it for me and bring it home with a red bow and all of that," she beamed.

He shook his head. "We in la-la land tonight, huh?" She was getting mushy with him, and he loved it but always kept cool.

Jackie ignored that comment and crossed her legs as she sat up in the bed. "Do you think the boys are smoking? It smelled like weed in the basement."

Good thing his back was turned to her because his face would have probably given the truth away being that the question caught him off guard.

"I doubt it, they good kids," he lied. Them lil niggas smoked liked chimneys. He stayed leaving them buds in the first drawer of their dresser. Sean told them to not cop weed from no one, he would gladly supply their habit as long as they didn't smoke with other niggas, cop from other niggas, mix shit with their weed, attempt to sell weed or go broke trying to get high. Those were all "hell-no's" in his book. Sean also let them know that if their mama found out it was on them. He would have nothing to do with it.

"Yeah, they good, but what that got to do with them smoking? You smoke," she reminded him.

"It's to keep me calm," he argued back, which was the truth. Without that herbal remedy, a lot of mother fuckers would be dead.

"Sean, whatever, that's a mind thing." She shook her head in disbelief.

He was for real though. "Nah, my therapist prescribed me some marijuana pills too." With a pair of boxers and socks in hand, he was headed to the bathroom to wash his ass so he could lay up with his Queen.

"Therapist? You have a therapist? For what?"

He didn't even realize he had shared that with her, especially since no one knew. It wasn't necessarily a secret, but it wasn't something he openly shared with niggas either.

In the African-American community, therapy was looked down on. People automatically assumed that if you saw a shrink, therapist, counselor or psychologist that you were crazy in the head, but that was not true. Everyone wasn't comfortable openly speaking about their feelings with family or close friends, and some people didn't wanna talk to the preacher man down at the church.

Sean had researched several religions and of course, he chose God and Jesus, but still...his therapist was the answer to his problems and his claim to peace. He trusted her and looked forward to their sessions.

"Nothing in particular," he finally answered, which was the absolute truth. There was no issue he was dealing with, but he enjoyed her. If she could take him off her calendar, she probably would. Nothing was wrong with him.

"Sean, I trust you, okay, and I trust you around my kids. So if you low-key dealing with some shit or you have some kind of mental disorder-"

He couldn't believe her right now. "What? You gon' leave me?" he wanted to know.

She took a deep breath and chose her words carefully. "Don't put words in my mouth."

"Well, say what you wanna say then." He was offended already, it was her best bet to speak with caution.

"Going to therapy is something you share with the person you're dating, that's not something you keep to yourself."

He went into the bathroom to lay his things down for his shower and then stood at the doorpost to address her. "Jackie, it's a lot you don't know about me. A lot I'll share over time, and a lot of shit I never will. I live a hectic life, I've seen a lot of shit and I do a lot of shit...that's not for you to know."

"But you think you telling your therapist helps? What if she go to the cops?"

"You think I'm stupid? She don't know shit about that life, and speaking on that, be mindful of what you tell your mother," he warned.

"Why? She know how this shit go-"

He didn't care. "You heard what I said. My business is my business, so don't tell her *my* business. Whatever she already know needs to be it." That wasn't up for debate.

Jackie knew he was for real, so she simply nodded her head and said, "Got you."

He was done with the conversation in relations to his therapy sessions and her mean ass mama, so he went to shower.

When he was dressed for bed, Jackie was already sleep, lights off and all. So, he climbed in behind her and pulled her close. When she spoke, he knew she wasn't fully knocked out.

"I don't want to ever feel like I don't know the person I'm with." She had more to say. "He kept so much from me, not enough, but a lot, and I don't want to be blindsided when it comes to you. If you going through something, let me be there, if you dealing with something, I'm here. You don't have to feel like you need a therapist."

She was jealous, insecure, worried and questioning her position in her life.

"If I told you my therapist was a man, would you still feel this way?"

She turned towards him, eyes barely seen because the room was dark. "The thing is, I know you wouldn't be pouring your heart out to another nigga, that's a fact, so was you about to lie?"

"Are you going to do this every time I tell you something?" he asked. She had trust issues.

"Not if you don't give me a reason to," she quickly shot back.

Sean was tired, no longer in the mood for sex. He kissed her forehead. "If I could erase your worries I would, but I can't, so all I ask is that you start fresh with me, Jackie. Don't bring that shit into what we got."

She knew he was right, but still...little miss therapist needed to be exed out of the picture. "Can I go to your next session?" she asked.

He shook his head. "No, if you wanted to go without being nosey then yeah I would love that, but to check her out? Nah. She's cute, I'll gon' and tell you that. She a foreign chick, big ass, nice titties, green eyes, all of that," he kept it one hundred with her.

Jackie wanted to choke him. "What else?"

He sat up and cut the lamp on that sat on the nightstand. "What else what?"

"You fucked her?"

He shook his head. "I don't mix business with personal."

"Why don't you have any kids? Why haven't you ever brought a girl over to meet us?" She started thinking about his life before she was attracted to his fine ass.

Kids? Sean didn't want kids, not now or ever. And maybe that was another reason he chose to settle down with Jackie, she was done with bearing children.

"I do have a kid, well I fathered a child. She got a daddy though. Now can we go to sleep? My flight leaves at six," he said.

"What you mean? All these secrets in one night...you're driving me crazy!" she spazzed.

"It's nothing." He was nonchalant as fuck, Sean had always been that way.

"What you mean it's nothing? You got a whole ass kid out here, and it's nothing?"

"It was a mistake, and her mama remarried. She got a good ass father. I fucks with homie," he told him.

"And does she know you?"

Sean shook his head. He didn't ask to be around or known. He had no reason to come and fuck up her life. He was good with how things were. And honestly, he wasn't one hundred percent sure the child was his. Half of him knew he needed to get a DNA test, but the nigga in him really didn't care enough to make that happen. Sean had no father and had no desire to be a father, at least not to a daughter. He had been breaking hearts since his dick could get hard and knew that karma was real. With Jackie's sons, parenting came easy. He kept it real with them and in return, they did the same.

"I don't even know you." Her voice was unsure and shaky as she peeled the comforter back to sleep in the guest room.

"Where are you going, man?" He wasn't in the mood for this shit.

She shook her head as she got up and put her robe on. "I need some space, I can't be around you right now."Jackie was lost as a mother fucker.

"Come back to bed, that room isn't even furnished," he reminded her.

"I don't care, I'll sleep on the couch." She was never too good to hit the floor either, Jackie had been homeless before.

He didn't want her kids to think they were beefing already. "Jack!" He got up and tried to grab hold of her before she placed her hand on the knob.

"What the fuck else are you lying about, Sean? Huh? Cus something tells me that it's more."

ŋ

New York was New York. He was a Southerner all day long, so New York was nothing to him. The weather was too cold, and so was everyone's personality. Every time he touched down he anticipated his return home. Jackie made him breakfast this morning, so that told him she wasn't too pissed at him. He called her when he landed, but she sent him to voicemail. She would be all right.

They hadn't been together a good year and the few things he had disclosed, she ran and told her mother, so Sean was slowing down with the late night pillow talking.

He trusted Jackie, but that trust didn't extend to her family. He couldn't blame anyone other than himself if shit blew up in his face. His freedom meant everything to him, and that was something he couldn't play around with.

Jackie wouldn't know shit else concerning how he moved. She already didn't know much, but the little she did know was for her safety. He planned on putting her through some tests to see where her head and heart was.

She was a lil' gutter, but he had to be one hundred percent sure that if shit the fan, she could hold her own. Sean was praying he didn't jump off the bridge with this relationship thing, but in due time everything would figure itself out.

The trash in his loft was stinking from the hallway, and he was surprised that the Homeowner's Association hadn't called or emailed him about the smell.

After he unlocked the door and turned the alarm off, he took the bag and tossed it down the chute.He lit a candle and cleaned out the fridge as well, the smell was making him sick to his stomach. He ended up opening the door to the balcony to let some cool air come through the place.

He had a few hours to spare before he had to meet up with his niggas, so he went back downstairs and crossed the street to have lunch and a beer before taking a much-needed nap.

When he woke up, he called Papa to see where they were linking up, but he sounded very unsure over the line.

"Is you alright, nigga?" he asked, never being one to bite his tongue, and Papa wasn't either, so he didn't know what was up.

"Did Nas call you?"

Sean told him that he just got in town and hadn't spoken to anyone.If it had nothing to do with business, he didn't really communicate with anyone.

"Oh, cus from what I was told, Polo didn't want you at his house, but I don't know, nigga, call Nas," he said.

Sean knew he didn't come up here for nothing. "Why didn't no one say that before I switched my whole week around? And fuck that nigga!" He wasn't holding his nuts over that slimy mother fucker. Sean did what any real nigga would have done, and that was handle the situation. He had no reason to bring Lauren into his beef with Nasir, if anything, he should have touched Jordyn, but Sean wasn't grimy. He didn't wish bad on anyone, and Jordyn had done nothing to him.

"I feel the same way, trust me," Papa told him.

Sean told him that he was about to rap with Nas and then hung up the phone. Nasir wanted his ass kissed, and Sean wasn't the one. He was waiting on the perfect time to cut ties with The Underworld and no, that wasn't right now because they were up right now.

Sean was having his way and getting a lot of paper, but didn't enjoy the set-up or dynamic of The Underworld. He felt as if he was at the bottom of the totem pole, though he did the most work.

What did Nasir do was always his question? He had never seen the nigga put in no time, yet his take was the largest. Shit didn't add up to him. And on many occasions, he wanted to ask the other members of The Underworld how that shit made them feel. They were all wealthy, but that didn't mean shit to Sean. He still wanted everything that was due. And it wasn't greed, it was fairness. Shit wasn't fair.

"What's this about I can't come to the meeting tonight?" was how he started the conversation.

Nasir rudely said back in the same tone that Sean used with him, "I'm having a good day, thanks for asking."

It was obvious they stayed out of each other's way, and that was cool. As long as the money kept piling up, Sean was good. He knew how to deal with Nasir.

Sean had no time for the pettiness. "I came up here for nothing, or is this a misunderstanding?"

"No, it's not a *misunderstanding,* and I was going to link up with you right after or tomorrow," he told him.

"What's the meeting about?"

"Did you call me on your other line?" Nasir asked, being that Sean was doing a lot of loose talking right now. Like, what the fuck was he thinking?

He pinched his nose, he was feeling really tried. "You think I'm a rookie or something? It's a burner," he told him.

"Oh, all right, but nah, I don't know what it's about. But he was clear that you wasn't invited."

No one really fucked with Polo, but did they have a choice? They did, but it was Nasir who chose to be a puppet in Polo's play.

"And he gets to make decisions and get a cut every month? Rightttt." Sean was sick of this shit.

"Gotta play the game sometimes."

"Nah, you just gotta kill a nigga sometimes, it's simple."

For years, Polo had been having his way, and it was bullshit to Sean. He didn't understand what kind of weird ass hold he had on Nas because everyone else had agreed that Polo and his ugly ass wife had to go.

"You and Papa need help, killing isn't always the answer."

Shitting me. Sean kept his thoughts to himself. "Hit my line, and I'll meet you."

"Cool, if you get bored MJ needs some help-"

He had him fucked up. "I'm off the clock, I don't get paid enough," he said sarcastically. He handled the Southern region by himself with no help, and he would be damned if he came up here and picked a brick up.

Nasir chuckled but said nothing in return because he knew he was right. "I'll catch you later."

When the call was over, he made a mental note to holler at Samira when he got back to Atlanta. Something had to give and soon. Sean knew he deserved more. He was capable of running an empire on his own. And no, it wasn't greed or a lack of loyalty. This possible career move was all business, nothing personal.

He was unappreciated and overworked and then to be sat out of a meeting was bullshit when he brought in a large piece of the pie every month. There was no one in The Underworld he was close enough to for them to tell him what really was discussed in the meeting....no one except Lauren, but he knew she wasn't going. However, Lauren and MJ were close, so he called Lo to put some shit in motion.

"Stranger."

Lauren giggled into the phone, "Mr. Carter, what can I help you with?" She knew he wanted something because he never called.

"I'm in love now, how you feel about that?" She always told him that he would settle down one day, and it wouldn't be with her.

Sean never understood Lauren. He had tried several times and failed miserably, so he fucked her and left her alone. He had to sample that pussy and although it wasn't planned, it was one wild ass night he did not regret. Nasir had done some crazy shit behind Lauren, and now he knew why, because that was some of the best pussy he ever had in his life.

"Are you in town?"

She told him she wasn't, that her boyfriend was fundraising in Dakota.

"Where the fuck is Dakota?"

"Nowhere near Atlanta," she laughed again. Her voice sent shivers down his spine. Lauren had roots on him, he was convinced. Jackie didn't even give him this feeling, and all homegirl was doing was laughing and shit.

"I'm up here for a meeting that I can't even go to," he smacked his lips.

Lauren couldn't care less about The Underworld, but she was bored, so she asked him, "Why? I know they ain't getting rid of you." She was probably the only one who acknowledged his hard work and dedication to the organization.

"Hell nah, Polo said I'm not welcome in his house."

His name caused her stomach to cringe. Lauren had overcome that battle, but still...she hated him and his fucking wife. "I wouldn't wanna go over there anyway, Sean."

He agreed, but business was business. "Yeah, I feel you. They can't be making decisions without me present." He didn't want to keep using the word unfair because it was a bitch move, but that's exactly how he felt.

And as if she read his mind, she said, "I'll call MJ and get the tea tomorrow, I know she will tell me."

He threw a fist pump in the air. "Damn Lo, good looking," he played things cool.

Lauren wasn't stupid. "Sean, don't play me, we better than that. I know that's why you called me cus you ain't stunting me," she let him know.

He laughed loudly. "Man, you done went vanilla on a nigga!" He was still shocked she had fallen in love with a white dude.

"And it's real good too," she said sexily, thinking about the love of her life.

"Don't let dude hear you say that."

She smacked her lips and rolled her eyes, although Sean couldn't see her. "Dude is blocked and will stay blocked." Nasir was apart of her past, but he was still in denial. He popped up on her often and not less than seventy-two hours ago, he ate her pussy so good she screamed out Simon's name, and he left. That was one crazy ass afternoon. Lauren considered him pitiful. She didn't want him which made him want her more, but those days were over.

"I'm happy that you're happy." He was honest about that.

"And I'm happy that you're happy too. Is this the same chick you brought to the club that night?"

Everyone was familiar with Jackie. He didn't bring women around The Underworld. They were on some real Sopranos shit, and everyone couldn't be trusted, plus the wives of The Underworld were stuck up as hell to him. The good thing about Jackie was that she was older, reserved, mature and not pressed for friends. She wouldn't come in trying to keep up or impress the wives. Jackie wouldn't give a fuck. She was her own person, and Sean dug that.

"Yeah, got her a house and made it official." He felt good about the major move they decided on together.

"Treat her right, it's hard to get a real woman these days."

He knew that to be a fact. "Shit, you know I know, Lo. I done had my share of tramps. I'm good on all of that." He was done fucking bitches. Sean had changed his number and everything. A few of his lil chicks felt as if he owed them an explanation because they were part of his weekly roster, and then them other broads got the hint once the operator said, *"The number you are trying to reach..."*

"My boyfriend is coming out of his meeting, I'll call you after I touch basis with MJ."

"Stay up," was how he ended the call.

Sean was good to go as long as Lauren came through. What he planned on doing was keeping cool until he spoke with her and then comparing MJ's play of the meeting versus whatever Nas told him.

He smoked a blunt and went back to sleep. All that road running and trapping plus the flight had a nigga feeling loopy. Sean slept the rest of the day away, woke up, ate, smoked and went back to sleep.

Jackie was working a double today, so he wouldn't hear from her until tomorrow, that's if she picked up the phone when he called. He didn't plan on being in the city long. After he chopped it up with Nas, he would be on the first plane back to the crib.

η

The Underworld

If they could get money without the rah-rah, life would be too perfect. So, this meeting with Polo had to happen because he had been too quiet. Malachi didn't understand why Nas couldn't go alone and teased as they waited on someone to answer the ringing of the doorbell.

"Nas, you scared?" he laughed, but Nas didn't think that was funny.

"Man, I would blow the cap off that-"

Papa cut him off. "Shut up, cus if that was the case we wouldn't be here right now." He was grumpy and wasn't in the mood for no meeting.

MJ remained quiet. She never understood why she was always summoned to the meetings. No one never acknowledged her or told her, "Good job" or anything. She had no interest in this shit and hoped they got into it so the meeting could end before it even got started.

Surprisingly, Noel was present as well, so that told her it was important.

Miko was on the phone with her man, but moved the phone from her mouth and asked, "Damn, does he not hear us knocking?" She had no patience.

Malachi, her brother, felt the same way. It had been almost three minutes.

"Nas, are you sure the meeting is tonight?"

They were getting on his nerves already. "I should've smoked," he mumbled under his breath.

Papa lifted his Nike boot and kicked the door a few times. "Aye, nigga, we out here!" He knew they were aware of their presence because if not, security wouldn't have let them through the gate. But these were the kind of games that Polo played.

"Why couldn't Sean come? Nigga feeling some type of way," Papa asked.

Nasir shrugged his shoulders. "Ask Polo, but for real, if you shot at a nigga would you want him in your house?" He understood where Polo was coming from. Even if Sean did that on the strength of his bitch, it wasn't Sean's place.

Papa didn't agree with Nasir. "He should've killed the nigga."

Finally, someone came to the door, Polo's wife, Mina. "We have the music up loud, my apologies. Come in," she told them and moved out of the way.

They all ignored her as they stepped in and waited on further instructions.

"Are y'all strapped?" one of the security guards on post asked.

"Wait, your big ass been right here this whole time? You ain't hear us ring the doorbell?" Papa wanted to know.

Chi told him to chill, they had just got there.

Mina laughed nervously. "They're security, not butlers, Papa. Relax."

Papa hated that bitch so much, but for the sake of everyone else, he would keep cool tonight.

"We don't have all night, Mina. Where is Polo?" Nasir was ready to start and end the meeting in less than an hour.

Mina hated the way things had transpired between Nasir and Polo. They had truly loved and viewed him as a son, but he always appeared to be so disgusted with them now. It pained her heart.

"He will be down momentarily, we have dinner prepared, come eat," she said happily. She would do anything to have things how they used to be with The Underworld. She had seen them all grow and start families and push her and Polo out.

Back in the day, Mina used to entertain all the time, it was her favorite thing to do. She could host a party of one hundred with her eyes closed. They were once the most talked about power couple of the streets, but they lost it all and were barely holding shit together these days.

The lies spilled from everyone's lips.

"I'm fasting."

"My wife cooked."

"Not hungry."

"I'm not eating meat."

Mina looked crushed, and Nasir couldn't care less. "Tell Polo we will be in the sitting room." He knew his way around their house, so he led the others to where he figured the meeting should be held.

Mina stood there with her mouth agape but said nothing as she turned on her kitten heels to retrieve her husband.

"Did she really think we was going to eat shit from this house? Bitch ain't about to poison me," Papa said and shook his head.

MJ agreed. She had to pee but would hold it in until she got home. She didn't trust Polo or Mina and didn't understand why they still broke bread with them. They had hurt one of their own, and that should have automatically been the end, but Nasir said no. MJ sat next to Noel and Malachi and crossed her legs.She had a lot on her mind and was eager to return home and meditate.

Nasir was on his phone doing something, not engaged in the conversation everyone was having about the new interest rates and shit.

Noel was talking when Polo finally appeared.

"My favorite money makers," was how he greeted them with his arms wide open and a smile on his face that no one trusted.

Nasir stood and dapped him up while the others remained seated. They had no respect for him.

"What's this about?" Papa cut right to the chase, knowing that Nas wouldn't do it. His nights of being out all night were over. He had kids to tuck in and a wife to fuck before she fell asleep, so Papa was ready to go.

"It's always good to see you, Papa," he said sarcastically.

"Baby, get them some cigars and champagne or something," he bossed Mina around.

Malachi told him they were good and were eager to begin the meeting. Nothing was necessary.

Polo looked at Nasir for confirmation of what they were saying and shrugged his shoulders. "We all had a long week," he lied.

Papa mumbled under his breath, "This pussy ass nigga."

Polo took a seat on the table, apparently having faith that his big ass wouldn't break the glass.

"Well, I'll get right to it. Y'all need a new plug, cus mine is retiring." He didn't know how they would take the news, but it was what it was.

"How long you knew?"

Noel chimed in, "He's telling the truth." Her mother kept her ear to the streets.

"And you just now saying something?" Miko asked Noel.

She shrugged her shoulders. "My bad."

"Cool, can we go now?" This was not bad news for The Underworld. Finally, Polo could be cut out of the pie.

"It's not that easy, we gotta find somebody to supply us. Do you know how much we cop? A fucking lot!" Nasir was pissed.

"All the money we make we should have been had our own connect. Ain't no way we still copping from niggas. Shit don't make no sense," Papa argued, and everyone agreed.

It wasn't that simple, and only Nasir and Polo seemed to understand that.

"Give me his information, I'm going to set up a meeting with him. Hopefully, we can work something out," Nas told him.

Polo shook his head. "Uh, nah, I can't do that. How do me and mine eat if that happens?" He wasn't stupid.

"All I've done-"

Papa stood up. "Man, fuck that nigga! We can figure this shit out on our own. I'm sure Farren know some folks."

Papa looked at Noel for confirmation, but she told him, "I don't know, maybe."

"Chill out!" Nasir yelled. He looked at Polo. "Put a price on it." Money talked, and bullshit walked.

"One billion."

Chi laughed, this man was insane.

Papa was pulling on his ponytail by now. *For a phone number?* "You're one greedy mother fucker!"

Nasir shook his head. "You done made so much money off of us."

"And I gotta keep it coming in, young bull." He winked his eye at his former son.

Chi was ready to be done with The Underworld anyway, so he said, "Let's talk about this amongst ourselves." He didn't want them in this man's house any longer. It was clear they were a check to him and nothing more.

"I'm with that," MJ said as she stood up, ready to go.

"How long you knew he was retiring? We just re-upped, and you never said nothing about that." Nasir wasn't done with this conversation. He felt played, and this was the last time this nigga got over on him.

Papa checked the time on his watch, it was time to go. "Nas, let's roll." He didn't understand why he was trying to figure him out. He had always been a snake.

Shit happens. It's the game, everybody you meet won't be one hundred. That's when you learned to decipher between the real and the fake. The Underworld wasn't who they claimed to be, they should have had their own connections from the jump. Nasir had grown comfortable with the prices that Polo had. He had anger and hate all in his eyes.

Mina returned with flutes of champagne. "Here ya go," she sang as she entered the sitting room with a gold tray that cost more than a rack.

They all looked at her stupidly.

"I'll be in the car," Noel said as she was the first to head out, and everyone else followed except Nas.

"It's business, Nas. If a nigga retire, that's what he do. I can't make him stay in the game just for y'all," he tried to get him to understand, but it was all bullshit.

Chi told Nasir and Papa, "I hate to say this, but I'm glad this shit happened."

Papa agreed. "It's a blessing."

Miko told them, "I'll crunch the numbers and get them to you tomorrow morning. We will be fine until y'all figure everything out." As long as there was enough money to do payroll for at least a month, they could take a break to get a new plan together.Miko was sure of that.

"You know what you can do?" Malachi said toNasir, but he already knew what and who he was referring to without him saying.

Nasirshook his head. "Not an option." Hewasn't giving that nigga the privilege or the power to think he was running shit. *Not fuckin' happening.*

Chapter 5

"Chasin' this money, I ain't gon' never retire." – Young Scooter

Sean went back to Atlanta two days later. Nasir never called, but the information that MJ shared with Lauren told him everything he needed to know. He didn't even bother reaching out to Nas, knowing he should have stuck to his word, and that was to call him. Sean knew what was really going on and would sit back and wait until they figured it out. He had product stowed away in case of a rainy day, his cousin Boo taught him that.

Sean was his most consistent client every month, and when he copped from The Underworld to distribute to the Southern region, he always bought at least an extra brick and put it up in case of emergency. One could never predict what would happen next, and Sean never wanted to be sitting around looking stupid, so he had plenty of product to last him for a while if need be.

It was a Friday night, and the old him would have been headed to Pinups, a strip club in Atlanta with the best lemon pepper wings on this side of Heaven, but instead he was having dinner with Boo and his wife, Samira, and Jackie, his girlfriend.

Sean had his hand resting on the nape of her neck while Jackie sipped wine. She told Samira, "I'm not much of a drinker, but this right here is good."

She looked at Sean and winked her eye in a way to tell him that she was no longer mad at him, and he could to return to their bed tonight to sample her pussy since it had been so long.

Sean smiled back at her silently telling her thank you for taking him out of the doghouse.

"You still ain't told me how the meeting went?" Boo said as he rejoined the dining room table after taking a phone call he couldn't let go to voicemail.

Samira's eyes lit up as her husband sat beside her. On her worst day, he was still the best thing that had ever happened to her. Boo was the light of her life, her sunshine, the beginning and the end of each day. Love wasn't love until she had fallen deeply into a pile of it when she met Boo.

It was amazing how they survived the bullshit, beat the odds and were still madly attached to each other. Samira looked at her cousin-in-law, wanting to know as well what went down, but he wasn't comfortable speaking in front of Jackie.

Jackie asked him, "Do you want me to step in the living room?"

Boo laughed, "Man, hell nah, he shouldn't have wifed you if he ain't trust you." He looked at Sean when he spoke because that was a major fact.

Sean bit his tongue, wanting to check the nigga but tonight was pleasant, and he appreciated the invitation and them welcoming Jackie into their fold.

"I didn't go," he stated, hoping they didn't probe any further.

"What did you go up there for? I thought it was an important meeting?" Boo was now confused.

Sean cleared his throat, and Jackie could sense that he was uncomfortable, so she removed the black linen cloth from her waist. "It's okay, really." She had no problem getting up. He was clear that he didn't want her in his mix, and she was cool with that.

"Jackie, really, sit down, girl. Sean, I'm listening. What's up?" Samira asked.

He felt like a child being prodded to tell the truth about something he did. "Look, I don't want to talk about the shit right now. Boo, don't do that no more," he spoke up because he was a grown ass man and could do that.

"Shit, nigga, I only asked a question."

"Someone told me that y'all peoples retired. Is that true?" Samira ignored them both and asked a question of her own.

Sean shrugged his shoulders. "Apparently, that's what the meeting was about, but I think that's a lie."

Boo was now confused. "I thought you didn't go?"

"I didn't, nigga, MJ told me."

"But why didn't you go, you slacking on your business?"

He shook his head. "Dude didn't want me in his house. You know he been hating me ever since I handled that thing, remember?" He really didn't want to talk about this in front of Jackie. *At all.*

Samira knew what he spoke of, but Boo smoked so much damn weed his memory was shot.

"What thing?" Boo needed to be refreshed.

"Lauren," Samira said, but kept her eyes on Sean.

"Well, you know y'all can cop-"

He shook his head. "I think he knows that's an option but doesn't want to give me that much control, so he rather suffer and let them starve right along with him."

"What power would you have?"

Sean smiled. "Oh, ain't no way they copping from my cousin and I don't get a bigger percentage or get promoted. Hell nah."

Boo felt where he was coming from, but he had to remind him, "It's still stupid to me that you fuck with them niggas. You could've been doing your own thing. Me and Sammy ain't with that team shit." It had always been just the two of them and then people under them. Sean had to move when The Underworld moved, and he had always been his own man.

He appreciated the benefits of The Underworld and the lessons he had learned along the way. It wasn't all bad with them jokers. Up until recently, things were going great, but now he wanted more, expected more and rightfully so desired more from the organization.

Sean wasn't looking for his exit route as of yet, but sooner than later, he would begin wrapping things up. Now, if they reached out to him for a meeting with Samira, he damn sure would open his mouth about how he had been feeling for quite some time, but Nasir's pride would get in the way of him ever asking for a favor from him.

"I don't know, we will see." He was trying to end the conversation or at least pause it until another day.

Jackie asked Samira, "Do you plan to retire soon?" She was such a beautiful woman, and she would have never suspected her to be dealing dope, but you can't always judge a book by its cover.

Boo chuckled and Samira giggled, tipsy off the wine. "We are retired." She was actually telling the truth, but no one ever really retired from the streets.

"Oh, okay." Jackie should have just remained quiet, but curiosity killed the cat.

"Sean, when are you retiring?" Samira asked.

He could have slid under the table and died, they were doing the absolute most tonight. "Are y'all niggas rolling?" He knew that now and then they popped a pill to turn the heat up in the bedroom and wondered if that's why they were so antsy tonight.

"Hell nah, the kids are here, we chilling. What's wrong?"

Sean was ready to go. They were high off of something or drunk. Either way, this night had come to an end.

"He's retiring very soon," Jackie answered for him.

Boo and Samira looked at each other and busted out laughing at the joke that Jackie had told.

"This nigga ain't doing shit. Don't listen to him, Jackie. Sean is addicted to money," Boo said with big eyes and all the golds in his mouth on full display.

"All right, all right, I'll catch y'all niggas later. Y'all tripping." He got up, and Jackie did the same.

"What's wrong with 'em bae?" Boo asked his wife.

"They don't think we funny. Jackie, thanks for coming, it was really good meeting you officially."

Jackie smiled and waved before following her man out to his car. Sean didn't even open the door for Jackie, she had to get in her damn self. He said nothing as they headed home.

"Sean," she said his name, expecting him to acknowledge her.

"Really don't feel like talking," he told her and turned the radio up, not wanting to have a conversation.

But Jackie wasn't with the shits, she reached over and muted the rap music. "What's really up with you? I don't want to hear nothing about you not trusting me yet. I want to know everything. Don't have me blindsided. Can some niggas run up in my house at any given time?" She had a million and one questions.

He slammed his Maserati on the brakes. "Do you really think I'm a dumb mother fucker? I would never put you or your kids in harm's way! What kind of nigga do you take me for?" He was offended.

"I don't take you for shit cus I don't know! So tell me, and what the fuck is The Underworld?"

η

The sun had come up, and he was on his second sack of loud, chain smoking and drinking Dos Equis in a glass. He never drank his beer out of the can.

Sean sat back and put his feet on top of the table and sighed as he pulled on the blunt once more. At this point, he was high out of his mind and gone far away from his thoughts. The sky was a pretty pink and orange mix. He had never seen it this way before, so he took it as a sign that a change had come or was coming.

He closed his eyes as the smoke hit his lungs and dared it to stay there until he coughed profusely.He reached forward and dumped the ashes in the tray and went in for another toke.

Jackie had given him a sorry ass ultimatum last night before bed and when she laid down, angry and all, he got up and had been on the back porch ever since.Lost in his thinking, he didn't even hear the door open or close. Jackie sat in his lap and took the blunt from him and smoked it herself. He had never seen her smoke, but didn't care enough to ask her what the fuck she was doing.

"You been out here all night?" she asked as she blew smoke in his face. He remained silent, eyes on the sky. "Sean, I know you probably know more about him than I do." She never said his name. *Never.* He didn't know if it pained her to do so or not. "But I wasn't dumb when it came to the life he lived, and I know you think you're untouchable, but bullets are real."

He looked at her with a fury in his eyes that wasn't directed towards her, but today she would probably receive the wrath. "You don't think I ain't been shot before?" he asked. She had to stop jumping to conclusions or assuming shit when it came to him .And this is what he meant when he said no one knew him. He lifted his shirt and showed his war wounds, things she didn't see when they were fucking, apparently. She ran her hands over the faint scars that told her he had a past. "I ain't no dummy," he reminded her. He believed she had no faith in him. "Hustling is what I know, Jackie."

She believed otherwise. "So what's the point in you opening the casino? The gym? The hair salon? Baby, you got enough money to get out right now. Sean, my kids look up to you, I look up to you." She wanted more for him.

"It's not that easy, Jackie. I feed a lot of ma'fuckas. My mama depend on me and about fifteen other niggas." He had his family on his back. Sean wasn't done yet.

She wouldn't go back and forth with him, his mind was made up. "I want to start a business then."

"All right, get me the business plan." He knew she was popping shit, so he would see how serious she was.

Jackie left him outside, and he sparked up the blunt again and went back to his thoughts. Minutes later, she returned and dropped a green folder in his lap. "It's all there. I gotta get to work."

He was surprised as hell but said nothing. He placed the folder on the table and got up to hug and kiss her before she dipped. Jackie didn't need to go to work mad at him.

The boys were still sleeping. On the weekends, them lil' niggas slept all day and stayed up all night. Sean went into the master bathroom and watched Jackie undress for her shower.

"I'm not mad at you," he told her.

"I don't care if you was, baby, I only want what's best for you."

He smiled at her jazziness, that's what he loved the most about her.

"You, Kevin and Jonathan are what's best for me, and that's on my mama."

That comment made her smile, and she asked him if he wanted to join her for a morning wash. He undressed and walked in behind her.

"I'm not stressed or no shit like that, Jack. Sometimes I get in my moods when everything be on my mind, even the things I have no control over," he shared with her.

"And what does your therapist have to say about that?"

She didn't sound like she was being sarcastic, so he told her, "She thinks I work myself about nothing and need to just relax."

"Yeah, I agree." She washed his back and then turned around so he could do hers, but instead he massaged her cheeks, loving the way her ass sat up.

"Ain't no way you not twenty-five," he teased.

Jackie laughed, "Boy, I ain't been twenty-five in a long ass time." She didn't care that they were years apart. What they had going on had nothing to do with age. If Sean was a childish man or didn't have shit together, she wouldn't be with him. Jackie was too old to be raising a grown ass man. Thankfully, he had everything in order. He was a great listener, hands-on with her children, an amazing lover and a beautiful friend. She had no complaints, minus his involvement with The Underworld.

"Damn, I still can't believe this is all mine."

She turned around and wrapped her arms around his neck. "It's really been yours."

He kissed her and slid his tongue into her mouth, releasing a lustful energy amongst the two.

She shook her head once he tried to move his hand in between the middle of her legs. "I can't be late."

"Girl, you got a whole business plan, fuck that job," he mumbled in between kisses.

Jackie laughed. "I've had that for a while, I only gave it to you cus I knew you didn't believe me."

"I really didn't. What is it for?"

"Restaurant, nothing major." She was always downplaying her cooking skills, but baby girl could really throw down.

"You know I support you with whatever you wanna do, baby. The world is yours," he told her as he always did.

Jackie's days of worrying and struggling were behind her. Never in life would she have to pray on a bill instead of paying it. He was in her corner forever, whether they lasted or not.

"Let me get in this real quick though." They could talk business and branding at a later date, he was horny as fuck and knew her pussy was the perfect recipe to put him to sleep for the rest of the day.

Jackie couldn't tell him no. The pouty look on his face told her that he needed her right now, needed her to take his stress away, needed her to put a smile on his face, to reassure him that she was where she wanted to be, and that was with him.

How could sex make all of that happen with the use of one muscle? Well, two muscles; her tight pussy and his throbbing dick. Sex could do more than serve as a physical release. Sex could do more than bring physical satisfaction.Why do you think most couples loved makeup sex? It's a form of an apology that might not otherwise ever come. It was the translation of "we in this shit together, you not leaving" but minus the conversation. Sex could do a lot of shit if you let it, if you didn't hold back. Sex is a tool. It's medicine. It's therapy .It's a vacation. It's a wake-up call. It's a remedy. It's a movie depending on who's in the starring role.

Sean needed her in the worst way. He had been having thoughts of The Underworld trying to kick him out after all he had done. He had nightmares of Jackie finding out his dark past. He was worried that the child he really hoped wasn't his, really wasn't his. He feared for his mother's life while she recklessly gambled and bragged on her son being rich. He didn't want to die or go to jail...or be alone for the rest of his life.

Sean had a lot on his mental right now, and he boggled himself on the back porch, using weed to stay afloat as the moon went away and the sun came out to play.

He was a nigga, no doubt, but even niggas had feelings. He couldn't wait to sit down with Dr. Robinson again. He wondered if he lackedconfidence in himself and his street capabilities.

Sean pushed his thoughts to the side as he made his way into his peace, his haven, his heaven, his solace. Jackie was warm and snug. She shuddered as he swelled inside of her.

He bit her shoulder and then kissed her to take away the bite. "Let me in," he begged for her permission to bust her down how he really wanted to. "Let me in, baby." He was stroking her middle and focusing on making her cum while using this session of sex as a mental block. "Jackie, let me get in this pussy!" he begged in a child-like tone as lust dripped from his every word.

"Have your way, baby, have your way."

Jackie gave him free reign to do as he pleased, knowing he knew what he was doing and would take good care of her.

"Fuck!" He had hit a hidden spot and dug deeper into that hole until he felt himself about to explode.

Jackie yipped out in pain and pleasure as her belly rumbled. "It's right there, I feel it," she told him her release was near. She was cumming in any second now.

Sean's eyes were glued shut as he tried to control his breathing and his rapid pushing into her warm place of peace and pleasure.

"Shit, Sean." She had cum suddenly, and it spilled all over his dick as he too felt his own coming right behind hers.

"Damn it." He pulled his limp dick out of her pussy and staggered back to the shower wall, not caring that the water was now falling all over his head and face.He was sweating anyway.

Jackie panted as she bent over to pick up her washcloth. She showered quickly. "I gotta go."

He wasn't tripping, he knew she had to get to work. Sean took a seat on the bench and turned the temperature of the water as hot as he could take it.He remained seated until he grew tired, rinsed his body and fell into bed, damp and all.Sleep succumbed him and if only for a few hours, his mind was able to rest. The Underworld needed him, that's what he told himself before he closed his eyes.

When he woke up, the smell of weed hit his nostrils as his stomach grumbled. Sean wiped his eyes and got up to piss and brush his teeth. He found his way to the kitchen and made a big bowl of Frosted Flakes and added a few ice cubes to the milk. He liked his cereal super cold. Sean took the bowl to the basement with him to check on the boys.

"Aye, your mama think y'all smoke, and y'all giving it away by not even closing the door to the basement or to this funky ass room?" He covered his nose because it reeked of weed, balls and dirty socks.

"Why you got your nose covered up?" Kevin asked him.

"Man, it stink in here, y'all need to light a candle or something," he told them and left the room.

Kevin and Jonathan both shared a laugh before pressing play to resume their music.

An hour or so later, the boys came into the den where Sean was chilling, something he rarely did.

"What?" he asked because he knew they wanted something.

"We found this in the laundry room," Jonathan said and handed him a gun.

What the fuck? He wasn't careless. "This must be your mama's," he told them because he would never leave a loaded gun around the house. He had no reason to. No one was coming out here to fuck with him no way.

"Can we go to the gun range?"

Sean shook his head. "Man, y'all better take y'all asses outside to that basketball court." He wasn't entertaining violence.

"What if somebody come in here, how do we protect ourselves?"

This was a bad attempt at reverse psychology. "Why would they come in here? This is a million-dollar house in this white neighborhood. Y'all go to private school, your mother is a nurse and I sell real estate?" he asked.

They were so tired of being treated like babies. "Man, we already know you in the streets, can we go to the gun range?" Jonathan decided to cut the funk.

"What streets?" he played dumb.

They didn't laugh or think it was funny. "For real, you always out of town, and Ma sleeps hard. We need to protect ourselves."

"I would never let nothing happen to y'all," he told them in all seriousness. They still weren't fazed. Sean took a deep breath, he didn't have shit to do today, so why not? "Don't tell your mama and don't be bragging at school. And I'm not getting y'all a gun so don't ask," he fired off rules and regulations. They had to know that this came with precautions. Jackie would go the hell off if she knew he had taught them how to shoot a gun, but the boys had a point, she slept hard as hell, and he was out of town often. It seemed right for them to be able to protect themselves in case of an adversity.

"Go take a shower, y'all stink. I'll meet y'all at the truck in thirty minutes," he told them and stood up to go get dressed. Them lil' niggas thought they was slick. Once you had a gun in your hand and pointed it at somebody, you had better fuckin' shoot it. That was the first rule Boo ever taught Sean. Maybe that wasn't the best advice to give a thirteen-year-old, but to date, Sean had no living enemies. And thankfully, he was able to sleep at night not worried about a nigga lurking in the trenches to seek revenge.

He didn't forgive those who did him wrong, *he killed them.*

η

"Where are you today? Because I've asked you three questions and you keep zoning out?" Dr. Robinson asked Sean. Not that she was being impatient, but she wouldn't waste her time or his if he didn't want to talk today. "Would you like to reschedule?" That was her second question after he didn't answer her first one.

He shook his head and put his phone away. "Sorry, Doc, I got a lot going on."

She understood. "Let's try for next Tuesday?" She pulled her planner out from under her notepad that she reserved for patients and tried to see if she could fit him in next week.

He didn't want to reschedule, he put his phone away and finally gave her his full attention. "My bad, okay where were we?" He was now prepared to talk and listen.

They only had about twenty minutes left of the session, but she would do all she could before her buzzer went off. Normally, she could allot more time for Sean, but not today. She had a full day of counseling and then her very own tonight around eight.

"So, you were saying that you finally told Jackie about the daughter you don't think is your daughter, but she probably is?" She was sort of confused with the trail of his thoughts today and was trying to get him organized so she could better help him, if possible.

He replayed her words in his head. "Uh, yeah kinda. I was trying to let her know that kids were not an option for me, and I hope they not for her either."

"And Sean, while we are on the subject, let me ask you this, why are you so sure you don't want children? You're still relatively young and very successful, who's to say years from now you won't want to settle down?"

He shook his head and sat back against the velvet couch. "I can put a million on that right now, I do not want children. I have no desire to burp kids, wipe asses, help with homework or none of that. I have no interest."

"Do you have godchildren? Nieces? Nephews?" she asked him.

"Of course, but that's different. I don't baby sit them, I just drop gifts off for parties and tell them to live right." He was okay with things of that nature.Sean didn't want to be a parent. He didn't see himself being a father, ever. And that was okay with him. It wasn't for everyone.

"And if I'm not mistaken, your current girlfriend has two sons?"

She was correct, but that was different. "They damn near grown, the hard part is over," he was convinced.

Dr. Robinson smiled at his ignorance because he had things backwards. "No, not hardly. The stuff that you think is oh so hard is really the easy stuff.

It's when they're older and able to talk back is when you ask yourself what the hell did I get myself into," she laughed.

He didn't care what she was saying, he didn't want children. And no, it wasn't no deep reason as to why. There were tons of people, successful people at that, who had no children.

"How was your relationship with your mother growing up? Describe it for me."

He pursed his lips together. "I know what you trying to do, not gon' work. She has nothing to do with it."

Dr. Robinson came from behind her desk and sat in the chair right next to the couch where he was sitting. "Okay, well can you please still answer my question?" She wasn't hearing him at all.

He took a deep breath and scratched his head. "I mean, she was all right. My mom ran the streets."

"So, did she raise you or no?"

He always felt like he raised himself, but with the help of his grandmother of course. "Well, we stayed with my grandmother and my aunt off and on, my mama never kept her own place long."

Dr. Robinson didn't want to assume she was on drugs, so she asked what the reason was for them not having their own home.

"She had a real bad gambling habit and had no problem gambling the rent."

"So, your grandmother raised you. Where is she now? And your aunt?"

"Dead and on life support." He cringed at those words. Losing his gammy was one of the hardest things he had to accept. She was the matriarch of their family and thankfully, no one fell apart too bad after she died, other than his aunt.

"Life support?" Dr. Robinson wanted more information.

He hated talking about the situation his aunt was in. He smiled, hoping that would help keep the tears at bay. "You know what...my cousin need to come see you. That nigga need help for real," he laughed. "My aunt has been on life support for years. He spends hundreds of thousands of dollars keeping her alive by the year because he can't let go.On her birthday he sings to her and on

Christmas he takes her gifts." Boo really needed to let go of his honey gal, but he couldn't. She and Gammy were all he ever had.

"And do you go visit her at the hospital?"

This is where it all came out. "She's at his house."

Dr. Robinson looked up at him. "Huh?"

"Yeah, I know right...she raised him. He refuses to pull the plug," he shared with her.

"And this is your mom's sister?"

He nodded his head. Dr. Robinson began scribbling things down rapidly on her notepad.

"Okay, let me ask you this, are you the only child?"

"Nah, I'm not...I got a sister."

"And where is she?"

"She doing her own thing." His sister got the hell on as soon as she graduated.

"Okay, back to my first question, how was your relationship with your mother growing up versus now?"

He was growing irritated with her line of questioning. "It was all right. I don't hate my mama, I don't blame her for nothing. She got a bad habit that's it, I love her."

"No drugs? What about alcohol abuse?"

He shook his head. "She drink, but no drugs... I love my mama."

"To the point where you'll consider her an alcoholic?"

"Nah, not at all. Man, I love my mama."

"And growing up, did you ever feel neglected?"

He took a deep breath. "Aye, I gotta go." He was ready to get out of there.

She touched his knee. "You can't keep running every time things get touchy. I'm trying to tap into something here," she begged with her eyes for him to work with her.

"I didn't feel neglected, Doc. I love my mama."

"Why do you keep saying that? As if you're trying to convince yourself that you really love her? Do you feel like you don't love her or something?"

She had her hand under her chin, looking like a fucking therapist.

And this is when he had minor breakdowns. This is when he questioned himself and why he was seeing a shrink. Nothing was wrong with him. What hood nigga had a therapist?

Sean jolted out of his seat. "I can't do this," he told himself and her too.

She didn't stand because she knew she was right and was pretty sure he couldn't handle the truth. "Sean...do you feel like you were alone growing up and just maybe...you had to love her because no one loved her or maybe...you feel as if you show her love she'll love you more than her vices?" She was getting somewhere. Finally. His chest was heaving up and down. Dr. Robinson thumbed through her notes. "March 2 you told me that you took care of her, and you had recently bought her a bigger house. Why did you get her a new house? Does she work? Are you her provider?" She had so many questions.

Sean had to go. "I'll catch you later, Doc."

She said nothing as he walked out of her office. Dr. Robinson was pretty sure she had left with him a lot to think about, and that was the point.

She wrote down in her notepad, *Mr. Carter is hiding something. For the first time I'm seeing pain, disconnection, weariness. Patient identifies with family but there is something else that hasn't been revealed. Will try again during next session. Mother is weak point for Mr. Carter. Noted.*

Sean sat in his truck for an hour before he pulled out. A blunt dangled in the corner of his mouth, but he never sparked it up. Sean wondered, did his mother love him for real? If he didn't have the money he had, would they have the super-cool ass relationship they had these days?

What he didn't like about therapy was the way he felt when he left. He never had a problem with his mother, he was cool with taking care of her. Isn't that what people worked hard for anyway, to boss up and make sure loved ones were straight? Sean hated that Dr. Robinson planted seeds of doubt and now he was second-guessing everything.

Yeah, his mama fucked up a lot of money over the years and had a bad gambling problem, but what single mother was perfect? She did what she knew was best, and that was to take risks. Sean wasn't pointing any fingers though, he turned out all right.

He took a deep breath and put the blunt in the ashtray and pulled off from Dr. Robinson's office. He hadn't been in a good mood all week and was hoping that meeting with her would take him off out of his funk, but it only made it worse.

A text message came to his phone, and it was from Jackie asking were they still on for lunch. He couldn't cancel. Jackie was getting used to their lunch dates when she worked the day shift, and he was a man who stuck to his word. He told her he would be outside as soon as her break started.

Sean headed to the hospital with the music off and the windows down, he had so much on his mind it was ridiculous; *The Underworld, children he didn't even have, nor did he fuckin' want, and his mama.*

He didn't even see Jackie approaching the truck until she banged on the door to get his attention. Sean reached for his gun, it was in his norm to expect something bad to happen. It was the life he lived.

"Sean!" she shouted his name.

He blinked twice and dropped the gun and then unlocked the door. "My bad, baby," he apologized.

She rolled his eyes and slammed the door once she was in. "You good?" she asked him. Jackie knew something wasn't right. He hadn't said much around the house, they hadn't had sex nor had he touched any of the food she had cooked in the last three days.

He nodded his head. "Yeah, what you got a taste for?" Sean wouldn't discuss his problems with her, knowing she wouldn't understand. Jackie and her mom had a great relationship, he was the one with the dysfunctional ass family.

She told him there was an Italian restaurant up the street they could dine at. Sean headed there while she fired off the directions. The couple parked in the front of the door and headed in.

"Table for two please." She held Sean's hand in hers as the hostess led them to a booth. Jackie already knew what she wanted, so she didn't need a menu, and Sean wasn't hungry.

"Talk to me please," she asked after the waitress took their drink and appetizerorder.

He shrugged his shoulders. "I'm good. How is work so far?" Sean was always putting everyone else before himself, that's all he knew to do.

Jackie reached across the table and grabbed his hands. "Talk to me please, don't shut me out," she pleaded.

His hardened eyes met her soft ones and even in the wash grey scrubs, she was gorgeous.

Sean loved the pixie cut she had been rocking the past two months. Jackie normally wore her hair cut and tapered, but she spiced it up and added a few pieces of weave in the front and had the rest of her hair shaved low. She rocked a gold diamond cross necklace, and he was sure it a gift from her late husband. He was thankful she took off the wedding ring. The day he noticed it he went to say something, and she asked him not to.

They were making progress, and for that he was grateful. Sean knew he could trust her, and he knew she loved him. Although she hadn't said it just yet, it was understood.

"Jack, I don't know where to start, let's enjoy lunch though, baby. I'm good."

"That's not true though, you aren't fucking good," she hissed, not wanting to bring any attention to their booth since the restaurant was crowded with everyone trying to eat during their lunch hour.

"What you want me to say?" He was getting mad because she was getting mad with him.

"Is it business? Is it me? The kids?" She was worried that this was too much for him. The other day, she asked him to pick up a prescription for Kevin from the pharmacy and then turned around and had two more favors. Jackie wondered was he really ready to help her co-parent.

"The kids? Hell no, why would you even me ask me some shit like that?" Sean loved her sons as if they were his.

"I know being a step-dad or whatever you wanna call it isn't easy."

Step-parent? Is that how she saw him? "We not using that word. We ain't been using it, and we not starting now." He didn't like that.

"Well, Sean, what you wanna call it?"

He didn't understand the need for a title. "I'm saying, if they not trying to put a label on me, why are you?"

She bit down on her bottom lip. "They lost their father..."

"Okay? So now I'm the step-daddy? No, don't put me in a box. I love your kids,Jackie, don't separate me with that stupid ass word." He shook his head, not even believing her right now.

"So if it's not them or me, then what is up?" She wasn't letting that go.

"Next subject."

She rolled her eyes. "I honestly could have eaten alone today." His attitude was salty, and it wasn't fair to her being that she was in a great mood.

"Well, get your shit to go then." He wasn't kissing her ass. Sean had enough shit going on.

"Oh nah, buddy, you can go. I'll walk back!" she snapped.

He grabbed his truck keys and told her, "Say less."

Sean left her ass sitting there alone. Today was not his day. He peeled off from the curb and slid into traffic. His head throbbed, and he knew he was officially stressed out.

Nasir hadn't bothered to give a nigga call or nothing. The Underworld was cooking something up and the fact that he wasn't in the kitchen water whipping with them didn't feel good. He felt as if he was on the outside trying to get a look in.

Boo called him, and he went on and answered. "Yeah?"

"Damn, nigga, you still in your feelings?" He had called him the other day, and Sean had the same dry ass tone.

"What up?" Sean asked him. Boo was the only person that didn't know how to take the hint and call back later. Boo took adeep breath. "Well, cuz, you was right."

Sean didn't know what he was exactly referring to. "About what?"

"Your folks reached out."

Where you at?" He didn't want to say too much over the phone.

Jackie had sent him the longest message in history, but he didn't read it. The constant vibration in his ear told him that she was still sending messages going off and most likely calling him every pussy ass nigga there was.

"Gammy's house."

Sean told him he would be there in less than twenty minutes. He checked his trap phone and still no call from anyone in The Underworld. They had decided without him, and that his cousin knew before him told him a lot. To feel unappreciated was the worst feeling in the world, especially when you worked hard and loved your job. To never get a pat on the back, a raise, recognition or anything wasn't cool.

Sean wanted to say fuck them niggas and do his own thing but knew that wasn't a smart move. He had the potential to make shit happen, but the connections via The Underworld were endless. Together, they were a unit. The Underworld was powerful. The Underworld was untouchable. They got shit done. If Sean went independent, he might be dead in a year. And that wasn't out of fear, but it was a fact.

He pulled up in Gammy's yard and finally glanced at Jackie's messages of her threatening to leave him and all kinds of shit. Sean knew her ass wasn't going nowhere, so he shot her back a quick, *"I love you too"* and got out of his truck.

He headed into the house and was surprised to see Boo's wife, Samira, over as well. She rarely popped up in the hood, but back in the day you couldn't keep her out of the streets. She credited her children to slowing her down and forcing her to retire.

"What's going on?" Sean asked them.

Boo looked at Samira and gave her a head nod to begin speaking. "I'm going to be one hundred with you, okay?" She wouldn't beat around the bush.

He nodded his head. "That's all I want."

"Okay, well in like an hour, your boss or whatever the fuck he is-"

"He ain't my boss, we all are a team," he interrupted.

"Well, that's not how he just kicked it to us." She shot daggers at him.

Sean looked at his cousin, wondering what the fuck was really up. "What you trying to say?" he asked, his arms now crossed, feeling the need to be defensive.

"I'm saying, what do you really do in The Underworld, cus according to them, your ass is a runner and nothing more."

"Them or him?" was his question in response to what she had said.

Boo looked at Samira, a look that forced her to chill out. He hated how they effectively communicated with each other without being verbal.

"Anyway, that's not my business, they're going to call you and act like shit is cool and…" She kept getting off subject. "And to be clear, I'm only telling you this cus you are family." At the end of the day, business was business, and Samira didn't play about her money.

"Oh, am I?" He was baffled.

Boo didn't like that shit. "Nigga, what's that supposed to mean?" He stood up.

"Man, fuck all of that. What y'all call me over here for?"

"You need to move to New York. That's what he's about to call and tell you."

"No!" Sean was not fucking moving to New York.

Boo came from around the table and stood right in front of his cousin. "Do you trust me?"

Sean looked at Samira, but Boo moved right along with his eyes and got back in his face. "Not my wife, nigga, me."

He blew out a deep breath of frustration. "You all I got. I trust you, Boo, you know that shit." Boo was his role model in many ways. He trusted that mother fucker with his life.

"All right then, move to New York. I got you, we got you," he said and pointed behind him to Samira who gave him a reassuring nod.

All Sean could think about was everything he was leaving and who he was refusing to leave without. Jackie and her sons had to come too, or he wasn't going. *Fuck The Underworld.*

Chapter 6

"No weapon formed against me, I pray that every night." – Meek Mill

One Year Later

"Who is that girl in there with Jonathan?" Jackie asked Sean once she came to bring him a beer and a blunt.

He shrugged his shoulders, eyes on the money while he counted almost a quarter million dollars.

"So, he just brought some random hoe in your house, and you don't know who it is?" She crossed her arms and stared at her man, anticipating and expecting an answer. He ignored her and continued to count the hundred-dollar bills. "I'm saying, Sean, he can't just be inviting girls over here whenever he feel like it and not tell me or you," she ranted. She was pissed.

He finally stopped and looked at her. "Bae, you don't see me handling something?" he asked her as if she should have already known. She didn't care though, not at fucking all.

"You been in here all day and night." *Never no time for me,* she thought to herself. Jackie hated New York and every chance she got she was going home to visit her church and spend time with her mother. She didn't understand why they had moved so abruptly, especially when it seemed as if Sean would rather be back in the south as well.

He had told her that this was business, and in business he couldn't always get his way, so this was him being a man and doing what had to be done.

In a few weeks, it would officially be a year since they made a transition, and Jackie was sure the only people happy to be up here in this cold ass place was her kids. They loved New York so much and the fact that they were dark skinned and had that southern hospitality and deep accents had all the "honeys" on them.

Her kids had been fucking everything left and right and had turned into little horn dogs, and Jackie hated it. She couldn't keep up with all the chicks they had over and now decided to put her foot down. She was too young and still trying to enjoy life to be somebody'sgrandmother.

Jackie had no grey hair on her head as of yet, but she was sure the moment one of her babies told her that they would soon be expecting a baby of their own, the grey hair would sprout out of nowhere, and she was not ready.

"I'm almost done, then we can do whatever you wanna do," he promised her.

Jackie still wasn't done with him though. "Like get married?"

She now had his full attention. "Say what?"

She smiled at him, blushing and all. "I'm serious." She wanted to become Mrs. Sean Carter. Jackie didn't want to wait another day.

"Why?" he asked, wanting to know why all of a sudden she desired marriage. Jackie seemed cool with them shacking up. Was she finally over her husband? Did she accept his death? For years, Jackie was in denial. What made her change her mind? Now?

He had a question, and that was, *"Why?"*

She rolled her eyes. "Fuck you, Sean." Jackie didn't have time for his shit. He could never be okay with whatever she proposed, everything came with a what or why.

The Underworld had fucked her sweetheart up. Sean was now more paranoid and had trust issues out the ass. When they first moved to New York, the wives of the organization that he was apart of had welcomed her with open arms. Although she had already met them a few times over the years, they officially invited her into their fold, but Sean was completely against it. He told her to not tell them shit and to keep her guard up at all times.

So, for a few months, this was done with no hesitation and ease, but eventually she saw that they were genuine souls. A little naïve, but they were all as sweet as her homemade peach cobbler. However, Sean didn't want to hear that shit, he considered them all vultures.

Jackie told him that he worried too much, but he felt as if he didn't worry enough, and that's why he was feeling as stagnant as he was.

"Jack, come here," he called after her once she was midway down the hallway.

"You keep rejecting me, how do you think you're making me feel?" she wanted to know.

He took adeep breath and wrote the count down so when he finished talking to her he could start back and not be lost.

Sean stood up and went to pull her back into his office. "You want the boys in our business?"

"What business do we have? They know your ass ain't never here," she complained.

"I'm making money. You act like I'm out fucking bitches."

"You think I care about that? What more money do you need, baby? Tell me what for?" she asked him.

Sean hated to say this, but he had to. "You need to find you something to do because you're bored." He knew that's exactly what it was.

Jackie stepped back and looked at him for a while before her lips curled into a smile, and she wagged her finger. "You know what...the house is almost done. I think am going back to work."

"Nah, I ain't say no late night shifts and all of that. You don't wanna open a store or nothing? I want you to be a boss, baby," he said as he wrapped his arms around her waist.

Jackie hadn't felt him so close in a long time. Sean was either out of town or in the streets, no in between. Every night, well early morning, when he made it home, she and the boys were already sound asleep. He would eat in the kitchen by himself, shower, smoke and go to bed.When he finally did arise, the house would be empty.

This routine had been going on for quite awhile, and today Jackie was putting her foot down. The house needed order, from the boys and from Sean.

"I love being a nurse, you know that. I put myself through school," she reminded him.

He understood all of that, but he had enough money for her to do whatever she wanted.

"What about your dream restaurant?"

Jackie sighed. "Sean, maybe a few years from now." She was scared to take on such a big project.

He kissed her forehead. "No better time like the present."

"Me being bored isn't why I'm ready to get married," she let him know.

Sean would rather talk about that after he finished doing what he was doing, and that was counting this money. "All right, give me like two hours, and then we can talk about all of that. You wanna go out to eat or you gon' cook?" He was with whatever she was with. The world was hers, he was simply living in it.

"Out to eat, I'm tired of being in here." She looked at the walls and shook her head.

"You did an amazing job though, baby." He kissed her lips this time, giving her praise.

When Jackie found the perfect house after living in his loft for a few months while she searched day in and out with his preferredrealtor, she told Sean that making the mansion a warm home for them would be her project since she wasn'tworking at the time. And lo-and-behold, their home was a sight to see.

They had already decided to move into a ranch as soon as both of the boys graduated. Jonathan was now a senior, and Kevin would be right where he was in no time. Jackie preferred a smaller place of residence, but Sean wanted land and a big backyard and so did the boys.

"Yeah, but now what? What do I do now?" She had nothing but time on her hands. Jackie had been volunteering every day, all day to stay busy.

"We will figure it out, as soon as I finish this." He looked behind him at the heaps of money.

Before she could give him a kiss and leave him to be, Kevin busted in the room. "Aye do you-" His eyes saw the piles of money. *"Holy shit!"*

Jackie reached out for her son to smack him in his mouth. "You better get out of here cursing." They were really forgetting what she had instilled in them.

Sean tried to cover the money up but couldn't find anything with material to do so. Kevin stood there with his mouth watering.

"Where all that come from?" he asked excitedly.

This was what she never wanted to happen. Her children would see the money and think, *oh that's the life I want to live*, but it wasn't that simple. The streets weren't for the weak. Jackie wanted her children to go to college and be better than their father...and Sean.

She dropped her head. "Kevin, I won't tell you again to get out of here," she asked him with the little bit of patience she had left in this day.

Sean apologized as soon as he exited the room.

"Sorry for what? That you brought that money here? Sorry for what?" She was irritated.

"Where else was it supposed to go?"

That was a dumb ass question for Jackie to ask. Kevin had no business barging into a room without knocking anyway, he knew the rules.

"Now what am I supposed to tell him?" She was mad.

He told her, "I will handle it, Jack."

She overreacted about the smallest of situations, and Sean had already sat them down and in so many words, but maybe not enough, told them that he was involved in a lot of different businesses.

"I bet."

Sean watched her storm out and slam the door behind her. This time he made sure to lock the door, not needing anymore interruptions. First thing in the morning, he had to drop this money off to Miko in order to receive the new batch of products.

The one thing he had to admit was that the system The Underworld now had in place was fucking amazing. Everything was running smoothly. Sean had to bite the bullet on several situations, but he knew all about being a team sport in order to win the ultimate prize. He rarely had an opinion about anything, and it would stay that way until he felt otherwise. Sean minded his business and made his money. He was either on the road, hustling or in the house.

His businesses were doing well, and his residuals were assisting in meeting his monthly financial goal every month. Everything else was in place the way it was supposed to be.

Sean had no complaints, but in the back of his head he felt that he had settled. Sean didn't feel a shift or any progression happening. Yeah, he was making money out the ass and surpassing his expectations financially, but other than those dollar bills, what else was going on? Nothing.

Maybe marrying Jackie would ease him out of this semi-dark hole of depression he found himself in. Or maybe he wouldn't be so down in the dumps whenever he thought about his life. Would marriage make him feel complete on the inside?

Sean pulled his phone out and texted Dr. Robinson. Because he no longer resided in Atlanta, they mainly spoke over the phone. Whenever he was in the city, he would stop by and chop it up with her, but that wasn't often because his trips back home were now all related to business.

Sean shot her a text message and then put his phone back in his pocket and resumed counting the money. "One fifty, two, two-fifty, three, three fifty..." He licked his finger to separate the bills and kept it going, "Four, four-fifty, five."

Money didn't even make his dick hard or his heart skip a beat anymore. Something had to give and soon. Depression was real, and not even money could cure it.

η

"So, we are celebrating our anniversary, right?" Jordyn wouldn't let him make a fool out of her this year. She refused, so before she made a million and one plans, booked hotel rooms and had the pilot gas up one of two of their private jets, she wanted to be one hundred percent sure that this year they were on the same page. With Mr. Nasir King, you never really knew what to get or expect from him.

Last year, he scheduled a meeting on their anniversary, and then when he made it home after midnight gave her a dumbfounded look and told her that he didn't understand why they were celebrating an anniversary if they weren't happily married.

Needless to say, the next morning Jordyn returned the five-thousand dollar gift she had purchased for him.

He looked at her with a confused look upon his brown face when she tried to give it to him. "Uh, Jordyn, why would we celebrate our anniversary?"

And this is the part of him that drew her to drink every night. He had déjà vu when it came to the fucked up things he had done in their marriage. If someone asked him was he a good husband, she was sure his answer would be, "I'm the best" but that was far from the truth. However, today she was in a good mood and had a full schedule ahead of her.

Jordyn's dentistry had expanded over the years into a cosmetic boutique, one that you've never experienced before, and she had recently launched an at-home line of whitening products.

Jordyn was the first African-American woman to have her own dental products which included a toothbrush, toothpaste, floss, mouth-wash and even chewing gum that fought against bacteria.

The one thing she would credit her dear husband for doing was pushing her to be the best she could be. Alongside Mr. King, she stood proudly as his wife being that she now brought millions of dollars to the table every year.

Their new home was in her name, and she was able to purchase it and not need a penny from Nasir. Ramone's tuition was paid in full, and that was another thing Jordyn didn't have to run to Nasir for. Thank God those days were now behind her.

"Okay, well I'll make reservations," she told him and then prepared to go back upstairs to get dressed.

But when Nas said, "Nah, it's on me this year. I will handle it," homegirl almost had a heart attack.

Spit bubbles formed in the corners of her mouth, and she just knew her ears were playing tricks on her. "Huh?" She needed him to clarify that.

"I'm for real, baby. I got this, and how about we invite Maude and her husband?" he suggested.

Jordyn knew it was too good to be true. "Sure," she told him and rolled her eyes. Everything he did could never be genuine or from the heart. He always had an ulterior motive.

Jordyn went upstairs to shower and get dressed so she could head on out. She peeped into Ramone's room, and he was still lounging around.

"What do you have planned for today?" she asked.

He shrugged his shoulders. "Probably riding with dad today." He was such a daddy's boy and now that he was older, hanging with mommy wasn't fun anymore. Ramone would rather be with friends or with his Pops.

Jordyn told him to have fun.She desperately wanted more children, but the way her business was taking off, she really didn't have the time these days anyway.

Jordyn stopped pressing Nas to attend doctor appointments and different consultations with fertility specialists. Ramone was a blessing from God and if she didn't have him, she would really be lost, so she was grateful for her son and left everything else up to God.

Over the years, things seemed to pan out, and she was thankful that she didn't give up on her marriage or herself. She still battled with her weight, but her self-esteem was now intact. The one thing she accepted was that men only treated you as good as you treated yourself, and Jordyn began to put herself first and in return, so did Nasir.

He was still a selfish manipulative asshole, but they had more good days than bad. Jordyn knew that she and Nas would be together forever, and it was sad to say, but as long as Lauren was out of the picture, she could survive and withstand the other trials and tribulations of their marriage.

She played her part and made sure home was always taken care of. Jordyn didn't question Nasir any longer, knowing he would do whatever it is that he wanted. The crazy thing was that she didn't think he was cheating anymore. It was now all business as he constantly expanded The Underworld. It felt good to be on the same page as her husband when it came to securing a better and profitable future for their son.

Jordyn sighed as she pulled her Bible from the first drawer of her nightstand and read Psalms 23. Nothing had changed in relations to her faith, for every storm she found herself in the middle in she constantly drew her strength from God. And that's how she remained standing to this very day.

"Babe, do you know where my gold cufflinks are?" Nasir appeared in their bedroom.

What would he do without me? He acted as if she had the answer for everything he ever asked and most times, she did. Jordyn closed her bible and said, "Amen" before going to retrieve the gold cufflinks. He had a habit of overlooking the smallest things. Jordyn searched every drawer on his side of the closet.

"Now I know I saw them..." She knew she wasn't tripping, so she stepped back, scratched her head and pondered over when the last time she saw the cufflinks. "Hmmm," she said aloud as she tapped her chin. "Gold cufflinks, gold cufflinks..." She looked again in the jewelry drawers that held her husband's things.

"I think I lost them." He had given up on looking for them.

Jordyn bent down and pulled the very last drawer out but wasn't expecting to see black folders where more clothing and other closet-related items should have been.

Nasir was still talking to her from the bedroom, but she had tuned him out. Her heart raced as she pulled one of the folders out and opened it. Black and white photographs of he riswhat fell out. Her and a man... a white man. And she was happy too. The glow was evident in the pictures. This was not new to her, but why was he still...

"J, you found them?"

She turned around with tears pooled in her eyes.

He took a deep breath. "Why snoop?" His accent was so heavy at times, mainly when he was guilty as hell.

"*Snoop? Why is she still your concern?*" she yelled and threw the many pictures in his direction. Nasir had already shared with Jordyn that Lauren was an asset and nothing more, but she didn't want to hear that bullshit. She knew things were too good to be true. "These weren't in here a few days ago, this is new...I swear."

"You swear what?" he challenged his wife.

"Every single time we take one step forward, you kick me a million steps back." She shook her head as she stood to her feet and walked out of the closet but not before dropping the gold cufflinks on the floor.

η

Growing up, he was always being lied to. Do you know how it feels to ask your grandmother where your mother is and why you haven't seen her in a few days, and she would look right at you and lie? It didn't feel good.

When he asked about his father, it was always a stream of lies.Sean vowed at a young age that he would be a man of integrity, a man who told the truth.He never wanted his name to be associated with no fugazy shit. He prided himself on being a nigga that always kept it one hundred thousand.

So, when Jackie asked him to be a man and sit her sons down since they now had a million questions about the money that Kevin walked in on, he knew he couldn't feed them any bullshit. Sean wasn't raising no dummies. They were growing into men, and he wanted them to be able to handle their own. He couldn't sugarcoat this shit.

"I'm a drug dealer."

Jackie's eyes went buck. "Sean, no... he's playing with y'all," she lied.

The thing about a lie was that if you told one, you had to tell another to keep up with the lie, and Sean didn't want to do that. "Jackie, let me talk to them by myself." He wanted her to gon' on.

She looked at her children and then eyed him with an, "I'm going to fuck you up" stare, but he wasn't bothered. He was the man of this house, and they were becoming men.

Kevin spoke up first once they were alone. "We been knew that, you used to work for my Pops."

Sean bit his tongue because he didn't work for that nigga. He worked *with* him, but that was here nor there.

"Yeah, something like that but listen, that's not to ever be repeated, do y'all hear me?" He was dead ass serious too. What went on in their house needed to stay in the house. He was sure that every black mother told their kids that at least once in a lifetime.

"Man, we not stupid, so what you sell?" Jonathan was eager to know it all.

"Everything. Listen, what I do isn't play-play, okay? It's for real. I'm taking real life penitentiary chances to provide for y'all niggas. It's not fun, it's not cool. This shit ain't no Grand Theft Auto ,it's real."

"Like *The Sopranos*?"

He shook his head. "Oh lawd." What he had gotten himself into?

Jonathan told his lil brother, "Nah, like *The Wire*. He in the streets, not in the mob, dummy."

The Underworld had surpassed both of those fictional television shows. "Uh, well..." He decided to not even go there. "The point I'm trying to make is to ummm..." Actually, he didn't know what the point was being that this was Jackie's idea. "Don't go in that room if I'm not home and if I'm home, knock first. Keep your mouth shut and be more mindful about who y'all let come over here," he finally found the words to say.

"Have you killed someone before?" Kevin asked Sean.

He damn near choked on the beer he was sipping. *You'd be surprised.*

"Haven't you asked him that before?"

"Go get washed up for dinner," he told them and sat back on the couch. He needed a blunt, more like two.

Jackie returned to the living room. "So, do they know you sell heroin, coke and everything else?" she questioned.

He pulled her arm down. "Watch your fucking mouth, man." He had never cursed at her before, but she wasn't scared of him.

"Don't you ever grab me like that again," she told him straight up. She would fight his ass if she had to.

He apologized quickly, but she needed to be mindful of what she said, for real.

"I'll be mindful when you stop counting millions of dollars in blood money in my house!" she spat.

"*Our* house, baby," he corrected her.

She wasn't stunting shit he was saying. "Technically, it's my house." She hated to remind him that the property was in her name.

Sean didn't want to go there with her. "Gon' on," he warned.

"Or what?" Jackie taunted him.

"If you want some dick, just take it." He already knew what his shawty was on.

But still, Jackie didn't know if their friends were in the room playing the game or what. She could have easily incriminated him by talking too loud and on shit she knew nothing about. Sean couldn't take any chances, especially when niggas was getting knocked left and right these days. The Underworld was tight, and damn near everybody at the police stations in all the boroughs were on their payroll, but in the blink of an eye a nigga would switch sides for their freedom, so he never got comfortable thinking he couldn't be touched.

That was the one small factor that set him apart from his comrades. Sean still moved like a nigga who didn't have a few million in the trunk. He took caution with everything he did and stayed prayed up. Life was worth living and not to be lived in a cage...Sean refused to ever end up in jail, *even if he was the dopeman.*

η

Malachi Morgan was at the mall, somewhere he hated to be, but for his kids he would do whatever.

"Daddy, they're only a thousand dollars? Can I get them?"

He was on the phone with a potential business partner, and the man laughed heartily, "Only a thousand? Your kids are blessed," he said to Chi.

To himself he thought, *More like spoiled.*

They had their mother's shopping habits, which was not a good thing. In fact, he was sure this was a mother's job. However, the last two runs to the mall had been on daddy's dime.

"Yeah," he whispered to his oldest daughter and then walked off but not too far away. It didn't matter if he did because he had two guards with him and his kids. You couldn't tell they were being paid a hundred bones to guard his family with their life, but they knew that shit, and that's all that mattered.

"So, what do you need from me?" the man from Turkey asked him, directing the call back to business.

He cleared his throat to speak. "Maybe ten mill starting off, I'm not at my desk to give you accurate numbers at this moment."

"That's in my alley, so hopefully it's not more than that."

Malachi wished he would start listening to his wife when she told him that things were done digitally these days, meaning all he had to do was download a few apps on his iPhone and it would be easier for him to float around and still get shit done. But Malachi Morgan was still old-school, pen and paper.

"I'm sure it's no more than that...for now." He had to reiterate that because the demand could go up which meant the price would change.

"When will you be home? I wanted to get everything wired to you before I go out of town. It's my wife's birthday, and I don't plan to discuss business while we are on vacation," the man said to him.

Chi understood that completely, but thankfully he and his wife were both work-a-fuckin-holics, and the grind didn't stop for them.

"In about an hour tops," he promised.

They ended the call right at the time where his kids were summoning him at the register. He didn't even want to know the price, he handed his bank card over to the lady.

"We did good today," Addison, his oldest baby, said with a big smile on her face.

"Yeah, I bet," he cringed as the long receipt began to print. He turned around and saw about fourteen shopping bags between the three.

"No more for y'all till Christmas, y'all breaking daddy's pockets," he lied.

His children didn't know the value of a dollar, especially not his oldest who thought money grew on trees. She was finishing up school and driving him fucking crazy. And the bad thing was, she loved hood niggas. Malachi didn't know how this happened. She went to private school her whole life, and he kept a leash on the collar.

Jade told him that's where he fucked up at, being the strict parent while her mother tried be her friend.

See, his wife and his baby mama were two different people; two totally different human beings, personalities and definitely mothers. Jade had no problem slapping the taste out of her kids' mouths, whereas Aaliyah babied Addison and made a million and one excuses for every mistake she made.

Jade didn't give her kids choices. It was her way or the highway. Addison was able to do her own thing. And it was sad to say, but his children with Jade were way more ahead than Addison, and they were younger than her. Malachi smiled at them and asked what was for dinner.

"Ma texted and said dinner was done."

"Well, let's ride then. Did y'all get her anything?" he questioned, but none of them said anything.

Chi shook his head. "Who raised y'all? You never come home with tons of bags and don't bring the main lady something." He backpedaled into the store and picked up the first he purse he laid his eyes on, knowing she had no problem taking it back if she didn't like it. One thing Jade didn't do was bite her tongue, though sometimes he wished she did.

He and his family piled into the back of the Escalade, and his driver asked, "Where to, Mr. Morgan?"

"Home sweet home." He had been out all day with his youngins and was ready to smoke and kick back. He and Jade were seeing better days, and he knew it was all God. There were a few times he dreamed about killing shorty, but he knew he would be sick without her, so he thought otherwise.

Sometimes he found himself thinking about all the fucked up shit she had done and what he did in return to make her feel the pain she inflicted upon him, but what was a relationship if you couldn't make it through the stormy weather?

He would tell anyone that prayer and counseling got them through that dark time. Jade had a problem with admitting her flaws and once she let that pride shit go, they were able to move forward.

Chi loved her more than she loved him, that much was quite obvious. Even now, she was still sort of reserved, and lately he had been putting in overtime to let her know they were truly good and he had forgiven her for real.

The elevator doors slid apart, and he smiled at the smell of something good in the oven mixed with cherrywood. He loved their place and was happy they decided not to move. They had been in their penthouse for many years, and Chi had no desire to be anywhere else. The top floor was where they had raised their children, and all they knew was high-rise buildings.

"Hey, y'all. Whoaaa, daddy broke the bank today," Jade commented once seeing the different designer bags they had in their hands.

"Yeah, about that, how do I keep getting chosen to take them to the mall?" he asked his wife as he gave her a hug and planted a soft kiss on her forehead.

"Cus they know not to dare ask me to take they young asses in no Gucci store," she laughed. "What do they have to look forwardto if you get them everything now? The Christmas tree gon' be empty?"

She had a point there. "Aye, bring them report cards to the dinner table!" he yelled down the hallway, but it was too late now.

Jade had thrown down tonight, and Chi was well-pleased as she listed everything she made.

"Hmmm, all right. I'm about to smoke real quick and then shower," he said.

"I love you."

He loved her too, but wondered where that randomly came from. "You good? How was your day?"

She smiled at him. "It was good, very productive. And stop overthinking. Everything is fine," she reassured her husband.

"All right, be back in an hour."

Jade watched her baby walk his fine ass down the hallway of their penthouse and make the first right into their master suite. She sighed as he disappeared from her vision. She would do anything to see that old glimmer in his eyes. Chi kept telling her that they were good, but she wasn't one hundred percent sure.

She had faith that they would be fine eventually, but when would that be? It had been year since her slew of affairs...and she still felt like she was paying for her mistakes.

Chi had always been a giver, so that never stopped, but it was the time and attention he used to give her that now felt obligated.S he didn't want them to go on dates or have sex because that's what they were "supposed" to do. Marriage was not supposed to feel like another thing on the to-do list. It was to be free and fuzzy. Malachi put too much thought into making her smile when he didn't have to. She wanted that old thang back, badly.

After dinner, the kids went up to the pool and left their parents at the dining room table by themselves. Jade was on her third glass of wine while Chi was still nursing a cup of chilled Belvedere.

"The man I was telling you about that your peoples introduced me to, he's on board for the project," he shared with her remnants of his day.

Her eyes were droopy, and the wine had her quite tipsy, but still she praised her man. "Salud to more success!"

He smiled lazily at her, cus he too was feeling wavy. "We fucking up right now, baby, way up!"

She definitely agreed with him. "Who ever thought a lil country girl from Alabama would be a world-renowned artist?" God had truly been good to her.

"I'm so proud of you," he beamed at her with pride.

"Touche, Mr. Morgan touché."

Malachi checked his Audemar. "How long do you think I have?"

She eyed him, not following his question. "For what?"

"To eat you until the kids come back."

And then there it was...every time she was wary of where his head was, he wanted to place it between her thick thighs.True enough, she had cheated on him, betrayed him and stepped out on their marriage more than few times, but there was never, there could never ever, be another man that made her feel the way he did. When she was stressed, down, up and happy, he took her higher. Malachi gave her an electrifying feeling that couldn't be found elsewhere.

"You know it don't take me long to drip," she eyed him sexily.

He moved some of the dinner plates around. "Well, bring that pussy to me." He licked his lips as he removed his white cotton Polo undershirt. Jade was messy, she was a wild squirter. Her pussy got disrespectful whenever he ate it, so he always removed his shirt.

She took her time walking bare foot to him. Her leggings were left on the other side of the glass table.

"I don't wanna break th-"

"Shhh, I got you," he promised as he placed her before him and laid her back on the cold table. She shivered at the temperature.

"I'm nervous," she told him.

"Don't be, baby."

He pulled her legs apart and rested one on his shoulder. Malachi used his hands to push those other lips to expose what he loved the most, and that was her pearl. "Damn, Jade." She was glistening and smiling at him.

"Tick, tock," she reminded him of the limit they were on.

Malachi didn't want to be disrupted when he started, so he said fuck it and picked her ass up.

"Chi!"

"To our bedroom we go." He smacked her ass and carried her to their bed. He plopped her down and went to lock the door. The lights were already off, so he all he had to do was drop to his knees and fulfill his craving. His wife tasted like the southern woman she was. He swore to God that her pussy tasted like peaches and ripe oranges.

"Baby, shit baby, oh my!" She could never take the wicked combination of pain and pleasure as he nibbled and pulled on her clit, but at the same time stroked her insides with two of his manicured fingers. "Right there," she coached him, knowing he really didn't need her help. He was a professional, no longer a rookie in the game.

Jade was older than him, but she would be damned if her man didn't teach her a few things over the years. Jade had no clue about working and controlling her pussy muscles until Mr. Morgan.

"Give it to me." He loved when she got buck and threw that pussy in his face. Jade was awakening the beast in him with that rough and aggressive shit. He wanted her juices all over his face and beard.

"Shitttttt, Chi!" She was sweating, panting and heaving all at the same damn time. It felt so good her stomachtightened up at the orgasm rumbling in the pit of her belly.

"Let it out, give it to me, bae." He knew what was about to happen. Years of making love to the same woman over and over again was a skill. One area they never lacked in was the bedroom.

"Okay, okay, I'm goingto cum," she shared with him. Jade said fuck her fresh silk press as she sat up trying to get a small glimpse of his head moving in and out and up and down as he dug her orgasm out of her.

"When was the last time you came?" he asked her. He couldn't remember because they had been so busy.

"I don't know, baby...fuck....I'm cumming, Chi, I'm fucking cumming!" she told him as it came. Hard. That pussy was thumping erratically. She sprayed her husband's face with a potent love juice he loved to drink. With his tongue, he hungrily lapped all of her up. "Hmmmm." Jade was exhausted. Working, cooking dinner, painting, consulting, working out and then this toe-curling head had her wanting to curl up with her thumb in her mouth.

"I love you, baby," she told him as he pulled his head from between her legs.

Chi smacked her thigh. "Go wash up, and I'm coming in behind you," he told her before he went to tell the kids to clean the kitchen up since he had just heard them come in.

Jade wobbled her half-naked ass to the bathroom. He didn't know why she was acting so tired because he was not done with her tonight.

The kids were thankful for the shopping spree today, so they hopped up and got the kitchen together. Chi locked their bedroom door and turned some music on now that they were no longer alone in the house. He walked into their massive shower and pulled her down on his dick as he took a seat on the marble bench.

"Ride me, Jade."

You never made love until you did it in the shower until the water ran cold. Jade conceived their children under the water, he was convinced.

"I'll do whatever you want me to do, daddy," she said and looked in his eyes as she climbed on top of his pole and slid down slowly, taking long deep breaths as she grew comfortable with him inside of her.

"You love me, don't you?" he asked, as if he wasn't already sure.

She nodded her head. "More than I can ever show you."

Chapter 7

"Pick a way you gotta choose, or you gon' fuck around and lose." – MoneybaggYo

In a casual Tom Ford navy suit, Sean stood in front of Jackie at the courthouse. They didn't do too much, their relationship had been on the low-low for so many years that she didn't bother with letting the world know she was getting married again. When she and the boys moved to New York with Sean, many people raised their eyebrows wondering how she could skip off to la-la land with her dead husband's best friend, but they all knew better to say it to her face.

Questions were posed in the streets such as, *Damn, how long he been fucking her? Did they set him up? What kind of an example is she setting for her children? Sean is trifling, how he gon' do that?*

Jackie's cousin had called her a few times with the tea but she quickly shut it down and told her that no one paid her bills or had been there in the way that Sean had, so they could all kiss her ass. No longer was she allowing anyone to control her happiness or her peace of mind.

Jackie wore a wrap dress by Diane Von Furstenburg and a pair of Fendi pumps. Her children wore navy, and the only invited guest was her mother.

Jackie asked Sean was his mom coming up, and he told her no. Sean hadn't spoken to her much since he moved up north, but every month he laced her accounts with plenty of money. And the crazy thing was, she hadn't tried to visit not once, so he did him while him she did her. Eventually, he would sit her down so they could have an adult conversation, but time hadn't permitted. Sean had a lot of shit going on but was giving his Queen a week of uninterrupted time.

After their quick nuptials, the family went to Ruth Chris Steakhouse and surprisingly, Sean telling Papa that he and Jackie had tied the knot sparked the interest of the wives, and they were there with roses and gifts.

Sean kept it cool, but it made him feel good that they came together to celebrate this milestone. Sean had supported all of them, so he wasn't sure why he didn't expect the same in return. He had some shit he needed to let go of, especially when it came to Nasir King, who was sitting right next to him talking shit.

The restaurant gave them the back room for free since Demi was a frequent customer at the establishment. Stuffed chicken, lamb chops and ten-ounce steaks were ordered by everyone, and the drinks never stopped coming.

Sean kept asking Jackie was she ready to go, but the twinkle in her eyes told him that she was having a good time so he relaxed.

"You the last one to get married, how do you feel?" Jade asked Sean.

"Bout time," he answered. He wondered would marriage life be different for the two of them.

"Any advice?" he asked everyone.

Jackie had been married before, but she wasn't going into this relationship with the same mindset that she had with Kentrell.

"Uh, don't cheat and come home early," Nasir told him.

Jordyn rolled her eyes. "And don't hide anything from your wife, she should know everything."

Papa shook his head, not agreeing with her ass. "Not everything," he chimed in.

"She should know enough," Jordyn countered.

Nasir rolled his eyes. "Make sure your wife stay in her place," he mumbled under his breath.

Jackie pursed her lips together. "Okayyy," she said as she finished the last sip of her champagne.

Demi had good advice. "Well, me and Papa married really young and so many people told me that we wouldn't last, including my own parents, but the one thing I can say that we made sure to do was to keep people out of our business. He's my best friend, and I'm his, and that's most important. Friendship before the relationship. I never felt as if I had to confide elsewhere, and I think I can speak for him and say it was vice versa."

Papa was beaming and blushing and reached over and tongued her down in front of everyone. "Love you, baby."

Demi looked just as in love as he did and from afar, it was beautiful.

Love was contagious, Jackie kissed her man.

Jade agreed with Demi, and she believed that's where the discord came in her own marriage.

"Business is business all day, but once you home, cut that shit off. The streets don't make it past my front door unless it's an emergency," Papa told Sean.

He nodded his head, knowing that was the one thing he really needed to work on.

"To love and happiness and married life," Jordyn proposed a toast.

She looked beautiful tonight, and Nasir made sure she knew it before they left the house, but apparently he didn't do a good job because she was still talking smack to him.

Everyone lifted their glass to celebrate a new union in The Underworld.

When the couple made it home many hours later, Jackie was in awe at how much money everyone gave them.

"It's vacation money," he told her.

"We didn't plan a honeymoon though."

Sean had been so busy leading up to this day that he forgot to tell her. "Damn, baby, it slipped my mind. We going to Aruba in the morning."

Jackie screamed and tossed the money from her hands as she got her thick ass up off the bed and jumped into his arms. "For real?"

He laughed. "Hell yeah, I gotta fuck you on the beach as your husband," he said while licking his lips.

Jackie was a beautiful bride today. He still couldn't believe he had married her. Ten years ago, he would have never thought this shit would have happened, but you can't help who you love.

Boo and Samira had their two cents about the impromptu marriage, which is the exact word that Samira used when his cousin passed her the phone.

Sean wasn't no dummy, he didn't make moves without thinking shit through. He wasn't a come-up to Jackie or a security blanket. They had real love, and he didn't feel the need to make them see that. As long as he felt it, he was good.

Sean kissed her in the mouth. "I love you."

She finally said it back after they shared vows earlier, and he was relieved because if she didn't say it he wouldn't have known what to do.

Her mother loved the house and told Sean to continue to make Jackie happy, and they would be good forever. The boys were happy and dapped him up after they said "I do." They were going to Aruba with them only because Sean didn't trust them in the house by themselves.

"I know I'm heavy, you can put me down," she told him.

Sean didn't wait a second to put her on the floor. "Hell yeah." Jackie was far from a light load, but he loved every pound on her.

"I need to start packing, my mama should have stayed to keep a look out on Kevin-"

"They going with us, but they got their own room."

She was relieved. "Family vacation."

He shook his head, "No. Honeymoon, Jack." Sean was cool with a dinner or meeting them for breakfast, but this trip was to celebrate their marriage.

"All right, all right, let me try to throw some stuff in a suitcase," she said and walked into her closet.

Sean grabbed his cell phone and went into his man cave to call Dr. Robinson.

"Congrats are in order, the pictures you sent were beautiful," she told him as soon as she answered.

"Preciate it, Doc. Quick question for you." She waited on him to continue. "Was I supposed to invite my mama? When I told Jackie I didn't tell her I was getting married, she gave me a look."

Dr. Robinson knew that Sean was in denial of the disconnect between him and his mother. "Do you feel as if today was important to you?"

He told her, "Yeah, I'm married now."

"So why didn't you invite her?" she asked him. Sometimes, Dr. Robinson wished she could shake him. Most of the answers he had were right in front of his face.

But that's where he was stumped. "I don't know, Doc."

She took a deep breath. "Sean, think back to maybe some of your other accomplishments, was your mother there?"

He seemed to be in denial but was okay with being that way because it was difficult for him to accept the situation for what it was. It was better for him to pretend that everything was okay; that he was busy, and his mother was his mother. No matter what, he loved her anyway, or did he? His mouth moved to say no, but his mind went from the conversation with his therapist to a talk he had with his mother many years ago, many, many years ago.

"Ma can you hear me?" It was loud in her background and his as well, but she could have controlled hers simply by asking them to turn the music down for a second or stepping outside of the gambling house. Of course, Neet would never do that, not even for her only boy.

"Huh?" she screamed into the cellular device.

Sean peered over his shoulder before walking further down the dimly hit hallway. His body ached, and his left eye had a gash so deep he knew it would be worse by morning.

"Yeah, my bad. Mama, I won!" he told her happily. Sean had consecutively defeated the same Light-Weight champion three times in a row. He was possibly well on his way to the big leagues. For the past nine months, he had been training in New Orleans, Louisiana hoping to make a dollar out of fifteen cents and live out his dreams of becoming a renowned fighter.

"Sean, you need to let that shit go before you get hurt," his mother told him, disregarding that he was actually good and winning all his fights.

He dropped his head, discouraged by the lack of encouragement from his mother. The one person who was supposedly required to care, nurture and be supportive, was selfish, unconcerned and rude. She lacked motherly love.

"I'm not going to get hurt, I know what I'm doing," he told her with confidence, but she didn't want to hear that.

Neet had heard her name being called and needed to get back to her weekly card party that she hosted in the hood.

"Baby, I gotta go, but Sean, find you something else to do...please. Your cousin is making a lot of money, you need to come back home and get on his level."

That was the last thing he heard her say before the call was disconnected. She had hung up in his face and went back to living her life while he remained posted on the wall replaying her words in his head.

"Nah, not really," he told her three minutes later after that one painful memory of his mother shutting him down replayed in his mind.

"And you've been there for her, correct?"

"Yeah, but if we taking it there, Doc, I've been there for a lot of niggas who ain't never did shit for me. That's just who I am." His heart was made of gold, and he had a hard problem saying no to those in need.

"And who's there for you?" She pushed further and asked, "Today was supposed to be a magical day, and I'm sure it was, but think about who was there for you today. The ones who show up when it's least expected are the ones who care, in most situations. It's who's clapping for you without you asking them to...that's who we celebrate," she shared a life gem with him.

Sean thought about The Underworld. As the years went by, he felt good about the progression they had made and then on some days, he wanted out and desired a life of independence.

"I need a real sit down with you." He pinched the bridge of his nose and took a deep breath.Was he going about life the wrong way? The Underworld definitely put a smile on Jackie's face today and surprisingly, his as well. Whereas, Boo and Samira didn't send a gift or nothing. Could he finally let his guard down and trust The Underworld? A knock at the door of his man cave took his attention. It was his wife.

"Baby, I packed a few things for you," Jackie told him.

Sean told Dr. Robinson that he would get in touch with her after his honeymoon as he stood up and went to open the door.

"Heyyy, husband," she cooed at Sean as she wrapped her arms around his frame and pulled him close. He smelled like weed and designer cologne mixed with strawberries from the cake that Jackie had made for the special day. Never in a million years did she think she would use that word again regarding another man.

"You got everything together?" He looked into her eyes and saw a glimmer of love and expectancy. How could he ever let her down?Although they didn't hand write their vows, he took the court-mandated ones very serious and would do whatever it took to make her happy and keep her there.

"Yes, ready for bed?" She was tired but not exhausted enough to have sex as husband and wife and hopefully, he was on the same page as her.

"Yeah, let me finish this blunt up, and then I'll join you." His mind was on a million and one things and if he didn't get higher, he wouldn't be able to rest peacefully.

Sean wanted to place everything on the back burner so he could really enjoy their vacation together because she deserved that, and he did too.

That sounded like a plan to Jackie, so she went to prepare for bed and left Sean alone to finish his herbal meditation. The word "unity" crossed Sean's mind, so he pulled up the word on his cell phone to get the real meaning of the word.

Unity isdefined as the state of being one;oneness. It's also defined as a whole or totality as combining all its parts into one, the state of being united or combined into one, as of the parts of a whole; unification. Unity is also defined as absence of diversity, unvaried or uniform characters. Oneness of mind, feeling etc. as among a number of persons; concord, harmony, or agreement.

The Underworld could go further in this street shit if they seriously got on one accord. It was as if everyone had their own end goal. For some it was the throne, going legit or passing it to someone else, but when Sean got back from vacation he would seriously propose that they laid everything out on the table and then come together for once and for all.

Things had to get better because Sean didn't want to feel some type of way about the people who were supposed to be the "closest" to them. For goodness sake, they broke bread together, and he wanted unity amongst the organization. And, he really didn't like how they treated the workers, mainly Nasir.

Sean would suggest a dinner for everyone, including the mules, packers, runners, even the niggas who looked out on the block. If everyone felt like they were showing love, then the silent fear of one person bringing the empire down to crumbles might go away.

Sean finished up his blunt and stuffed it in the ashtray to kill the smoke. He heard the sounds of R. Kelly playing in the hallway leading to the master bedroom and could only imagine what tricks Jackie had up her sleeve.

He opened the door and was surprised to see white petals all over the floor and tea light candles spread around.

"White represents new beginnings," she shared with him from the middle of bed where she looked like an angel; his angel, his wife.

Sean locked the door behind him and removed his clothes. He saw her chest heaving up and down. Like a dog in heat she was anticipating him touching her...licking her...fucking her...and then making sweet love to her until the sun rose.

"I like this," he commented on the white La Perla lingerie set paired with white furry heels that had to be about six inches.

She reached up and pulled him down on to the bed and top of her. "Love me now." Jackie was far from aggressive and had no problem allowing her man to be the dominant while they were sexual, but tonight didn't come with any particular rules or instructions. She wanted him in the worst way and didn't want to talk any longer. They had danced, talked and wined and dined all night and now, her body needed proper taking care of.

Sean kissed her forehead, nose and then lips before attacking her neck with no remorse.Using his lips and teeth to sink into her skin, he placed marks as reminders of what he would do to her coming forth.

"Seannn,"she moaned as he magically made his fingers into his favorite place and broke the dam. She spilled all over their sheets.

"You ready for this dick?" He was always asking questions he already knew the answers to.

She nodded her head, happily and hungrily wanting whatever he was going to give to her, whether it was dick in her mouth or her pussy...and if they were really doing things in a new way, he could have her ass too.

"I want you now," she whined.

Sean didn't have to be told twice, always wanting to give Jackie the desires of her heart. He lifted up a tad to see where he was heading and then decided to not play around anymore and inserted his rock-hard penis into her tunnel of love.

Inside of her nothing else mattered. Gone were the thoughts of his mother, lack of unity in The Underworld, lack of support from his cousin and every other lil' fucking thing he could complain about. Jackie's body had a way of taking him in and making him feel complete.

She yipped out in pleasure as he stroked her middle in ways no one had ever done before. Sean was a silent lover, holding in his satisfaction while she was too, but tonight she refused to hold on to her bottom lip. She moaned loudly, knowing the boys were in front of video games and R. Kelly served as an extra layer of drowning her out.

"Yes baby, yes, baby," she encouraged him to dig deeper into her soul and pull out orgasm after orgasm.

Sean dropped his head into the sheets to keep from howling like a wolf. Jackie was moving her hips under him and tightening her pussy on his dick. He couldn't give up so soon, so he pulled out and flipped her over, arching her back in a way for him to enter her until he was balls deep into her pussy and only his nuts hanged, clapping her clit.

"Lower," he told her, pushing her body down, forcing her belly button to touch the bed while her ass was in mid-air. Jackie rested on her elbows as she got comfortable for this position that Sean seemed to love second to missionary.

"I love you so much," she looked over her shoulder and told him as he stroked her slowly.

"And I fuckin' love you too, baby."

She refocused her attention on preparing herself to cum again and again. The couple made love until he nor she could take it anymore. And when it was time to head to the location where the private jet awaited them, Jackie was limping to the plane.

"Ma, what's wrong with you?" the boys teased, already knowing what went down last night.

"Shut up and mind yo' business," she rolled her eyes at their jokes.

Sean joined in on the laugh and then smacked Jackie's ass. "Leave them alone, they know you a married woman now," he said as if married women could have all the sex they wanted and single women weren't allowed to. And boy was last night beyond amazing. It was sex on a whole other level, and Sean knew he was about to have the time of his life in Aruba. Jackie only had permission to eat and suck his dick, he joked with her this morning after they finished making love in the shower.

She turned to him and smiled instead of hitting him back. "Yes, I am." Married.... Jackie was married to Sean...her husband's best friend.

η

The next morning, Demi was wide awake and ready to start her day after running five miles, as she did three times out of the week, and making sure the children had breakfast and were doing something productive and not destructive. She lived her life on a strict schedule, every second of the day was accounted for. The children were all actively involved at school and in the community. If they weren't at swimming lessons, then they were at soccer or Spanish lessons, or the math tutor was at the house. Plus, her girls all danced, so she was always busy.

But this life...she loved it so much. There was nothing Demi would trade out if she could. From her clingy kids to her almost senile husband, she was happy. And it wasn't always this way, it took her many years to discover peace and to be content with where she was and the many loads she had carried. Demi struggled with seeing her peers from high school travel the world alone while figuring shit out and finding themselves. She didn't always know her purpose or what she was supposed to do in the world, but it was her children. No longer did she pity herself for choosing love right after graduating high school over everything else. No longer did she beat herself up for always being pregnant or turning down events because her children needed her home. This was her life.Demi was a mother and a wife, and nothing came before those two major responsibilities and roles.

Her husband was still sound asleep so she tiptoed into their bathroom to shower before one of her babies came looking for her .Demi could never go too far away without one of them needing her to do something or for a hug. Her children loved hugged and kisses, and they got that from their father.

Tattooed, rude and rugged, Papa was the sweetest man she had ever known, and the only man she had ever loved unconditionally. Not even her father could compare to Papa.

She closed the bathroom door, not wanting to wake him up before his body was ready. She undressed out of her gym clothes and turned the shower on. Demi was natural and rarely wore her hair pressed because she sweated a lot while running and doing other activities, so for the most part, her hair remained in a bun on the top of her head in its natural state.

But according to her schedule, today was wash day, so she untied the knot and allowed her wild and curly hair to fall way past her shoulders. She had cut her hair a few years ago while dealing with life and the death of her son, but Papa begged her to let it grow back and to never cut it again.

She ran her hands through the untamed mess knowing it would take her about two hours to wash, shampoo, condition and detangle her tresses.Demi stepped into the shower and took a deep breath, it felt so good under the hot water. Her body was thankful for the pressure of the water hitting her aching muscles. She moved her head under the water to wash her hair.

Papa rolled over, but wasn't surprised to see that the bed was empty. Demi went to bed early and woke up even earlier. On most nights when he made it in, she had texted him hours before apologizing for not being able to wait up for him.

Many years of being together, Demi had finally accepted that her husband's definition of, "Baby I'm on the way home" was not ten or even thirty minutes away, more like hours and hours.

Demi trusted her husband and without trust, they wouldn't have made it this long. Mainly because he kept such late night hours, and it was nothing for Papa to have to run out of town and come back days later without a hint of communication.

Security and trust went hand in hand, and Demi trusted her man because she was very much secure in their relationship. She was confident that there was only one Demi. She didn't have a problem seeing him go somewhere without her, which was rare being that they thoroughly enjoyed each other's company. No husband wanted to dread going home, and no wife wanted to cringe when the alarm went off and their husband came through the garage door. What kind of way was that to live with the person you claimed to love?

Everything wasn't always perfect, but they had more good days than bad, and to Demi that was worth fighting for.

Papa sat up and stretched, instantly regretting not rolling his normal "wake and bake" blunt. Papa groaned as he got out of bed and went to take a leak.

The bathroom in their estate was oval-shaped. The shower was in the middle of the floor and was big enough to hold about ten people, literally. On each side of the bathroom were two infinity sinks which gave them a total of four and a vanity desk. When you entered the bathroom, the lights instantly came on, and the floors were heated.

Papa smiled at the sight of Demi's ass and her curls trailing her back.

"Goooooooodmorning, baby!" He was well pleased with what was before him.

She turned around, not bothering to cover herself because she loved her body, and Papa did too. Plus, they had been together so long, it was nothing he hadn't seen a billion times before.

"Hey, baby!" she shouted over the water. Papa slept naked every night and with every step he took, his dick swung to the left and then to the right as he made his way to the toilet. "How did you sleep?" Demi asked him that every morning, no matter what. His well-being was important to her. She was always encouraging him to detox and to practice self-care because he neglected his self all the time for the sake of everyone else.

No one worked harder than her husband, and she was thankful he was a great provider. But the best thing she ever did for herself, other than having her children, was go back to school to get her degree. Demi always felt like something in her was missing because she didn't have her certifications. And no, school didn't always qualify you and wasn't required to succeed, but Demi wanted her children to know that college was an option for a better future. It was something she did for herself, and it felt damn good.

"Yep," he told her after flushing the toilet. Papa brushed his teeth and then joined her in the shower. She moaned as he took over her hair washing duties and massaged her scalp.

"I feel like you just washed your hair, or am I tripping?"

She shook her head. "I did last week," Demi reminded him.

Papa couldn't keep up with Demi, she was such a busy body. "Can I ask you a question?"

She nodded her head, not caring what he wanted to know as long as he didn't stop touching her scalp the way he was. It felt amazing.

"Did you mean everything you said yesterday about me?"

Papa was a man, a hoodlum, some might even argue that he was a killer, but Demi would never want to hear that. He was rough around the edges, well to be honest, he was just a nigga; a real, street hood nigga who would blow your fucking head off but...he had a weakness: Demi Westbrook-Huffington was his soft spot.

She was his, "don't push me cus I'm close to the edge" kind of thing. Demi was the one person who could get away with hell. She was the only one allowed to check him and tell him when he was fucking up, anybody else just might get pistol-whipped. She was who he listened to. She was his mentor, therapist, superior, wife, baby mama, best friend and his number one supporter. Demi was who got him together, and at the same time, she was why he struggled with who he was.

He never felt good enough for someone of her caliber. To this day, whenever he attended events as her date, people whispered. Beautiful Demi with the man with sagging pants, worn Chuck Taylors and tattoos from his forehead down to his ankles, is she really married to him? Demi's world of dance was a judgmental universe, and Papa had been judged on several occasions but she always had a blind eye to the hate.

Papa cared more than she did. Demi loved him and didn't care what people had to say. She turned around and touched his face gently.

"Baby, you know I meant it. What's wrong?" she asked, seeing the faraway look in his eyes.

"Nothing, I'm good. I love you." He didn't want to seem so emotional and shit first thing in the morning.

Demi would have probed him for more, but in due time he would tell her whatever was on his mind. "It's me and you, right?"

He nodded his head. "Always."

Papa was a nigga, but he had feelings too and never wanted her to think there was better out there because he wanted to be all she ever knew. Demi had only experienced him, and he wanted it to stay that way forever. He would kill a mother fucker if they ever tried to convince her otherwise.

η

"Hey, babe, you forgot something," Jackie told Sean right before he was about to head out to meet Chi at MJ's house.

He backpedaled into the room and patted his pockets while doing a mental check of everything.

Phones?

Gun?

Cash?

Keys?

She walked towards him with her fist balled up, and Sean was now confused. "What did I forget?"

Jackie dropped something in the palm of his hand. *"Your ring."* She had a slight attitude.

"It was on the counter in the bathroom," he told her as if she didn't know.

Jackie nodded her head. "You're absolutely right, and not on your finger, so put it on." She folded her arms and gave him all her attention.

Sean didn't want to wear the ring. "Is it a problem if I don't?" He sounded scared to ask the question, already knowing it would be an issue.

She snaked her head back in pure disbelief. "I wear mine. Is it a problem if I was to take this off and say I'll be back later?"

He laughed because she was a character. "Jack, that's not what happened. I told you I had to leave back out hours ago."

"But you *just* went in there, used the bathroom, got dressed and took your ring off." She was low-key pissed off. It hadn't been a week since they returned from their memorable honeymoon, and he was back in the streets every fucking night.

"That's not how that went, I was washing my hands cus they smelled like weed," he explained.

"Sean, put the ring on, it's not up for debate." She wasn't arguing with her husband about wearing the ring. He *had* to wear it. Point blank period.

Sean smacked his lips. "I'm not a ring person. It's not my thing, baby."

"You don't get to say shit like that, you don't get an option," she let him know.

He really had to go, so he tried to hand her the ring back. "Here."

She shook her head. "I swear to God," she warned.

Sean would pacify her now, but she didn't run shit. "Bye, man," he told her after he slid the ring onto his finger.

"Love ya!" She was pleased that he made the right decision because if he hadn't, homeboy would have been on the couch tonight.

Sean left out, and Jackie spent the rest of the night doing research on a cookbook. Her husband gave her free reign to do whatever with his money, but she wanted to make the right decisions and think this business move through.

Jackie was contemplating opening a restaurant and a cookbook, or both. She had also stumbled across something about food trucks being the new thing, so she planned on doing some more research on those as well. She had too much time on her hands, so she could do it all if she wanted to. Jackie's sons would both be out of the house before she knew it, and it seemed as if Sean wasn't letting up any time soon when it came to The Underworld. Jackie had to find something to do, or she would be returning to work as a nurse.

On the other side of town, Sean was smoking a blunt with Chi and MJ, who hadn't said two words to them since she let them into her house.

"I think this blunt is stale." Chi kept spitting or flicking something with his tongue.

MJ shrugged her shoulders. She knew it was stale, but she wasn't saying shit. She preferred to smoke in a bong anyway.

"Hell yeah," Sean definitely agreed.

A surprise knock came, and everyone reached for their guns, including the owner of the home. From the look on her face, she wasn't expecting any guests.

MJ was off. Sean had always felt that way about her but even more so now. Ever since that nigga died in that plane crash, she barely spoke, and she didn't fuck with The Underworld too much. In fact, Nas had demoted her, but MJ couldn't care less about standing up on her feet all day cooking dope and shit. She was done with their asses and wanted them to set her free.

"Who is that?" Chi asked MJ.

She rolled her eyes. "Nigga, do it look like I know?"

She went to open the door with her gun in her hand. Whoever it was had to know her because she didn't take customers after five. Yeah, it was a trap house, but she also laid her head in this house and treated her shit like a real operation.

She had business hours, and they were in stone. MJ made no exceptions because that's when you set yourself up to get robbed or killed. There were times when niggas thought she fucked with them on the cool tip and would come knocking on her door at nine or ten o'clock at night, and she would be sitting right in the living room, smoking or doing whatever it was she did at night and wouldn't move a muscle to let them in. And no, she didn't run to turn her lights off or none of that shit.She didn't care if you knew she was home or not. That's how you demanded respect and remained professional.

"It's me," the person said as if she were a frequent visitor.

But all three of them knew who the voice belonged to...especially Sean.

Lauren Howard was Lauren Howard. She alone was an adjective. She was a verb. A action. A sentence. A complete thought. She was *that* chick. The epitome of "bring her home to mama" and the definition of, "Everything I ever wanted in a woman" plus so much more.

Her radiant smile shone through the dimly lit living room in MJ's house.

"Oh wow, I should have called," she said through clenched teeth.

Malachi shrugged his shoulders. "We still family, Lo. How have you been?" He stood up to give her a hug, but she really didn't fuck with any of them. However, she was raised right and knew how to also be fake when it was sort of necessary, so she hugged him back.

"Hope all is well, Chi. How has Jade been? And the kids?" She took it an extra step and asked questions she couldn't really give two fucks about.

He told her everyone was good, real good actually.

Sean watched Lauren as he sat back comfortably on the couch. The room was filled with smoke with all the blunts in rotation.

MJ commented on how nice Lauren looked, and of course, she downplayed it as usual. That's Lauren Howard for you though.

"Girl, I threw this on," she told MJ in response to her compliment. And knowing Lo, she probably really did throw it on, but she still looked as if she was fresh off of someone's runway.

The grey sweater and denim jeans were casual, but most likely designer, and the Moschino boots she wore were brand new, that much was obvious. Lauren had her real hair French braided to the back, and she had on diamond earrings that could blind someone if they stared too hard. On one hand she worea simple silver Rolex, and the other hand she wore the ring, the infamous ring that was an heirloom of Nasir's grandmother.She hated him truly, but never took the ring off. It was special to her.

"Is that a wedding ring on your finger? Say it ain't so." She was shocked as she spoke to Sean.

He looked down at the Cartier silver band that he was forced to wear. "Yeah, still in the newlywed phase," he said and smiled at Lauren.

She nodded her head, giving him a silent stamp of approval. "She's a very lucky woman."

"Nah, I'm the lucky one," he told her and winked his eye.

Lauren asked MJ did she cook and in fact, she did. The two of them went to heat up whatever was in the fridge while Sean and Chi smoked. Business had been handled, but it was a ritual to smoke at MJ's house when you first arrived and when you departed.

"Hey, where did y'all park? I didn't see any cars when I pulled up," Lo asked out of curiosity.

Sean told her he parked up the street, and Chi shared that he was dropped off by his driver.

"I see some things still haven't changed," she told Chi of him always being chauffeured. She went back into the kitchen with MJ.

Chi saw Sean's eyes on her ass and said, "You can look but don't touch, nigga. You married now."

He didn't laugh, and Sean would have appreciated him saying it in a joking manner whereas not minding his own fucking business.

"Happily married, but I'm not blind," he said.

Sean had no plans of steeping out on Jackie, but damn, it was just a fat ass. Was he wrong for looking? He had tapped that already anyway.

"I never looked at her in that way," Chi said.

Sean thought to himself, *Good for you, nigga.* Instead of responding to his comment, he passed him the blunt.

"Have you ever kept something from Jade?"

Chi thought about his question before answering. "Nah, I can't think of nothing."

"So you tell her everything?"

Chi asked him, "What's everything? Like street shit?"

He shook his head. "No, your past stuff you did before y'all got together."

"For what? That's irrelevant, and I don't wanna know nothing about her either."

Sean nodded his head. Half of him wanted to pour his soul to Jackie, and the other half of him planned on dying with that one big secret.

Chi saw the look on Sean's face and warned him, "If you gotta think that hard about it, don't tell her." He then said, "Y'all are married now, don't fuck that up by saying something she probably don't care about anyway."

But it wasn't that easy. Shit was complicated. He knew Jackie would care. She would be hurt and betrayed.

Sean stood up. "Let me get home." He needed to hold and make love to her. That's the only thing that would keep his mind off of that.

Chi was about to leave as well. "MJ, come lock the door, we out," he shouted.

"Why must you yell? It's not that big in here." She hated when people raised their voices.

"Man, come lock the damn door, Erykah Badu," he teased.

Lauren stood with a mug in her hand. "Take care, Sean, and congrats again."

He blushed, hating how Lauren Howard still had some sort of effect on him. Good pussy was unforgettable, he knew first hand.

Chapter 8

"No one wins when the family feuds." – Jay-Z

Chi was in the gym going in as he did every morning when his chocolate cupcake stood before him with a scowl on her face.

"What's wrong with you?" he asked her, scanning his brain wondering had he fucked up...but he hadn't done shit. Plus, they had sex last night, and she was on cloud nine when she rolled over on her side of the bed and said goodnight. What possibly happened from then to now?

"You tell me."

Women expected their men to do everything and be everything. Today, Jade wanted him to be a mind-reader.

"Uh, you cramping?" he took a wild guess.

She rolled her eyes and smacked her lips. "The first day I get on this stupid ass social media shit, and I get a DM from some bitch saying that you her man, and you don't really want to be with me," she finally spilled her guts.

Chi pressed stop on the treadmill so he could get off. This was some unbelievable shit. "Say what now?"

Even when he moved out for that brief time, he wasn't pillow talking with other bitches and discussing Jade. He would never discus her with another woman.

"It's old, but I don't care," she added.

He realized then. "Oh, all right." Chi put one foot in front of the other, prepared to get back on the treadmill and finish his run, but she wasn't done with him.

"What you mean, oh all right? Who is this hoe?" Jade didn't curse much, but she was pissed the hell off. She didn't cuss in front of their children, but they were alone, and she was two seconds from kicking his ass.

"Man, you just said this shit was old, so what you want me to say?"

She couldn't believe him right now. "I want you to tell me that you don't know the hoe."

Jade was tripping. "But that could be a lie. I probably do know her, so now you want me to lie to you?" This was a pointless conversation to him.

"Chi, why is this girl messaging me? I am your wife, they shouldn't even have this kind of courage."

He wasn't in the mood for this shit. "Jade, what are you on there for anyway?"

"My publicist thinks it's a good idea for me to create a social presence. We have to go with the wave, Malachi," she schooled him.

He was in the streets and didn't fuck with social media. He believed that's how niggas got caught up, posting pictures and shit. The FEDS were always lurking. He had no desire to post anything he had or where he went. No one would ever be able to keep up with him or his family.

Chi constantly preachedto his oldest daughter to keep her ass off of there and to not take any pictures of him or where she lived with her mom, and definitely not at his house.

Addison knew not to even think about posting him on Father's Day. People speculated that she was a secret child to some famous rapper or basketball player. At one point, they even accused her on some gossip site of being a whore. Addison cried and cried, wanting Chi to hire a private investigator to get to the bottom of the rumor, but he refused. His only suggestion was to get off social media. She wasn't doing nothing but flexing and belittling people anyway. He didn't understand her reason for being on there. She wasn't making any money or promoting black excellence.

"Hello!" She mushed him in the forehead once she realized he was not listening to her.

"Aye, don't start that shit." Lately, she had a bad habit of putting her hands on him whenever she got mad, and he was sick of that shit.

"She told me I was a bitter hoe!" Jade shrieked.

"And what you say back?" Chi laughed. This social media shit was crazy to him.

Thank God he wasn't cheating because he would have been caught the hell up with these young bitches not knowing how to play their role and wanting to post everything for folks to see.

"I told her she would be a dragged hoe if she ever messaged me again."

He nodded his head. "Good job, baby."

His lil mama was from the country. Jade used to play with pigs and shit growing up, so he knew she meant every word she said about beating the girl up.

"And you still don't wanna know who she was?"

He shook his head as he stretched his body so he could lift some weights before he went to shower. He had a meeting with The Underworld today. Surprisingly, Sean had called it, and that had never happened before so Malachi was eager to hear what he had to say.

"She irrelevant, baby. It's all about you...always has been, Jade."

She hated when he pulled her back in under his spell with those smooth words and long eyelashes.

He looked at her to see if she had anything else to say because if not, she could go back to doing whatever she was doing before she interrupted his session.

"What?" she asked him.

"Is that all?"

According to his tone, she knew the conversation was over. "Bye, Chi. You act like you be so focused in here."

"I am. You want me to stay this fine, don't you?" He was a gym rat and obsessed with his twelve pack and buff arms and legs.

"Not if more Instagram thotties gon' come out the woodworks."

Here we go with this shit. Chi knew then and there he had to get her ass off of social media before she drove him crazy and their marriage in the dirt. They had worked too hard to get on the same page again, and he would be damned if some virtual bullshit messed them up and set them back.

η

The Underworld

Money made his dick hard. It made him happy and kept him at peace. Honestly, money was the reason he woke up so early in the morning ready to start another day.

His mother asked him the other day over lunch, "How much longer, baby? What's the end game for you?"

She wanted to know when will it ever be enough.And that was a real ass question because truth be told, he told himself when he was about twenty-one years old and counting through his first mill that he only wanted nine more million dollars, and he was done.And then two years later, before he knew it he had made ten million, and then he said that wasn't enough, he needed twenty-five more million.

Well, twenty-five million turned into needing one-hundred million, and one-hundred million went to five-hundred million, and then he decided that once he made his first billion dollars, he would retire.

That was four years ago, and Nasir was past rich. He was floating in money. He could shit a hundred dollars three times a day and still have tons of money. And he didn't just have a lot of fucking money, but he also had stocks, real estate, investments and businesses that brought him in more money. At this point in his life, he didn't want or need anything and neither did his family, including his son.

Ramone was a multi-millionaire, and he didn't even know it. Nasir and Jordyn separately had money put up for him, so he would forever be straight.

So what now? When would he let this shit go? He had no idea. The Underworld gave him a hard-on. The thrill of getting shit done and being in charge...the power was why he couldn't stop just yet.

After a shower and a reading of some book that Jordyn had passed on to him since they were both book-worms, he went downstairs to make a smoothie so he could head on out.

The way their house was designed, each room on the first level had floor to ceiling windows. Nasir wanted to be reminded of home as much as possible. St. Lucia was near and dear to his heart and always would be. His favorite part of the house was between the library, his man cave and the backyard that resembled a mini-resort. Palm trees, an infinity pool and an outside kitchen and living room were key exponents of the backyard.

Nasir stood at the counter while his kale and banana smoothie blended in the blender. Jordyn was already gone, leaving hours before he even woke up and Ramone as well. Nasir enjoyed the peace and quiet of the house and almost hated to leave, but today there was an Underworld meeting.

They didn't meet often and most times, well really he was the only one to call meetings being that he was the head honcho, but today Sean wanted everyone to get together, and that was all he said.

Nasir couldn't wait to hear whatever this nigga had to say. Hopefully, he would announce his retirement being that he was a newlywed. He believed in giving a nigga credit where it was due, but Sean had been a thorn in his side for quite some time now. First, it started when he began to make decisions concerning who could cop in the South without clearing it with him first. Then out of nowhere he befriended Lauren and had her doing shit for him that he could have found any other chick to do it. Nasir had warned him to fall back, but Sean grew even bigger balls and fucked his bitch. That was the final straw, yet he still spared his life. Sean kept pushing him, kept putting himself where he didn't belong.

Polo struck against Nasir by trying to damn near kill Lauren and instead of letting him handle it, Sean played captain-save-a-hoe and caused problems when Nas had a plan. Apparently, he didn't move fast enough, so ever since then, they had been at odds. He stayed out of Nasir's way and vice versa. It was obvious they weren't close, and that was cool with Nas. As long as that money came in on time, he was good to go.

The house phone rang, and that was a rare occurrence so he answered. "Hello."

"It's all about to come crumbling down."

"Who is this?" Nasir asked.

The line clicked, and the call ended. Nasir tried to call the number back, but the person had calls blocked.

What was crumbling down? Surely not The Underworld. He wasn't even bothered by the call, the only thing that had him in question was, how did they get his home phone number? And how did they know he would be the one to answer?

After this lil' meeting, he was going to check in with his security and tell them to beef up on guards with his son and wife. Nasir also needed to stop by his attorney's office and see what was going on. And then lastly, a visit to Ms. Howard, who was responsible for keeping him in the loops with any possible pending charges.

Nasir let Lauren do her thing since she claimed to be so in love with this Simon cat. He was still confident that he could bag her if he wanted to, but truth be told, Lauren had moved on. For real.

Nasir finished his smoothie and then went upstairs to get dressed.

After he was looking and smelling good, he turned the alarm on and waited on his driver to pull up so they could ride out. On the way to his meeting, he phoned Jordyn.

"Yes," she answered on the second ring, sounding as if she was so busy.

Nasir rarely called her throughout the day, but this was important. "Hey, I just left the house. Has the house phone been ringing a lot lately?"

"Uh, what kind of question is that? I don't know. We all have cell phones," she told him.

"Okay, well if it rings while you're there, answer it, J."

Jordyn was now worried and wanted to know was there something she needed to know. "What's going on?"She got up from her desk and went to close her office door.

"Nothing, can you do that for me?"

She told him, "Yeah I can, where are you now?"

"Meetings all day, I'll try to make it in early."

Jordyn had a long day too. "I don't want Ramone to keep being home alone."

"It's tons of people there," he reminded her of the full staff of security they had.

"Not his family," she spat.

Nasir didn't have time for this shit. "All right, I'll scoop him from school, and he can ride with me."

"Don't have my son around no foolishness."

He was half listening to her as he scrolled through his email on his other phone. "Yeah, all right, have a good day."

"You too, I love you." She always made sure he knew that.

"I know," was his stark response, and then he hung the phone up. Sometimes he was in the mood for that shit, and other times she just had to chalk it up and know that their love was understood, even when he barely said it back.

The sting no longer hurt. Jordyn was numb to it. She had married a man whowas addicted to the hustle more than his wife.

It is what it is, was how Jordyn felt.

η

Miko hated that this stupid ass meeting with The Underworld fell on the same day as her umpteenth appointment with her fertility specialist. Nash couldn't be in two places at one time and unfortunately, he was losing hope with these different doctors promising his girlfriend they could perform miracles and really couldn't.

What he wanted her to understand was that there was no amount of money that could change what God had planned. Miko kept trying to find the most expensive specialist thinking they would have a different outcome. That was not possible.

She sat in her silver Porsche truck with a tear-stained face, her mascara and eyeliner running into each other and down her red cheeks. She was defeated at this point. The one thing she really wanted out of life was the one thing that damn near seemed impossible. She would do anything to conceive. And no, adoption was not in her plans. Miko wanted to experience labor and motherhood first hand. Nash deserved that, and she did too.

He called her phone over and over again, but eventually the calls stopped and she knew that was because he probably had to run on set to handle his obligation. She appreciated that he wanted to be with her, but she told him that business came, and she would be okay. It wasn't like Miko had any friends to support her on this journey, so here she was crying her eyes out, all alone. And what pissed her off even more was that she had to pull it together, wipe her face and go into this stupid ass meeting.

Miko stuck around with The Underworld because she was too scared to tell Chi she wanted out. She knew they talked about her all the time and not in a good way, but the one thing they could never say was that she slacked on her job. Miko was always available via phone for any last minute things they needed done.

She handled payroll on time and always made sure the numbers were accurate at the beginning and end of each month. Not that she didn't care about the well-being of the organization because she handled her business, but her focus was elsewhere. Miko made sure Nash's empire was constantly growing. Because of her, he had transitioned from just a rapper to a business mogul as well. The Underworld had a tiny, tiny place in her heart. That would never change, especially since she was still getting paid a pretty penny from being with The Underworld. So, in a way, it still had its perks.

In fact, a few months ago one of Nash's crew members ran into a sticky situation, and Miko made it go away in less than an hour because of the connections she had made via The Underworld. She told the dude to not tell anyone, including Nash, or she would have him fired being that she ran Nash's company. They were taking over together and staying focused.

Nash had become a legend right before her eyes, and she was so very proud of her man. She told him every day how blessed she was to be in love with him.

Nash sent her a long text message, once again claiming to love her more than anything in this world and how a baby wouldn't change that. But an interview he recently did had hurt her to the core, although he wasn't being mean or rude when the interviewee asked him why he had no children and did he want one. The sad and hopeful look on his face had crushed her. Miko prayed so hard that day, her womb needed to be anointed. Seriously.

The one thing her now distant friend, Lauren Howard, had taught her was prayer changes everything.

Miko tossed the paper the specialist gave her of things to do to conceive to the back seat of her car. She had a million and one of those fact sheets, and nothing on there ever worked. Miko had tried it all and failed every time.

She took a deep breath and tried to pull it together before heading into this meeting. Miko didn't want anyone to ask her what was wrong because then she would cry again, so she slid a pair of pink Gucci frames over her face.

She grabbed her gun, knowing things could easily go left in these meetings. Miko didn't have time for no shit today. She was already in a bad mood. She locked her doors and looked both ways before crossing the street and walking into where the meeting was held, of all places a bowling alley. But that's just how The Underworld was; unpredictable.

She was the first to arrive which was nothing new. Years were put in working at The White House, and that was the one thing that could get you fired, not being prompt.

Miko sent Nash a text message back saying she loved him too and was ready for him to get home. She was hungry and hoping they wouldn't be here all morning, she had other shit to do.

"Sis,"Malachi, her half-brother, walked in minutes after she did and greeted her with a warm hug.

"You don't need to lift another weight thing or whatever they're called."

Her brother was basically busting out of the cotton t-shirt he wore along with a pair of basketball shorts and sneakers.

"Man, gotta stay in shape so I can be ready to knock these lil niggas out for trying to talk to my daughters." If he could keep his kids locked up forever, he would. Malachi never took the old folks serious when they said to be mindful of what you did because you had to have kids one day. Chi had dogged several bitches out back in the gap, and he was now paying for it.

She laughed at her brother now going through the raising teenager blues. "They're good kids. You raised them right, and you know Jade don't play," she spoke of her sister-in-law.

"Speaking of my wife, you need to give her a call. She needs to know if Nash can do the thing again that he did last year for raising money for art programs in the inner-city schools." He had just remembered.

Miko added a note in her calendar. "Gotcha, I'm sure he is though." That was one thing she admired about her man. He was always giving back whether it was his money, time or his talents. Nash had remained true to who he was.

"What is this about?" she questioned.

Malachi had no idea. He shrugged his shouldersand told her, "I don't know, Sean called this meeting."

"Sean?" She was super shocked to hear that.Miko rarely heard him talk. "He's probably retiring," she assumed.

Chi was thinking the same thing. "We shall see."

They chopped it up for another twenty minutes until Papa and MJ arrived together. Their friendship wasn't the same, but they were back hanging out, and Papa missed the old MJ. He told her that she wasn't alone in dealing with the loss of her beau, but MJ was done trying to show him what she meant when people went home. She still had to deal with that emptiness.

People only cared for so long, and then you were left to grieve by yourself. It had been years since he passed, and she still hadn't been able to accept his death. Maybe because she blamed herself. She wanted to run far away until she finally felt a breaking in her spirit but didn't even know where to run to.

"Hi." Miko got up to hug MJ, and then she spoke to Papa.

"Hey, girl, you look nice." MJ was always paying people compliments.

Miko sat back down and looked at her watch. "Okayy, so we are waiting on Nasir, Sean and Noel, who's probably not coming anyway." But to her surprise, Noel was standing right behind her.

"Uh, hello to you too, Miko." She didn't appreciate her comment.

Miko's face flushed in embarrassment. "I didn't mean it like that, you know you live in Cambodia or wherever the hell you stay," she tried to fix it.

Noel rolled her eyes. "Yeah, whatever." She hugged MJ and the others.

"I am high as fuck," Papa finally opened his mouth. His eyes were the colors of fresh ripe cherry tomatoes.

MJ shook her head. "You are so dramatic, yo. We smoked two blunts," she told Chi.

Papa swore he was floating. "I can't feel my hands or feet." He sat down and took a deep breath.

"I can't smoke in the morning no more like I used to," Chi said. Noel, MJ, and Papa definitely didn't have that problem.

"Shittin' me!" Noel laughed. She smoked all day, every day.

Miko was on so many medications, she had stopped drinking and smoking, but Nash still smoked.

"Where these ma'fuckas at? I need to lay down," Papa complained.

Surprisingly, Sean and Nasir pulled up at the same time. Sean in his Bentley, and Nasir hopped out of a truck after his driver opened the door.

Sean didn't get who these niggas really thought they was? Neither Nasir nor Malachi drove. Papa was always on his bike if he didn't have his kids, and

Sean was a sucker for foreign whips and old school cars. He dapped him up, and they walked into the bowling alley together.

"Did y'all plan this?" Miko asked.

Sean was elated to see that all members were present. "Let's get started." He hoped they at least heard him out and gave him a chance.

"Who bowling alley is this?" Noel wanted to know.

"I bought this for my wife, it will be a restaurant soon," Sean shared with them.

Chi nodded his head. "Good looking." He enjoyed her food the one time he did have it, and shorty could throw down for real.

Nas didn't speak to anyone, that's just the type of rude fucker he was. Sean cleared his throat and turned all his phones on silent so he wouldn't be interrupted and lose his train of thought.

"All right, so just hear me out. I have sat on this for a long time but couldn't do that anymore," was how he started the conversation off with The Underworld. Everyone was all ears, and he had their attention. "We need to come together, all of us. And not just us, but the entire organization; the workers, the runners, the mules...everybody." No one said a word, waiting on him to continue. "I want us to have one big kick-off to let them all know that we appreciate the sacrifices they're making to help make us rich."

"Them niggas eating good too, come on now." Papa already wasn't with the shit.

"And we've survived this long because we aren't touchable, now you're saying to stoop down and be their friends? No, not happening." Chi definitely didn't agree.

"You be on the block though," Sean reminded him.

"Yeah, with niggas I know, not no petty motherfuckers that can get jealous and snitch at any time."

They weren't seeing his vision.

Nasir told him, "I'm still listening."

He took a deep breath. "It's all about unity right now. We gotta come together and remember why we started in the first place. It's like we all got our own goals, and we not working together."

"What makes you say that though? Cus at the end of the day, we all trying to get some money, so as long as that shit don't stop then what's the issue?" Papa asked.

MJ shook her head because they were missing his point. "Y'all won't understand what he saying cus y'all not in the field, y'all don't do shit," MJ chimed in. And that was a fact.

"Who don't do nothing?" Chi asked her in all seriousness, because he knew he put in work, or so he thought. MJ considered all of them rich and privileged.

"None of y'all. Me and Sean are in the trenches with them, so I get what he's saying, and I think it's a good idea." She had never in her life spoke up or had an opinion about anything in relations to how The Underworld handled shit, but she was tired of these lazy fuckers not doing anything but collecting a check every month.

Sean worked hard and ever since he moved to New York, his work load had tripled, and she never heard him complain. Not once. He came up here and got straight to grinding. MJ wanted him to know that his hustle hadn't gone unnoticed.

"Yo, I don't even know what you on right now." Papa wasn't about to let MJ piss him off or blow his high.

She said what she had to say.

"Sean, what are you asking us to do, specifically?" Noel wanted them to stick to business and not let personal feelings get involved. She didn't fly all the way to America for no bullshit, her time was not to be wasted.

"I want us to take a second and regroup. We need to revisit the mission of all of this. We can't be so uppity where the niggas that rock with us don't fuck with us."

"Who's to say they won't stack they money and do their own thing?" Nasir finally had a question. "But ain't that what you want to do?"

Sean knew he was trying to fuck with him. "You never heard that come out of my mouth, so miss me with that." He wasn't about to let him switch the motive of this meeting. Nasir could play them mind games on another dummy.

"This is possible," Miko nodded her head. She liked the sound of something new happening for the organization. Maybe it would spark her interest and enthusiasm.

Chi wasn't with it. "This system has been in place from the beginning, and change isn't always good."

"And then sometimes it is," Sean argued.

Papa stood up and said, "All right, let's vote then, that's fair right?"

Miko conducted the vote. "All for change raise your hands."

MJ and Sean were the only ones that wanted to see change, and that's because they were the only two working for real.

Noel told him, "I get what you're saying, I just don't think it's fair that I say I'm for change, and I'm not around. I don't even live here," she tried to explain to him, but it wasn't about her.

MJ shook her head. "Idiots." She was so over them it didn't make any sense.

He really wanted Nasir, Papa and Chi to get where he was coming from, but he kept his game face on. "Cool, well thanks for hearing me out."

Papa was about to go back home and sleep his highness off. "Yeah, nigga, we ain't letting them niggas get close to us and take our traps, they workers for a reason." He held his hand out for Sean to dap him.

He was pissed, but he wouldn't let them know. He dappedhim up. "Be safe."

Everyone said their goodbyes, and Nas didn't bother saying adios to anyone.

Sean sat down once they all left. They were making a mistake by not changing shit up. Eventually, niggas would get knocked and would tell, but if they would have listened to him and at least tried to meet him halfway, then today would have been a good day. Sean wondered if he did a good job explaining it or were they already in cahoots against him before he even opened his mouth. All he wanted them to know was that when you showed love and gave respect to niggas, it was easier to get it back.

If one of them got knocked today, there wasn't that much loyalty or love shown in the organization for a mother fucker to be like, "I'll die for The

Underworld." None at all. Niggas had no problem dropping names because to them it's like, "What have they done for me?"

Sean, however, was always showing love and looking out and in return, niggas fucked with him the long way. He had to make some moves, whether that was retiring and letting this shit go, or doing his own thing. Ignorance was bliss, and today showed him that none of them were on the same page as he was.

$$\eta$$

Ramone looked at his watch, the time on his cell phone and the clock on the radio of his dad's driver truck.

"I'm hungry, Pops," he said again. Nasir ignored him and continued reading his pocket novel. Had he known they would be sitting outside of an old apartment building for the past hour, he would have asked to be dropped off at the crib.

His Pops was always talking about being busy and tired from work, but everytime he rode with him the nigga never did shit. Ramone had friends whose fathers would come home super muddy, sweaty and visibly exhausted but nope, not his father. The only time he had ever seen him drained was coming from a run or meeting with his personal trainer.

"She has arrived, sir," his driver, Jimbo, finally announced.

He had never seen his Pops nervous or anxious for anything. Nasir finished the page he was reading and folded the top corner before closing it. He picked up his cell phone and checked the time. "I'll be back in about twenty minutes," he told his son.

Ramone shook his head. "I'm coming with you."

Nasir would never let that happen. "Coming right back, then we can grab whatever you want to eat," he sort of bargained.

"I'm not five, Pops, let me come up," he begged with his eyes.

Nasir sighed, knowing that Jordyn would shit bricks if she knew he had Ramone around *her*.

"Don't tell your-"

His son cut him off, "I know, I know." He was already hip to his dad possibly having something else going on. Ramone loved his mama, but he really looked up to his Pops, so if having a wife and a girlfriend was his thing, then when he got older he would have the same. His father was his idol.

They hopped out of the truck and crossed the street to what looked like a mill or factory of some sort. Nasir pushed four digits into a key panel, and a brown gate opened.

"Whoa!" Ramone was in awe. From the street, you would never know this was behind the gate. It was an entire eat, pray, live area that most likely housed about twenty units consisting of two and three bedrooms.

"This is dope." He wanted to move over here one day.

Nasir kept walking, forcing his son to catch up. Once they made it to the elevator, Nasir told Ramone, "She has a smart ass mouth. Don't say nothing back to her, even if she tries to talk to you, just ignore her."

He nodded his head in understanding.

"Do you have any headphones?"

Ramone told him, "Nah, I left them at home."

Nas prayed he didn't have to go there with Lauren today, especially not in front of his son.

They walked down a hallway and then made a right. Surprisingly, the door was unlocked, so Nas pulled out his gun for safety measures.

Ramone was thinking to himself, *What in the fuck?*

"Come in," Lauren told him from the kitchen where she was slicing up a watermelon.

Nasir pushed Ramone in before him and closed the door behind them, locking it.

"I'm starting to think you forgot what you've taught me?" She came from behind the wall with a knife in her hand decorated in different color watermelons. Her heart stopped beating when she saw Ramone.

"Oh, hello," she smiled at him, still in disbelief that Nas was really raising a son. Hopefully, he ended up nothing like him.

Ramone looked at his father who told him to go take a seat in the living room.

"You taught him to not speak when he walks in someone's house? How cute." She rolled her eyes and went back into her kitchen.

"No, I told him to not talk to *you*...he has manners," he said as he took a seat at the bar.

"Can I go outside? This balcony is playa," Ramone came up and asked.

Lauren told him, "Yes, sure. Would you like some tuna fish? And I made strawberry lemonade," she offered him lunch since it was no telling how long his pyscho ass daddy had been waiting on her to get home. Lauren kept Nasir on the block list, but it seemed to not bother him.

He was starving. "Yes, please, thank you."

"Oh, the baby does have manners," she said and smiled warmly at Ramone.

Nasir shook his head. "We gotta work on a few skills. You never let a pretty face and smile knock you off your square."

Ramone had the biggest, goofiest look on his face. He was very attracted to Lauren and couldn't hide how smitten he was.

Lauren thought it was too cute. "Your dad used to be the same way." *Oh, the good old days.* They were now long gone. "I'll bring it to you in a second." Lauren began to make him a sandwich. "What kind of chips does he like?"

Nasir ignored her and asked his own question since that was why he came over. "When was the last time you talked to your boy Sean?"

Lauren decided on a bag of plain Lay's chips. "Uh, it's been awhile."

"Before or after you stopped by MJ's house?" He knew everything. He always did. Nasir could tell Lauren things about her that would probably blow her mind.

"I rather you ask me what you came to ask me instead of beating around the bush, because today I don't have time." Gone was her southern charm, now the bitch had arrived. Lauren wasn't even in the mood for Nasir and wished he would stop popping up on her.

"He called a meeting today," Nas said as if he had no rights.

"Okay, he's a member and a leader of the organization. What's wrong with that?"

"Leader? Let's not use that word." In his opinion, Sean possessed no qualities or skills that reflected a leader. He was good at picking up and dropping off, nothing more, nothing less. It took a lot more than that to run a billion-dollar empire. Sean lacked decorum and tact. He could never lead The Underworld. Nas hated that Lauren used that word to describe him.

"Look, whatever you wanna call it, he holds the right to call a meeting," she argued back. Nasir was so bossy and controlling.

He didn't agree. "According to who?"

She was not about to let him get on her nerves today. "Okay, fine. He's not a leader, what does that have to do with me talking to him? Which I haven't," she added.

He watched her move around the kitchen and for a second he forgot why he was there. "Can you imagine yourself making lunch for our children?"

Those kind of thoughts no longer crossed her mind in relation to him...she had moved on. "Yes, me and Simon have been discussing children a lot lately."

Nasir chuckled. The idea of them together was still hilarious. "How does it feel living a lie, Lauren?" He said her name with so much haste in his voice.

"The only lie I'm living is the one with you. You have a whole family, but yet you keep finding your way to my house and into my life-"

Ramone appeared. "Is the sandwich ready? Sorry, I'm starving," he said, batting those long and thick eyelashes.

"Yea, baby, here you go." She handed him a wooden tray with a "S" on it.

"Superman?" Ramone questioned.

Lauren smiled in Nasir's direction. "Yep, my boyfriend is a hero."

"Oh, what does he do?"

Lauren licked her lips. "He puts bad people away."

"Ramone, head to the truck, you can take the sandwich off that cheap ass tray." Nas stood up from the bar stool he sat on.

Lauren went back to slicing the watermelon, knowing she had ruffled his feathers. After the door slammed, he reached over the counter and grabbed her neck.

"Stop fucking playing with me!" he warned her, and today would be the last time.

"Let me go." Lauren was going to stab the fuck out of him the minute he did.

He commanded her to, "Drop the knife." He wasn't stupid.

She rolled her eyes as the knife fell to the floor. "Nas, this is my last time begging you to leave me the fuck alone."

He shook his head. "Not an option."

Lauren hated him with everything inside of her. "I don't know shit about nothing, why don't you believe me?"

"Because he's not smart. Sean is a dumb ass nigga. And he has his cousin who pumps life into him, but no, I don't think it was the cousin who put him up to try to change what the fuck I've built. I think it was you. My theory is that you want him to take over and put me away, but Lauren, that's not possible."

He was losing his damn mind. She stared at him with tears welling in her eyes, wondering how the sweet, angelic boy with so many hopes and dreams that she had fallen in love with before the money and power had changed into a monster. Nasir needed help.

"I pray God's mercy on your soul," she told him and meant every word.

Nasir wasn't moved by her dramatics. "No more conversation with Sean."

"I do not talk-"

"Shut the fuck up, and just say okay. That's your problem now, you talk too fuckin' much!" he snapped.

She took a deep breath, praying he would leave her house immediately.

"What's going on with Simon?" was his next question. Lauren knew nothing about that either. "So no update, is that what you're saying?"

She nodded her head. "That's what I said."

Her slick ass mouth and sarcastic responses to any and everything would never change, Nasir was finally convinced.

"Okay, well that's not acceptable, so get one. Someone called my house today, and I'm wondering does that mean a case is pending."

"That's what your lawyers are for," she mumbled under her breath, not understanding how she still had ties with him and she was out of The Underworld and he was married. Why couldn't he let her go and let her live her life?

Nasir didn't want to let her go, that's why.He loved her very much but had a weird way of showing it.

Lauren massaged her neck. "I'll see what I can do," she told him after his silence and cold stares had her shaken up.

"I will be in touch." Nasir headed for the door.

She picked up the knife and was about to wash it off and try her hardest to forget that he ever stopped by. She wanted to act as if he didn't choke her or that he didn't threaten her either.

"Lo," he called her name.

Lauren took a deep breath. "What?" He had fucked her whole day up.

"You do know that I love you, right?"

Chapter 9

"Link with the connect and we collect them blocks." – Meek Mill

Home was where the heart was, and Atlanta, Georgia would forever have a hold on him. Sean made sure that as soon he, Jackie and the boys touched down in the South, their first stop was JJ's Rib Shack. Sean was a country nigga, and the barbecue in New York had nothing on JJ's.

He ordered two slabs of ribs with extra sauce, baked beans and grilled corn. Jackie stayed in the car. Everyone knew they were in town visiting, but the main person she was excited to see was her stylist. Since they moved, she had been doing her own hair, claiming she'd had the same beautician for almost twenty years, and she was the only person who could touch her hair.

Sean told her that she barely did a good job, but he was a man and didn't know shit about slaying a short cut.

She honked the horn, wishing he would stop running his mouth so she could go get her car and get in traffic. He looked over his shoulder and threw up one finger, telling her to hold on.

She rolled her eyes and smacked her lips. "I got stuff to do, how do y'all feel being home?" she turned around and asked her sons.

They were cool with seeing their friends, but had low-key fallen in love with living up North.

"I told grama we would stop by before we left," Kevin said.

Jackie pursed her lips together at the thought of her mother-in-law. She didn't really fuck with them, they had turned their backs on her when he went missing.

Jackie rarely asked them for anything, but the few times she did, they never told her they could help. She wasn't going with them. Kevin and Jonathan were old enough to go over on their own.

"Don't tell her shit about what we got going on, it's not their business," she reminded them of what they had been taught their whole lives. Jackie knew her in-laws had been talking shit about her moving to New York. No one really knew she had married him or they really would have dogged her out.

"Yes, ma'am" they nodded, understanding what she was saying.

Jackie honked the horn again. Sean was really tripping at this point.

"Mannnn!" He jogged to her side of the window and handed her what looked like a big ass bag of trash, that's how much food he ordered.

"What did you get?" She wasn't even hungry.

"This for my cousins and shit at my Gammy house, we just gotta stop and get a pack of sodas," he told her.

Jackie shook her head, she didn't come all the way back home tosit in the hood all night. "Uh, no Sean, drop me off to my car, I got things to do."

He was surprised she had plans. "We gon' be playing cards and shit, baby."

She wasn't going over there. "Okay, y'all have fun. Come on, I really gotta go home, get changed and all of that," she reiterated.

He told his homie, "Pull up to my Gammy's house, I'ma be over there, let me drop my girl off," he said.

Finally, Jackie thought to herself.

"What you gotta do tonight?" Sean asked her since she had no friends in Atlanta. He was now wondering what she had going on. He was rolling a blunt and taking a shit while she showered.

Sean kept his homes in Atlanta because he knew they would be back and forth as much as possible and didn't want to be staying in hotels. The other places he owned were now being rented out, creating another source of income for him. Sean was all about his coins at the end of the day.

"My co-workers from the hospital, is that okay with you, daddy?" she asked him sarcastically as she stepped out of the shower and wrapped a towel around her body. "You stink, can you at least flush the toilet?" She covered her nose and walked out of the bathroom

"I'm just making sure you ain't trying to be cute while you out here, that's all," he joked.

"Cute with who? You the one in your old stomping grounds, not me," she reminded him of what was really good.

Sean had tons of bitches in Atlanta, that was a fact. "I'm good, I got who I wanted," he told her.

Jackie knew that and wasn't worried. She made him happy and kept home together. And yeah, niggas still cheated even when you did everything right, but he knew the risk of losing her, and Sean didn't want that.

After he used the bathroom, he hopped in the shower so he could head out right behind her.

"You look real good, baby," he complimented his wife as she stood in the mirror applying a red coat of lipstick.

Jackie didn't feel like she was all together. "Not my hair," she complained as she fluffed it up, hating that Sean made her miss her hair appointment, but her stylist told her to be there first thing in the morning.

"I'ma mess it up tonight anyway," he smiled and came behind her and kissed her neck before going into the closet to throw something on.

Jackie was going to hit a few lounges with some of her nurse friends, and Sean would be posted in the hood until she called and said she was headed home, that's when he would peel out.

"All right, I'm ready." He threw on a pair of jogging pants and a Polo shirt.

"Oh no, sir." Jackie put the comb down on the counter and looked her husband over.

He didn't know what she was talking about or what was wrong. "Huh?"

"You not about to be all in the hood with your dick swinging."

Sean busted out laughing, "Man, you hell!" She was so crazy at times.

"Am I funny right now? Sean, it looks like you don't even have draws on."

"I can't help I got a big dick." He grabbed his stuff and blew her a kiss.

She wasn't with that. "Can you put on some jeans?"

Sean hugged his wife. "Why you acting like that, baby?" He squeezed her ass and then kissed her lips. "This yo' dick, and you know that," he reminded her with another kiss.

Her body heated up, but she had somewhere to be. "I gotta go," she whispered.

"I can't get none of my pussy before you go?" He would have loved a lil quickie before he got his night started.

"Nope, cus then we gon' end up in the bed, I'm going to fall asleep and you're still going to go to the hood." Jackie was learning his ways.

"Damn, you got me," he chuckled. She was correct.

"Yeah, that's what I thought. Let's go."

Jackie and Sean headed to the garage where her Lexus truck had been parked for a few months.

"You got gas?"

She turned the truck on. "Yeah, I'm good."

He made sure she had her seatbelt and shit on. "Have fun and be safe. Keep your phone charged and if I call, pick up," he ran off the rules.

Jackie nodded her head. "Gotcha, baby."

They kissed again, and he watched his wife head out for a night she needed and deserved. All she did was see about him and the boys. He wanted her to get out and enjoy herself. Jackie had to get a life because it couldn't continue to revolve around them.

Sean made his way to the hood, and everybody was on the block. Despite the shit that went down with The Underworld this week, he was still in a good mood. This weekend trip back home was for him to rejuvenate and reset. When he returned to New York, he wanted to be refreshed.

At the time, he didn'tknow what he was going to do, but he knew his time with The Underworld was coming to an end. His only prayer was that it wasn't too late.

η

The one thing Nas enjoyed about being married was when date night included other couples. Jordyn was amazing, she truly was, but sometimes being with her was boring, so whenever she came home and told him they had plans with Nia and East, he would be more eager to go out instead of canceling and staying home in his man cave, alone.

Nasir and Jordyn were headed to meet them for dinner and a movie. He was jamming to whatever was playing on the radio, and Jordyn was still working via email.

"I'm glad I'm not insecure," Nasir told his wife.

"Oh, good for you. I'm glad I never made you feel like you've made me feel over the years," was what she shot back at him.For every shady comment he had, she now had three or four.

"How have I made you feel? I've been going good," he said, thinking he had truly done a one-eighty.

She laughed. "You coming home early and fucking me more than once a month is not doing good, Nas. Marriage is more than that."

Well if that was the case. "Well, what are you doing differently?" he asked.

"Me?" She was now baffled at his line of questioning.

"Yeah, it ain't like I'm coming home and you got your mouth ready to suck me all night, and you don't even cook no more." He could go on and on with what she no longer did.

"Are you for real right now? I work-"

"Exactly." That was the word he was looking for.

Jordyn now had a life; she had goals, dreams and aspirations. Basically, she had shit going on. Once she got her first whiff of her own money, it turned her into a robot.Damn, she was working right now.

"Our marriage has always been my first priority, don't even go there."

He shook his head. "Not no more, but I'm cool with that, baby. That's the difference between me and you."

Nas didn't trip on Jordyn, he was all for her getting her money. She couldn't throw that in his face any more about him being too busy because now she was busier than him.

"Okay, so what do I need to work on?" Jordyn closed the Gmail app on her phone and gave him her full attention as they headed to the restaurant.

He gave her a quick glance. "First off..." He was ready to tell her everything and could tell she was prepared for the worst. Jordyn looked magnificent tonight, and he couldn't remember if he told her or not. "You look sexy as shit."

She blushed in a million different ways, and her cheeks pushed her eyes tight because she was smiling so hard. "Thanks, Nas." She tried to keep it cool, but on the inside she was doing cartwheels.

Jordyn had been juicing and doing Zumba three times a week. She felt damn good when the pink dress she purchased a few days ago from Zara fit perfectly. She paired the mini dress with leopard pointed toe heels and had her hair curled loosely.

Nasir always matched her fly without trying too hard. He had on all black, but his shoes had leopard shoe strings, they were on beautiful couple.

"Yeah, so I want more head, more sex, more love, really more everything," he said.

Jordyn was surprised. "Do you really?" From the beginning they had never been that type of couple, so why now?

"I'm getting old. I want more love and shit." He was being honest. If he was seriously going to slow his lifestyle down, he didn't want to not be home. Home should be a pleasant place plus, Ramone would be going off to college soon, and it was obvious he was their glue. Nasir wanted them to get it together without their son being the main reason why.

"What else?" Jordyn asked.

"Trust issues, we gotta work on that."

That was simple to fix. "Are you cheating on me?"

He shook his head. "No, and you know I'm not." He was being for real. Lauren was the one person he fucked off with, and it had been a while since they took it there. In fact, the last few times they did link up, he would end up leaving a few minutes later after threatening her or some shit.

Lauren stressed him out. Jordyn didn't. Cheating took too much energy. Jordyn now had her PhD in Nasir King, she always figured shit out. She had her own shit going on these days and would probably leave his ass if he cheated on her again. Nasir didn't want those problems. He appreciated coming home to his family.

"Well, I trust you then. To be honest, baby, we only had one problem, and that was *her*." She never said her name. *Ever.*

Thankfully, they arrived at the restaurant so the conversation ended. Nasir rarely drove, but when they had date night is when he pushed his whips.

He got out first and walked over to help his wife out of the car. Hand in hand, they walked into the restaurant and asked if Nia and East had arrived. After being told that they hadn't, Jordyn suggested they get a drink at the bar to get the night started. She ordered a Ciroc and pineapple, and Nasir ordered a Dusse double.

"Wow, I've always wanted to see what you looked like up close?" some chick said to him.

Jordyn was shocked that she was being so bold, but she decided to let her husband handle the bitch.

"Do I know you?" Nas didn't recognize her face.

The woman smiled and held her hand out for a handshake, but he had never been friendly. "No, you don't, but you will. I'm going to arrest you one day," she told him.

"Excuse me?" Jordyn stood up, but Nas looped his arm around her waist to calm her down.

"Enjoy your dinner," she told the couple and walked off.

Nasir's blood was damn near boiling over. Arrest him? What in the fuck was going on?

"Who was that?" she asked him.

He ordered another drink. "A shot of Hennessy please." Nasir ignored her and downed the one in front of him. His forehead was sweating and so was his back, so he took his jacket off. "Stupid ass hoe."

He would never ever forget her face. Nasir ran his hands over his face. Something was up. He had to get in touch with Lauren again, she wasn't doing her job.

Nasir pulled his phone out and texted her, "*Tick tock.*" She couldn't fuck this up.

Jordyn wanted to ask him so many questions, but he was irritated, and she didn't want him to say anything rude to her and ruin the night any more than it already was.

"Damn, what's wrong with y'all?" Nia approached them and asked. Both of their faces were sour.

Nas went to the bathroom to get his head together while Jordyn filled her best friend in. When he returned, they were at the table.

Nia was telling Jordyn, "I'm so happy that East got out. I will be praying for y'all." She meant that wholeheartedly.

East had made his money and over the years, he had doubled, tripled and quadrupled those funds. Along with his wife's income, they were doing great and weren't hurting for nothing. East never had to return the streets again and didn't plan on it.

Nas kissed Nia's cheek and dapped East up.

"Don't kiss my wife no more," East teased. Nas smiled, although his mood was still shot. "You ain't know her?" he asked Nas.

He shook his head. "Never seen her in my life."

"It's probably nothing."

That was some bullshit. Nasir was a kingpin, no one played around with arresting a nigga. She meant what she said, and it was a warning that things were about to get real. The phone call that came to his house came back to his mind. Was he missing signs? Nasir was about to switch some shit around real quick.

"Y'all wanna go to St. Lucia in a few days?" He needed to go see his mother .Nasir had to make sure she understood the plan if anything was to happen.

"Uh, yeah." Nia looked at her husband to see if he was down.

"What, Nas? We just got back from Africa," Jordyn reminded him. She knew he really wasn't in the mood for a vacation. Something was brewing.

"Two days." He only needed two days to do what he had to do. They would fly commercial since he didn't want to use his private plane just in case they were watching him.

"Sounds good." East could tell that Nas was shaken up about that lady approaching him tonight and could only imagine how that shit felt, not knowing what your fate was. He hated to think about being so blessed and getting out when he did, but right now, that could be him stressing out as well.

Nasir ordered another drink in an attempt to drown out his worries, but he knew he wouldn't sleep tonight or the day after.

Lauren texted him back, *"I'm on it!"*

He read that in her voice and knew she had an attitude, but he didn't give a fuck. Jail was not for him or for anyone in The Underworld. Why were they fucking with them anyway?

η

MJ asked the private investigator that Lauren had her put in touch with, "When were these last taken?"

"Five days ago."

She thumbed through the photos again, not believing that her daughter was a grown woman now. And she was beautiful.

"If that's all, I'm going to head out? My wife gets mad when I'm late to dinner."

MJ had no one to cook for anymore, but that wasn't here nor there.

"Let me go get your money."

"Oh no, Ms. Howard paid me graciously, let me know if there is anything else I can do for you," he told her.

There were still good people out in the world because he could have easily been a sleaze ball and took MJ's money knowing he had already been paid.

She asked him, "Please, let me at least tip you." MJ gave him a thousand dollars before walking him to the door and letting him out. She sat back down on her couch and crossed her long legs.

If she could go back and do things differently, she wondered, would she? An adult child. Her daughter was grown. MJ felt old, she had tears in her eyes but still giggled at the thought of her actually being a grandmother one day.

"The fuck?" She shook her head and held those tears back. She was lonely and weary. MJ desperately wanted to experience life all over again. At night, she held herself wishing Donovan were still alive. He didn't even have to be alive and with her. She wondered about his children every night and his wife who hated her. MJ understood why, she blamed herself for his death and had yet to bounce back from that horrid day.

She leaned back and rested her head. *I hope she knows I did what was best,* she thought to herself.

MJ had a million questions for the private investigator but couldn't form her mouth to ask not one. She had a blunt behind her ear and lit it. All she knew how to do was hustle and smoke, oh and cook whenever she was in the mood, which was rare these days.

Many men had tried to court her over the past few years, but she declined every time. Her heart couldn't take another heartbreak. MJ felt cursed. She would rather die alone than bring pain upon herself again.

A knock at the door came, and she swore she wanted to get the hell on sometimes. No one ever respected her privacy. She wasn't in the mood to talk or do anything tonight.

"Who is it?"

"Open the got damn door, you got a window."

For the most part, Nasir respected MJ, so she opened the door only to curse him out.

"You rotten mother fucker-"

He ignored her and made his way in. MJ could tell he had come from somewhere important because he was dressed nice and smelling good.

"Has anyone driven by here that you haven't recognized? Phone calls? Have any of the girls called out for anything?" He fired off tons of questions she didn't have the answer to.

She shrugged her shoulders. "I haven't sat in that window in so long."

For a very long time after Donovan passed, she used to sit there and wait all day for him stop by, hoping and praying his death was a bad dream, but he never came. That window sill hadn't been touched since.

"What you mean? That's all your ass used to do." Nas didn't believe that shit.

"And I just told you I don't do that no more, what's going on?"

He saw the pictures on her coffee table and picked one of them up. "Who is this?"

She ran over to him and snatched the photograph out of his hands and picked the others up. "None of your damn business!" She wouldn't let him know shit about her child.

Nasir was evil and when he didn't get his way, he had no problem going to extreme measures to make it happen. She knew about a lot of trifling and horrible things he had done to people. He was the devil.

"She looks just like you, MJ," he told her.

"What's going on?" She got back to business.

He took a seat and picked up the blunt in her ashtray and wiped the tip off, not wanting to put his mouth on anything she touched but needing to smoke.

MJ rolled her eyes. "My mouth ain't been nowhere yours ain't been," she let him know.

"Shut up, man." Between her and Lauren, he didn't know whose mouth was worse. "Look, so we need to buckle down."

That's all he said. MJ needed more than that. "Okayyyy, why?" All she needed him to say was what she had already predicted would happen one day so she could pack her shit up and go find her daughter.

MJ wanted to be completely done with The Underworld because she had reached out to her child. She didn't want anything haunting her or tainting her new life.

"I don't know yet, so keep this between me and you." He gave her a hard look, silently swearing her to secrecy.

He was such a liar. "Whatever, nigga."

"And you need to get a phone, MJ." He had been begging her to carry a cell phone for years.

They were supposed to be family, but here he was knowing shit and not speaking on it. This is exactly what Sean was talking about when he spoke of lack of unity in the organization.

MJ had made tons of money and had rarely spent a fraction of it. Tomorrow morning, she was going to the bank and switching her shit to an off-shore account and putting the majority of her money into an account that she had never closed for her brother. She had also never touched the money Donovan left for her, so she was set.

"I gotta go make some more runs, keep your eyes open, MJ," he told her before he left.

MJ wondered what the hell that meant. She was calling Lo first thing tomorrow morning. Lo was fucking the district attorney and should be able to give MJ the heads up about what was going on. She had probably already told Nas, and she needed to be in the loop as well.

Fuck the rest of them. She had to make sure she made it out of whatever was about to pop off...alive, and not locked up. Those weren't options for her.

η

Jackie was at the hair salon bright and early the next morning, catching all the tea while getting a deep conditioner. It felt so good to be back in her stylist's chair. She was on her third mimosa and couldn't stop laughing as everyone filled her in on what she had been missing.

"And then what happened?" she asked as her phone vibrated in the pocket of her blush Gucci hobo.

A blind woman could see that Jackie was back popping like in the days when her husband was taking care of her. She ended up driving Sean's Range Rover to the shop because her car was on E when she made it home last night, and he didn't want her to stop late at night to get gas.

Jackie was iced out, from the two-carat diamonds in her ear, to the gold Audemar watch and stack of Cartier bangles that were priced at six-thousand dollars each. And then her wedding ring, oh my, the bitch was blinging. Her ring was so big that the diamonds struggled to stand upright and tilted to the left every time she moved her hands. Jackie was flossing without trying, and there were a few people in the salon hating.

"Hello," she answered her ringing phone.

"You took the truck?" Sean's groggy voice brought a smile to her face.

"Yeah, I'm coming right back, I needed gas."

"All right, bae. You making breakfast when you get here?" He was going back to sleep but would be hungry whenever he rolled over again.

Jackie giggled. "No, I wasn't planning on it, but for you I will."

"French toast and bacon," he requested.

"Got you." She would have to stop at the store but didn't mind. Anything for her husband. Jackie loved cooking anyway.

After they ended their call, one of the chicks in the shop said, "Girl, you got a new man and don't know how to act."

Jackie assumed she was joking so she laughed it off. "You know how it be." She took her attention from the woman and back to her hair. "This shampoo feel so good." Her beautician was scratching the shit out of her scalp.

"So, did you wait until after Sean made a lil more money to fuck him cus we all know he ain't always been ballin'."

Her beautician couldn't even warn the girl. She'd been knowing Jackie for years and knew she was fireball.

"Bitch, do you know me or something?" Jackie was out of her seat real fast.

"I know Sean, and you ain't even his type."

"I'm his wife. He ain't got no damn type, and you shol' not it." Jackie was all in homegirl's face.

"Meka, don't come in my shop with that shit. Jack, she about to go, let me finish your hair so I can get you out of here on time."

She stared her down, and Jackie wanted the bitch to jump if she was feeling froggy because she had no problem mopping the floor with that hoe.

The girl wanted no problems, so she left. She had started that shit for no reason. Jackie knew people were probably talking about her, but they needed to mind their fucking business. She had worked for hers and had no problem returning to get her own check. Her man did not want her to work, so why hate? Her chest heaved up and down as she sat back and reclined in the chair to finish getting her hair washed.

Tears of anger rolled down her eyes, and her beautician bent down and whispered in her ear, "Do not come out of character for these hating ass hoes."

She was pissed. Jackie didn't say another word for her duration at the shop.

When she made it home, she smoked the rest of a blunt that Sean had left in the kitchen. A lot was on her mind.

"No food?" He woke up an hour ago and searched the oven and stove and then the microwave, thinking maybe she had put his plate up.

"Who is Meka?" was all she had to say.

He didn't know who that was ."You been smoking?" He smelled the weed, and her eyes were red.

"Who the fuck is Meka?"

Sean snaked his neck. "You better watch yo' mouth. I don't raise my voice at you, and I respect that in return. And I don't know who Meka is," he told her truthfully.

"I can't even get my hair washed without bitches confronting me about being with you cus you got some money now."

He was unfazed. Bitches were going to talk forever. He had wifed her up over a million other hoes, of course they were mad. Sean chose Jackie, his patna's wife, who was way older than him. And guess what? He didn't care. He loved the shit out of her old ass.

"And my thing is, I been had money, and everybody know that, but I'm a gold digger? How? They whispered about me like I was a hoe or something!" she cried.

Sean had never seen her so concerned with what people thought, and that's how he knew they had gotten under her skin.

"You want me to go find this Meka hoe?" he asked her.

She shook her head and wiped her face. "I hate we even moved up there. We should have stayed low-key."

That shit hurt. "You regret marrying me?" he asked her, his voice breaking with every word he spoke.

"Did I say that, Sean?" she shouted at him.

"Shit, baby, you ain't saying nothing right now. You mad about some hoes hating on you. Who gives a fuck?" He needed her to boss up and wear that shit with confidence. He took a seat beside her and pulled her chair in between her legs.

"It's nothing no one can tell me about you, not no fuckin' body. You don't think my cousins made jokes about me wearing a wedding ring last night? But I don't care. I'm with you cus I'm with you." He held her chin in his hand.

"I almost dragged that hoe," she told him.

He laughed, "Oh, baby, I can only imagine. I don't know shawty though, that's on my Gammy." Sean would never lie to his wife. Meka was most likely the cousin or friend of someone he used to fuck. That's the only thing he could think of, because any bitch he ever fucked knew better. They knew to never approach Jackie. Sean had everyone in check, even his old hoes.

He wiped her tears. "We ain't shedding no tears over no bitches, we living life, baby," he said and kissed her lips.

Sean always made everything better. "I love you, I'm sorry for cursing at you."

He knew she was mad, he wasn't tripping on that. "So since you ain't cook a nigga nothing to eat cus of *Meka*, what am I going to eat?" Jackie asked where the boys were. "They ain't come home last night." He figured they would stay out anyway.

"Oh, well in that caseeee…" She stood up and lifted her sundress over her waist. "Bon Appetit!" she laughed.

Sean had no problem eating his wife for breakfast. "All right, when I finish your ass still need to cook," he let her know. He followed her to the bedroom, and that's when she remembered. "Nah, never mind. I'm about to go to the store so I can cook."

He was already hard just thinking about some good, mind-blowing morning sex. "What you mean never mind?" She never denied him of his pussy.

"I just got my hair done, Sean. I'm not about to let you sweat my shit out."

"Man, what!"

Jackie knew he wouldn't understand. "You know how bad I been wanting my hair done, I can't even let you mess it up, baby."

He smacked his lips and got into bed. "Bye, Jack." Sleep was his only option because he was not about to beat his meat.

"You wanna ride with me?" she asked him. He ignored her and playfully began to snore.

She went over to his side of the bed and kissed his forehead. "Be right back, love you."

Sean couldn't fall back asleep after his wife left, so he called his cousin to see what the move was for today.

"Shit, we probably going out on the boat if y'all wanna come, you and your wife," Boo extended an invite.

"Man, she just got her hair done so she probably not going to want to do that." He would figure some plans out for them.

"Your mama stopped by right after you left saying she ain't heard from you"

Sean wasn't stunting her. "Yeah, cus she only call when she need some money."

Boo chuckled. "That's Neet for ya." He never called her auntie. He barely tolerated her, so he knew how Sean felt.

"Has she met Jackie?"

"Yeah, years ago with dude, but not since we got together."

Boo hated how fucked up their family was. "Well shit, cuz, if y'all wanna join us today, y'all definitely can. How much longer you gon' be in town?"

"I don't know. Some hoe tried to roll up on Jackie today at the salon. So before anything else go wrong, I rather get her back tucked in the city." He could only imagine who else was salty about him settling down with Jackie.

"You know these hoes hate to see a nigga happy."

Thankfully, Boo had been with Samira for so long that he didn't have much drama besides the few times he had cheated, and the one time she thought she was sneaky enough to mess around on him. Boo killed the nigga, and Samira vowed to never do that shit again.

"Yeah, but we doing good. I don't need the bullshit." Sean was able to get Jackie to let that situation go this morning, but he wouldn't have too much grace with her. She already felt that he was this washed up ass nigga, these girls would only confirm that.

They ended the conversation, and Sean got up and hopped in the shower. He cleaned up the bathroom and the bedroom, having nothing else to do.

"Did you leave anything in the store?" he asked his wife once she came back with a million and one grocery bags.

"Well, I got breakfast, something for tonight and then breakfast and dinner tomorrow," she told him.

"We could have gone out to eat."

She wasn't stunting him. "If that was the case, why didn't you suggest that this morning when you was whining about wanting French toast?"

She had a point, but Sean came back with a good comment. "You know I love to see your fine ass in the kitchen cooking a nigga a meal." He kissed her cheek and smacked her butt.

"Hmm-hmm, I bet." She moved away from him and started putting everything up.

"Can I get some later? From behind, no effort on your part, so it's no need for you to sweat," he reasoned.

She gave him a quick kiss. "We will see, baby."

Sean left her in the kitchen to whip up something good and went back to bed. These few days in Atlanta were all about resetting and relaxing. He had no clue what was brewing back in New York. No idea at all.

η

Simon woke up to breakfast in bed, which wasn't new. That's the type of girlfriend Lauren Howard was; loving, attentive, caring and all of that. She loved to keep a smile on his face and in return, he did the same for her.

On this particular Saturday morning, breakfast consisted of scrambled egg whites, wheat toast, sliced Avocado and turkey bacon...and a pregnancy test, a positive pregnancy test.

Simon's face lit up at the signs on the stick. "Is this real?" He had been wanting a child with her for quite a while.

Lauren had problems conceiving, but prayer changed everything. Together as a couple they had fasted and prayed, demanding an outpour from the Heavens. The one thing Simon constantly thanked her for was instilling a prayer life in him. That was their morning and nightly ritual, starting and ending their days with God.

Simon sat up in bed and immediately thanked Him for this blessing. Lauren wiped tears from her face. She wasn't twenty-one anymore, so she had to take it easy while carrying this baby. Lauren would do everything right to ensure that she had a safe and healthy pregnancy.

"I love you so much," he told her over and over again.

Lauren wiped her tears away after they finished hugging. "Eat your breakfast." She got back into bed with him.

"I'm so happy, baby, I can't even eat," he laughed.

For the rest of the morning, they went back and forth on names. Simon wanted a girl, and Lauren wanted a boy. She didn't think she had the patience to deal with a mini replica of herself, and Simon wouldn't know what to do either.

"Or what about twins? A boy and a girl?" His eyes lit up. Life felt complete for him at this moment. He was excelling in his career and had the world's greatest woman at home, and now his child would be here in nine months. What more could he ask for? Simon was ecstatic.

"Twins? Babe you work too much for two children at one time," she told him. Lauren was definitely right about that, and things were only about to take off from here.

"Speaking of work, I have a big meeting Monday."

Her interest was piqued, but she had to play it cool. "Oh, really? About what?"

"Don't know yet, I think it's going to be big though, like game changer big." He then got up to take the tray in the kitchen. "You wanna join me in the shower?" He gave her a sexy look that only his white ass could do.

Some nights when he fell asleep before her, she stared at him wondering when he would find out the truth and would it tear them apart. And now that a baby was in the picture and he was the District Attorney of the United States, what would happen now? Simon had enough leverage to take her child away if he wanted to. Lauren didn't want him to find out who she was, or rather, who she used to be from someone else other than her.

"Do you trust me?"

"Hell yeah, baby," he told her without hesitation. Simon loved the shit out of Lauren. "Come on, get up." He wanted her in the shower, from the back. Lauren's mind had a way of going left, and he wanted her to enjoy this day.

She peeled the comforter back and rolled over, placing her feet on the floor.

"I can't wait to see you fat." His face lit up at the thought of her carrying his first child.

Lauren rubbed her flat stomach. She had carried a child many years ago. "Me too, baby." This was a blessing. God had truly touched her this time around, and she had confidence that everything would work out in her favor.

They undressed each other while the water ran, and Simon moved out of the way so she could get in first. Lauren had her own place but was rarely there. Simon's home was her home, she had a key and everything.

"Noah for a boy, and Simone for a girl."

He took her face in his hands. "I love those names."

It was something about the woman you loved more than anything blessing you with a child. He felt something he had never felt before and wanted to shower Lauren with nothing but affection and attention.

"Noah...I like that a lot. I want a boy first so he can protect his sister," he told her.

Lauren nodded her head before turning around so he could wash her back. She only wanted one child, two at her age was pushing it. Noah was a strong and noble name. She was praying for a boy.

Simon kissed her shoulder before taking the loofah and washing her body. They said nothing else as they made sure the other was clean.

Lauren asked him, "Simon, hold me. Make love to me, baby." She was overwhelmed with emotion, mainly guilt, because she had a lot she needed to tell him and wanted to do so right now.

"What's wrong?" he asked, picking up that something was off.

She dropped her head. "Nothing, baby."

He lifted her head by her chin. "Whatever it is, give it to God. Ain't that what you taught me?"

Lauren knew she should give all her problems to God and hated to even think this way, but could God protect her from the wrath of Nasir? Once he figured out she was carrying a child that was not his, he was going to lose it.

Chapter 10

"It's all for the love of the money, what did y'all think?" – ASAP Ferg

Being in the middle of some bullshit never felt good, especially when it was between his wife, whose good side he wanted to stay on to keep the tension out of his home, and his baby mama,who knew how to make his life a living hell simply by being a bitter baby mama.

Aaliyah never really got over Malachi. Although she had been married twice since he left her, that didn't matter. She had thrown her pussy at him on several occasions until he got sick of having to tell her to respect Jade, and then he gave up and started sending his driver to pick up his daughter.

Now here he was with a throbbing headache and a blunt that he hadn't been able to spark because every time he went to light it, Jade was asking him a question, and Aaliyah was constantly blowing his phone up.

Malachi didn't know what to do or what to say. He understood where Jade was coming from as a protective parent and a parent who demanded respect, and then at the same time, he felt what Aaliyah was trying to say being that if her husband even thought about putting his hands on Addy, the nigga would be dead.

Malachi rubbed the side of his head and asked his wife, "Can you bring me an Excedrin?" He had been getting crazy migraines lately due to lack of sleep.

Jade stopped talking and rolled her eyes at her husband, but she did as he asked and returned to their bedroom with a cup of water and two pills.

"Thanks, baby," he whispered as he downed the pills

"You probably shouldn't smoke until you feel better," she suggested.

But he thought to himself, *The way y'all been on my nerves all day, I'm definitely getting high.* He wouldn't dare not smoke before going to check on Addison, he would be an idiot if he didn't.

Jade went back to presenting her case. "Baby, if someone is steadily running up on you and getting in your face telling you that you not gon' do shit, what would you have done?" she asked him again.

Chi took a deep breath. He understood her, but still, at the end of the day Jade was the adult in the situation and should have not popped Addison and in return, Addison should have known better. Jade was a loose cannon, she had anger management issues and clearly his child had caught her on the wrong day.

"I get you, baby. It's not me who don't get it, it's her mama," he told her for the millionth time.

She couldn't care less about that deranged thot. "Are you mad at me?" she asked him.

He shook his head. "No, but only because I know my child, and I know her mouth so I can only imagine what all she was saying but Jade, for real, you gotta work on that hitting shit cus you hit me all the time, and you done spazzed out and slapped the kids. Like, you gotta control that anger, baby." He was always extra careful as to what he said to her because of her anger, but in the case of his children, she had to learn how to control her attitude.

According to Addison, she was minding her business when Jade told her to wash the dishes. His child swears up and down that every time she comes over Jade is bossing her around and treating her like the maid instead of her step-daughter. Chi really didn't believe that because Jade has been around Addison since she was a little girl and loved her as if she came from her womb. Chi knew that for a fact.

From there they got into an argument, and Addison popped off at the mouth, and Jade, who already wasn't in a good mood, slapped her ass, and they tussled until one of the kids walked in and sort of broke it up.

Addison threatened to have her mom beat Jade up which only infuriated her more, and now here they were. Aaliyah was threatening to call the cops on Jade and all this bullshit. His daughter blocked him saying that if he chose Jade over her, she would never talk to him again. Honestly, it was all too much.

Chi had enough shit going on, and dealing with this minor situation only annoyed him further.

"What do you want me to do?" She controlled her anger to the best of her ability, but if people fucked with her on purpose, then what was she supposed to do?

Addison was a fast little girl, and Jade had been telling Chi that for quite some time. Every time she came over, her clothes were tighter and skimpier, and her mouth even more fly. Addison was too hot in the pants, and Jade blamed her mother for being so laid-back. It wasn't fair that she and Chi preached dignity and respect and going to bed on time and having a curfew, but when she went home, all of that went out of the window.

Jade had been asking Chi to get custody of Addison for years, and now she felt like the girl was a lost cause, and she couldn't care less how she turned out honestly. All the time and nurturing Jade had put into that child was out of love and genuinely wanting to see her bloom, but it was always taken for granted. Jade was done trying with Addison, last night was the final straw.

Chi didn't expect to come home to all of this. He had been down in San Juan handling some business and was looking forward to returning to a home cooked meal and some pussy. But his lil mama was fired up and ready to go to war.

"I don't know, baby." He laid down and stretched his legs.

Jade saw the tension across his forehead and decided to drop the subject for now. She crawled on to bed and took his Nike socks off to massage his feet. "So, how was the trip? Ooh, baby, you need a pedicure! Look at all of this dead skin. Gross, Chi!" She wanted to puke.

He chuckled, "Do me one then." He probably needed one for real. Chi was a nigga that wore sneakers in the summer and boots all winter. His feet were the last thing on his mind.

Jade scanned their penthouse mentally, trying to think if there was a pedicure tub in the closet somewhere. "Be right back." She remembered exactly where it was.

Chi sat up and lit his blunt. His head was still killing him, so hopefully smoking would help decrease the pain.

Jade returned twenty minutes later with everything she needed to get her man's feet in order. "Come on," she told him, motioning her head to the sitting area in their master bedroom.

Chi followed her to the couch and sat down on the love seat while Jade poured Epsom salt and lavender oil into the pedicure tub. He exhaled loudly as she placed his feet into the hot water. "Oh yeah, I needed this," he said once she turned the massage option on the tub to kneading.

Jade got comfortable on the floor with her nail kit in hand, prepared to doctor on her husband's feet.

"So, the trip went good? Did you go alone?" she asked.

"Me and Papa."

Jade and Chi discussed the beaches in San Juan compared to the ones in Mexico, and he preferred Puerto Rico.

"When is our next trip?" she asked, in dire need of some fun in the sun and drinks galore.

He looked at her as if she should already know the answer to her question. "Whenever you wanna go. Come on now, Jade." Had he not shown her that her only wish was his command? If baby wanted to get up right now and go the Bahamas, he would make it happen.

"I'm for real, Chi. At least forty-eight hours, and get Miko to watch the kids," she thought aloud about it further.

"Say less." He peeled his phone out of his pocket and called his sister. Jade watched him handle business and make shit happen for her in less than thrifty minutes. "Are you done?" he asked, referring to his pedicure.

She examined his toes. "They look better than they did before, but remember, I am not a professional."

Chi thanked her and then told her, "Pack a bag. Pilot will meet us in two hours. Miko said leave the kids in the lobby, and she will come scoop them".

Jade was about to say, "Oh hell nah" but Chi busted out laughing. "I'm fucking with you, we gotta drop them off." He was too tickled at the look on her face.

"Are you going to deal with Addison before we leave?"

He told her, "No, I need a break. I'll stop by when we get back."

These two days away with his wife were very much needed. It had been a while since they had gone out of town without a group of people or the kids. Quality time was about to be on and popping, and he was counting down the minutes until they boarded the private plane that The Underworld owned.

η

"Do you like it?" Sean asked his wife. He got a crazy ass deal on the bowling alley, only giving the Jewish man fifty-thousand dollars for the almost twenty-thousand square foot building that was equipped with a kitchen and bar.

Of course, they would have to tear all the bowling alley shit up, but Sean had a dope idea for a chicken and waffles joint while bowling. No one was eating good while bowling, and it would be twenty-five and up to keep the place upscale and jazzy.

She looked around again, remaining silent as she took it all in. Jackie didn't know if this is what she wanted. She had never had a business before, what if she fucked it up? She didn't know how to hire people, order equipment, do payroll and what about taxes?

"What if we adopt twins?" she suggested.

Sean had no clue where the hell that came from, but shawty was tripping. "I buy you a building, and you want twins instead? What's up, Jack?" he asked her.

Ever since they got back from Atlanta, she had been putting in applications for hospitals saying she wanted to go back to work part-time, so Sean felt as if this was the perfect time for him to show her the alley.

"No, it's not that. I love it, I really do, I just don't know if I'm ready for such a huge responsibility," she admitted.

"What do you think twins will be?" He prayed she was just bored because adoption, having kids and raising kids from babies was not on his agenda. Sean didn't want to deal with that

"I love children, it will be fun and easy." Her eyes lit up at the thought of starting over.

He ran his hands over his face. "You wanna go on vacation or something to clear your mind? We can go wherever you wanna go," he told her.

She shook her head. "Stop throwing shit at me. I can't be bought, Sean!" she shouted at him.

He bit down hard on his tongue, not wanting to snap on her because apparently she had some shit on her mind that had nothing to do with him.

Jackie held her mouth, he could tell she didn't mean to say that but it was too late.

"Let me drop you off, I got shit to do." He walked ahead of her and headed to his truck. Sean wouldn't keep going the extra mile to keep a smile on her face if everytime she shot him down with her hurtful words. He was low-key sensitive, and she still hadn't figured that out.

Jackie slid into the passenger seat and slammed the door. "Sean, you took what I said the wrong way. All I'm saying is, I don't think I'm capable of running a restaurant by myself."

"Cool, I'll sell it," he told her, ending the conversation by turning the music up.

She took a deep breath. He couldn't keep shutting down every time she was honest with him. That's not how a relationship worked. She reached up and muted the music.

"I feel like I can't talk to you. Every time I do, you get mad at me and ignore me for days," she opened up.

"And I feel like you shoulda stayed single cus you don't know how to be married," he shot back. *Ouch, that hurt.* "You know how many bitches wish they had a nigga to invest in their dreams?"

Jackie wasn't concerned with other bitches. "You don't get it." She was defeated by this point, but so was he...

Sean chuckled, "You right, baby, I don't. But you can bet your last dollar I'm done with trying. You wanna work? Cool. You wanna be independent? All right. The mortgage is $3500 a month, light bill about $700. Let me know which bills you wanna pay, and I'll leave them on the nightstand for you."

Sean was angry, and he was tired of feeling rejected. What was the point of working hard if you couldn't spoil the one you loved? Sean wasn't grinding day in and out for nothing. He wanted her to have several businesses. He wanted her to have whatever she wanted out of life. That's who he did it for, her and her sons, but she was ungrateful, and he no longer cared.

"You don't know what I've been through!" she spazzed.

Sean was so tired of that story. It was getting old. "Jackie, you ain't the only woman who got cheated on, stop using that as an excuse." He was over it.

"It's more than that. Every time he got mad at me he would threaten to take it all away... I refuse to let you-"

"Do you really think I would do that to you?" he questioned. No, actually, he stopped on his brakes and looked at her.

Jackie turned around to see if any cars were coming. *"Sean,"* she tried to get him to go.

"Answer me!" He was dead ass serious.

Tears were now coming out of her eyes. *"Gooooo!"* There was so many cars speeding around the corner.

"Tell me, do you think I'll leave you and take everything back?"

She shook her head. "No," she finally answered. He took his feet off the brakes and peeled off. Jackie's heart was beating so fast. "Don't ever do that shit again," she told him.

"I'm your husband, you need to trust me. Jackie, I never planned on telling you this, but I got you. Even if you leave me right now, you good to go. Why you think we ain't sign a prenup? Both Kevin and Jonathan have a million dollars in accounts for scholarships and another million once they turn twenty-five." She was in awe. Her mouth was wide open. "And to be clear, that was before I even got with you."

Real niggas were rare. Jackie didn't have a clue on who she had married. No fuckin' idea.

"So, are kids out of the picture for you?" she asked him once they made it home.

He kept the truck running because he didn't plan on coming in. He needed a drink. Solo.

He shook his head. "That was one of the reasons I knew I wanted to settle down with you. I was under the impression you didn't want any more children."

He was correct, but still..."I didn't, but they're about to be out of the house. I don't want to be here by myself. All you do is work."

"And that's why you need to open this restaurant," he reasoned.

She took a deep breath. "Let me think about it, Sean. I have to do that because I want to and when I'm ready. Please don't force this down my throat," she asked.

He nodded his head like a robot. "Roger that."

"And I'm going back to work to give me something to do."

"No overnight, you are married. I want my wife home when I get home, not at work on her feet." He wasn't bargaining on that.

Jackie felt as if his greedy ass just wanted something to eat on the stove when he made his way home, but she wouldn't argue with him on that. "Gotcha, day shifts only. What about overtime?" she asked him sarcastically.

He eyed her. Sean was not playing with her today. "Don't push it, baby." Working was one thing, but overworking? No. Not at all.

She reached over and kissed his cheek. "Give me a real kiss," she asked, but he wasn't fucking with her today.

"Nah, you hurt my feelings."

Jackie thought he was joking, so she tried to kiss his lips but he dodged her. "Are you for real right now?"

He was dead ass. "Yeah, man, get out. I got somewhere to be. I'll see you when I get back."

"What you gotta do? Cus at first you said today was our day."

Before he could answer her question, his phone rang. The other phone....his *Underworld* cell.

"Yeah?"

"I need you," Papa told him.

Sean didn't ask any questions. "I'm on the way, where am I coming to?"

Jackie sensed it was urgent, so she grabbed her purse and unbuckled her seatbelt. She mouthed, "Love you, be safe" and then opened the door.

Sean grabbed her arm and pulled her close with the phone still glued to his ear. He kissed Jackie in the mouth and even slid a lil tongue in there. "Cut the alarm on," he told his wife, never ever wanting to get too comfortable, even if they did live in a million-dollar neighborhood.

Jackie nodded her head and got out. Sean watched her get in the house safe and then pulled off.

Papa, of course, said nothing else about what he had gotten into, and Sean prayed he could get back home by dinner time.

He didn't recognize the address or the old barn he was staring at after he drove through about three miles of trees and shit. His main phone had given out since it was barely any reception, so all he could do was honk the horn. Sean's gun was on his lap and off safety in case this shit was a set up. He had trust issues out the ass.

Papa came out of the barn and waved him over. His hair was all over his head, and Sean really wished he would cut the shit. For goodness sake, who still rocked braids anyway?

Sean turned his engine off and hopped out of the truck. He didn't see any other vehicles other than an old school Corvette which was probably Papa's.

"Nigga, what is you doing? Ain't shit out here to look at?" Papa came back out of the barn and yelled at Sean.

He jogged to the entrance of the barn, and that's when he noticed Papa's face and hands covered in blood.

"What's going on?" was his first question.

Papa pointed a knife at a chair where a battered woman sat. "You know this bitch? Cus she say she know you, and that she work for you?" he asked him.

Sean had to walk closer to get a better look. He shook his head. "Nah." And that was the truth.

Papa mumbled, "Lying ass bitch." He pulled his gun out and was about to shoot her.

"Sean, it's me...Sunshine."

Sunshine? He hadn't used her as a mule since he fucked her and she didn't tell him she was on her period. Sean was so turned off by that nasty shit that he cut all ties with her, business and personal.

"Man, do you know her or not?" Papa was ready to kill the hoe and go home.

"Yeah, I do. Damn, Papa..." She was barely recognizable. Her forehead had a deep gash down the middle and all of her front teeth had been knocked out.

"I fucked around and shot a cop, but this hoe was with him."

"What?" He said he shot a cop as if that was a normal thing to do, and then he said it so nonchalantly.

"I ain't know he was one, chill, nigga."

Sean paced the floor. This careless, reckless shit was what he was talking about. Papa would be the cause of the organization crumbling. Sean saw it happening right before his eyes. He was always doing some dumb ass shit, and this right here was icing on the cake.

"You do not just shoot a cop? And it's broad daylight outside? Are you fucking for real right now?"

Papa backed up from him before he got mad and shot his ass. "Say, homie, you better cool it," he warned.

"Me? Nah, nigga, you! I got too much shit going on to go to jail over some bullshit. Control your mother fuckin' temper," Sean told him.

"Why is she here?" he pointed at Sunshine, who didn't deserve the brass treatment he had dealt.

"If you stop bitching and listen, I can tell you," Papa said. Sean took a deep breath and was now all ears. "Somebody been driving past my uncle house all day two weeks straight, got him paranoid and shit. So, I roll up over there and start busting, you know how I get down."

Sean turned to Sunshine. "What are you doing in New York?"

She coughed up blood. "Working for this girl," she struggled to say.

"Doing what?"

Papa already knew what was going on. "Selling pussy, nigga. What you think?"

He prayed she hadn't stooped that low. Sunshine had goals and shit, she just didn't know how to budget her money.

"Why was the cop at his uncle's house? Do you know?" he asked, and Sunshine began to cry. "I'm trying to help you, Sunshine. Tell me what you know."

Papa moved around him and got in her face, yanking her head back. "What did he tell you?" he barked.

She was now hollering from being in excruciating pain and out of fear.

"Papa, man." Sean wanted him to calm down and move out of the way. She was a good girl, and he knew he could get it out of her.

"Stupid ass hoe, you want me to go to jail, bitch?" He pistol whipped her in the face.

"Papa!" he shouted, but it was too late. He shot her in the head and then had the nerve to spit on her.

"What the fuck, man?" Sunshine was young. Papa was ruthless. Sean didn't see how he could just kill niggas and not blink twice about it. Yeah, he had killed tons of folks but for good reason. Papa was way too wild and hot-headed. She had her whole life ahead of her.

Papa couldn't care less. On his face was zero remorse. "No faces, no cases," was all he said to Sean before walking away and calling the clean-up crew.

This was not how he imagined his day to go, but in the life of The Underworld, shit was never predictable. He sat in his car for an hour trying to figure out how he could find out information on the cop without calling Boo and Samira.

Sean felt like a child every time someone fucked up and he had to call them to fix it. He was tired of going to them for every little thing, but killing a cop was like hanging yourself, and Papa didn't seem to realize that. Sean could only hope the cop wasn't a FED. And if he was a FED, why was he watching Papa's uncle house? It was all too much to process, but Sean had to follow through on this shit.

The cop world, much like The Underworld, those boys in blue stuck together. They wouldn't sleep until they had answers.

Sean rolled down his window and asked Papa, "Where is the cop body?"

Papa looked at him with a disgruntled face. "Fuck I'ma tell you for?"

He clearly was tripping. "We gotta get rid of it," Sean told him as if he was stupid.

"Nooo, I gotta get rid of it. Not you...me. And my uncle handled it for me."

"Your uncle?" Papa's uncle was old as shit.

"Sean for real, gon' about your business, cuz," he warned him once and wouldn't do it again.

At this point, Sean wanted to hop out the car on that mother fucker, but he would play shit cool and pull off. But again, here was another sign for him to get the fuck on out of dodge and to do his own thing.

η

"What is this for?"

Jordyn was in the middle of getting dressed for Sunday's morning worship service at the church she had been attending since she was a young woman in her early twenties.

Her Pastor had been a bright light in her dark life over the years, and she truly honored and thanked God for sending her to a church whose mission was to save souls.

Jordyn credited her peace of mind to the life groups at her church, the weekly bible study, Monday morning prayers and those Friday night healing services. She would be lost if it wasn't for God. God was at the head of her life and in her house.

Ramone had no choice but to go to church every Sunday. As he grew older, he didn't understand why he had to go to church and his dad got to stay in bed and sleep, but she told him to pray for Nasir.

Jordyn really believed that with all the stuff her husband was into and had escaped, he needed to be at the altar every Sunday, but she was done begging him to get right with God. Even her pastor told her that she had to give her husband to God and let him handle that.

"Did you even see what it said?" he asked her after he finished peeing.

Jordyn pulled her stockings up and slid a navy peplum skirt over her bottom half before actually opening the envelope. She almost cursed on the Lord's day when she saw how many zeros were after the number seven.

Jordyn went into their bedroom where Nas was climbing back into bed to go back to sleep. "Seven million dollars for what, Nas?"

He was always giving her money to give to the church, although he hadn't been since their wedding day and that one time Ramone got baptized when he was twelve.

"I had a doctor's appointment Friday morning, and my prostate was great, so yeah..." he explained.

Jordyn took a deep breath, he would never understand but again, she would try today. "How about you come to church and praise God for that blessing and put the check into the offering plate yourself?" she suggested. He began to playfully snore. "Nas, baby, I'm serious. I'm sure pastor would love to see you," she tried a different approach.

"Tell him to meet on the golf course next week." Now, that was the one thing he didn't mind doing with the man of God, playing golf. Nasir actually enjoyed his company but refused to go to church.

"Come today please."

He sat up. "What if I told you that I had to run someone over last night?"

She blinked her eyes rapidly, not knowing how to process his revelation.

"I don't feel right going to church knowing I've sinned so much in my life," he admitted to his wife. And that was the truth. Nasir had done some evil shit, some real fucked up shit to a lot of people, and he knew that church was full of judgmental folks. Nas rocked with J's pastor though. The nigga was cool, but today wasn't the day for church...for him. Maybe one day, but not today. Nas didn't want to play with God.

Plus, if he told Jordyn he had been researching on other religions, she would probably burn his library down. It was Jehovah and Jehovah only for Jordyn King.

She walked over to his side of the bed and sat down on the edge. This could possibly be the breakthrough she had been praying for. "And God forgives, He just needs a contrite heart, Nas."

He shook his head. "Pray for me." Nasir reached up and kissed her forehead, hoping she would go back to getting dressed so he could return to sleep.

Jordyn dropped her head. She had tried and failed again, but would extend the invite next Sunday, knowing one day he would get up and go with her.

"Love you," she told him minutes after she was prepared to head to church.

Nasir rolled over and winked at her. "I know." That was his favorite thing to say back.

Jordyn stopped holding her breath for him to say he loved her too. Every blue moon he would tell her those words without her saying it first or during sex, but even that was rare. As long as she stayed focused on God, Ramone and her business, she could deal with his weird ways.

Ramone had his headphones on the entire way to church because his mama tended to pray very loud and speak in a funny language he still didn't understand.

When they made it to the third row, praise and worship had just started which was perfect because Jordyn was already wrapped up in the spirit. She had filled out an envelope with Nasir's check in it before she left the house and planned on putting it directly into her Pastor's hand, knowing he wouldn't share the amount with anyone other than his wife.

Jordyn never wanted to be looked at differently for what her husband did which is why she kept it under wraps. The people that knew were the ones whose husband were in the streets too, which were the wives of The Underworld and her best friend, Nia, whose man was retired from The Underworld. Jordyn's other best friend, Maude, was married to a judge and completely clueless to who Nasir really was.

She loved the circle she was in off the strength of being friends with Maude and knew that if they were aware of her husband's status as an international kingpin, they would cast her out, and Jordyn really appreciated the friendship she had with them, especially she and Maude's, who had quickly become more than her best friend, but more so a long-lost sister. Jordyn prayed for everyone during praise and worship. She wanted God to continue to show up in all of their lives.

Back at their estate, Nasir was groaning loudly because his phone never stopped ringing. He ignored Papa's four calls and some other unimportant mother fuckers, but when he saw his mom's call he decided that sleep wasn't in the plans today and answered the call.

"Yes." He had an attitude, and Nadia definitely picked up on it.

"Good morning, son."

He had learned and practiced the act of forgiveness, not with many people, but with his mother. The turnaround of their relationship was a sure testimony because years ago he despised everything about her existence. However, now they were low-key inseparable. He had to thank Lo for pushing them together. She always saw the good in people whereas he assumed everyone was full of shit.

His mother was the coolest, and he looked forward to her visiting New York whenever she was in the mood to deal with the Yorkers. She and Charlotte, her long-time lover, had moved back to the Island, and she had been on cloud nine ever since.

"What's good?" he yawned into the phone, not even trying to stifle it. He was so rude and completely oblivious to his behavior.

"I handled everything you asked of me," she told him.

"Thanks, I'll make sure my lawyer knows to tell Jordyn if it ever gets to that point."

His mother was silent for a few seconds. "And why not Lauren?"

Nasir hated that his mom never even tried to get to know Jordyn. She was so stuck on Lauren being the one. But she wasn't...anymore.

"Lo is in love with a man from the other side, she's not deemed trustworthy right now. I have to feel her out some more."

"You know she's trustworthy, more than your wife," she argued. Nadia didn't get mad about many things, but her son's stupidity irritated her.

"Jordyn ain't going nowhere, and she would never cross me...she know better," he added with much confidence.

Nadia wanted him to open his eyes. "I prefer you to leave everything with Lauren and me. I don't trust Jordyn...Nas, I just don't."

"What you think she gon' leave her son high and dry? Ma, she stares at the nigga while he sleeps. Everything is good."

"No, no that's not what I refer to." Her accent was coming out now. "This island, the resort. Son, you employ half of the people here. I don't want her to sell it in case you go away."

St. Lucia was near and dear to his heart, and Jordyn knew that, but did she care was the question? He could vividly remember when he first took Jordyn home with him and was eager to show her his hometown and share with her the history of the island. She was more concerned with the beach and pina coladas. But not Lauren, she even had a tattoo of the island. That's how connected she had become because of Nas. So, his mother had a point.

"You may be right, ma. I'll get on that ASAP," he promised her.

"And one more thing."

He waited on her to speak up but she didn't. "What, ma?"

"I had a dream, and you know my dreams be real. Do you think Jordyn may be pregnant and not telling you?"

He knew for a fact she wasn't the one pregnant. "I told you she can't have kids, period."

Nadia would let it go then. "Well, I could be tripping, no more smoking before bed," she laughed.

He was in deep thought now. If Jordyn wasn't pregnant, and his mother dreamed it…"Ma, let me call you back," he told her and hung the phone up.

He hopped up and made the bed, his OCD wouldn't let him leave the house with the bed unmade. Nas showered and threw on a jogging suit and running shoes. He knew that Lo went to church on Sundays, and he knew the church she went to.

Nas hopped in his Bentley and headed to her place of worship. Lauren was on her knees boo-hoo crying, thanking God for being who He was in her life. She was forever appreciative for God's presence in her life.

Her phone kept buzzing, breaking her concentration. Who was calling her back to back? It had to be an emergency. Lauren wiped her face as she dug into her clutch. She wondered if it was Simon being that he was out of town. Maybe he had a quick question about something.

Homegirl's eyes rolled so far to the back of her head when she saw those familiar ten digits flashing across the screen under the label, *ten missed calls.*

Ugh, what does he want? She texted him since she was in church and couldn't pick up, *"Church."*

He responded back immediately. *"Come outside."*

Was he serious right now? It was Nasir King, of course he was serious as a heart attack.

He double texted her. *"Now."*

Lauren got up and grabbed her things and walked down the aisle to the nearest exit.

"Everything okay, sister?" one of the ushers asked.

Lauren nodded her head. "Work called, be blessed Sister, see you next week." She hated to lie in the place of worship, but that's what Nasir King did to you.

Lauren marched down the steps, and he pulled up right to the curb and told her to get in. She slid in the passenger seat and slammed his door so hard.

"I was actually enjoying church, you should have come in," she told him.

He ignored her as he drove away from her church and turned onto a side street before placing the car in park. Nasir observed her, mainly her stomach.

"Are you pregnant?" His eyes never left her womb.

Lauren swallowed so loudly, he heard the gulp. She wondered how he even knew. Lauren fingered her hair and then pulled it back behind her ear, something she did when she was nervous.

"Nasir." She never said his whole name.

With those two moves, his biggest fear was confirmed. His mother was right, someone was pregnant, and it was fucking Lauren Howard.

"How could you?" He was hurt. Nasir felt betrayed. "I let you love him-"

"*You let me!*" she yelled.

He had tears in his eyes, and she wished she cared or understood how he felt, but she didn't. Lauren deserved love.

"You crossing the line, man." He couldn't believe this shit.

She threw The Underworld out the window. Lauren fell in love with Simon. She wanted to be with him...not Nasir.

"You married her, you chose her, Nas. What did you expect me to do?" She would be a fool to wait on him any longer.

He laid his head on the headrest. "A baby?" If only this were a joke.

"Nas, you brought your son to my house."

"He's not-"

She held her hand up. "Don't you dare not claim him! You love him, I saw it on your face. Don't do that to him," she threatened.

Nas knew how to throw a nigga under the bus or downplay a situation, but she wouldn't let him deny Ramone for the sake of pleasing her. That shit wasn't cool.

"You fell in love with the enemy." He was disappointed.

Lauren reminded him, "He don't even know you exist!"

"Lo, if they come after us, what are you going to do? Now a child is involved. Did you even think about that, dummy?" She was stupid.

Lauren unlocked the door. "Take care, Nas."

He grabbed her by the hair so she couldn't get out and then locked the doors. "Listen."

Lauren was shaking, she was shaking so hard she was close to peeing herself. "Why do you hurt me every time you see me? What does me being in pain do for you? Are you satisfied now?" she asked him with tears in her eyes. He had turned into a monster.

"I don't want you to have this baby."

Lauren thought to herself, *Over my dead body*. She was having this child *and* raising it with Simon.

"This time you don't get what you want," she told him through clenched teeth and shoved him in the chest. "And don't put your hands on me anymore, Nas!" she yelled.

He wasn't in his right mind, she had fucked him up with her revelation. "You don't have a clue what loyalty means." He was disgusted.

Lauren was done with him. "Let me go, let me live my life with Simon. The same way you and Jordyn are all hee-hee, ha-ha at dinner and stuff, me and him will be the same. Nas, I don't owe you anything." She finally decided to cut ties with him for real. No play-play. There wasn't a bone in her body that craved another touch from Nasir.

"Not an option, baby girl." There was no walking away from The Underworld. Him? Cool. Be with that bitch ass cracker, but she still had an obligation to the organization.

"I'm not going to tell about shit. He's not even concerned with y'all."

"Yet," Nasir mumbled under his breath.

Lauren was confused. Did Nas know something she didn't? "Wait, are y'all under investigation?" she questioned.

He laughed, but there wasn't shit funny. "That's your fuckin' job, so you tell me!" he snapped, banging his fist on the steering wheel. He wasn't going to jail. Nasir refused to allow everything he worked for to be taken from him. Lauren had better get it together.

"He hasn't brought up work in so long, all we talk about is the baby," she told him the truth.

"Well, make him bring it up."

Lauren didn't get to play dumb with him, he had taught her well. She knew what to do. If she didn't, Nas wouldn't have given her the assignment of meeting Simon.

"All right, I'll try my hardest," she sighed.

He shook his head. "Nah, no trying. Make that shit happen." Nasir dropped her back off in front of the church. "I'll be in touch," he told her.

She said nothing back in response to that, but she did ask him, "Who told you I was pregnant?" Lauren hadn't shared it with anyone yet, not wanting to jinx herself.

He could have easily told her that his mom had a dream, but he needed to pump some fear into her ass. "Don't worry about it, just know I know everything," he told her and peeled off from the curb.

Nasir thought he was tripping, but he wasn't. Someone was following him. He pulled his gun from under the seat and tried to get a better look in his rearview mirror, but their windows were partially tinted. However, he only knew one woman that had a mole on the tip of their nose.

"Why the fuck is Mina following me?"

Chapter 11

"These streets is all you know, it's hard to tell who's a friend or foe."

– Jeezy

The fact that Jade kept using the two words, "Checking me" is what pissed Malachi off. He was two seconds from tossing her ass out the bed.

"I'm checking you because I asked you to spend some time with your man and stop scrolling fucking Instagram? Are you for real right now?"

Over the past few months, her obsession with social media had grown into a frenzy. Jade couldn't even get dinner on the table in a decent time frame because she was on Instagram. At every red light and stop sign, she was on Instagram. Malachi wasn't even getting a good fuck out of her because her phone was dinging due to a notification from fucking Instagram. He was sick of it.

Today, his personal partner and Mayor of the city, Trent Washington, sent him a text message with simple words but a deeper meaning, *"Tell your wife to lie low."*

Instantly, Chi knew it was regarding her social media. Shorty went from using her page for business purposes only to posting morning selfies, mid-day off-guards and all kinds of shit. He didn't understand how Jade thought it was okay for her to be on social media at her age. She was old as shit!

If he didn't want his kids who lived in the digital era of posting every move on social media for the world to see, Chi didn't get how Jade thought it was acceptable.

"You are so annoying." She shook her head and went right back to scrolling.

Ten, nine, eight, seven... He attempted to count so he could cool out, but that was an epic fail. Before he knew it, her phone was snatched out of her hand, and he had tossed it across the hardwood floors where he knew it had shattered.

Jade hopped out of bed and ran to her "poor baby". "I can't believe you!"

She was so shocked, but he couldn't care less. Jade had better stop fucking playing with him. His nerves were shot because he felt as if someone was hiding something from him...someone such as Nasir King.

They hadn't moved much product, and his reason made no sense. Since when did they take a break and relax? All of them were money hungry as hell, so why relax if they weren't planning on retiring now?

Chi had started spending more time with Trent to keep his ear to whatever he had going on. Trent was a cool cat from the hood, but had turned his life around and went political. All those years of Chi helping him out had finally paid off because he now was an asset and not a liability.

"Chi, you need to get a life," she crossed her arms and told him after inspecting her phone.

"Damn, so riddle me this, if I get up and leave right now and go lay with up another bitch, how would you feel, ma?" The lack of attention right now was ridiculous, and she was in denial.

"Do what's best for you, wouldn't be the first time." She didn't bat an eyelash either as she spoke.

Chi shook his head, she was pitiful. "We can be doing so good and then you'll-"

"What? I'll do what? Not suck your dick until my jaws break? I'm not a toy. I don't want you to play with me all night for your entertainment."

He didn't have to be here right now. Home on a Friday night? Chi could be anywhere, but after a long week, the only place he desired to be was home with his wife, kicking back and watching a movie.

"What does Instagram do for you that I can't do?" he asked her.

Jade hated him sometimes. "It's not that seriousssss," she told him again.

"But to me it is, Jade." He was always begging her to do something with him. This shit ain't feel good. "Are you cheating on me again?" This time around, he would kill her ass...for real. Jade didn't get to play him like a fool again.

"No I am not!" She couldn't believe he had even asked her that.

"Come fuck me then." And of course, he was serious. Chi pulled his pants down and plopped his dick out of his Burberry boxers.

Her pussy was nowhere near wet. Jade lied and told him, "I need a wax, I'm super furry." She wasn't having sex with him after he had just cracked her screen, told her he would go lay up with a bitch and then had the nerve to accuse her of cheating on him. Chi could kiss her ass tonight because he wasn't touching her.

"We married, baby. I don't give a fuck about no hair," he told her truthfully.

Jade knew that his nasty ass had eaten her on her worst days down below. He loved her dirty draws, literally. And lately, he had a weird fetish of fucking her right after she left the gym. It was as if her being sweaty and musty turned him on. He would lick her face and tell her that he loved her dirty pussy. The first time they had sex after she left the gym, Jade complained the whole time he hit her from the back that she was stinky, but he only seemed to go harder. Chi was weird like that.

"Jade, why do you get mad at me for wanting more of you?" He didn't get her sometimes.

"I wish we could go back to the old days...you know, like how it used to be so much fun...us sneaking around and stuff." Her face lit up as she reminisced on the old days while his lips turned into a scowl.

"You mean when we snuck around while you were still married?" He was confused. Before she could say anything else, he reminded her that, "We've been together almost twenty years, and you telling me you wanna go back to being secret?"

Their counselor did tell him that she believed Jade thrived off of thrill and adventure, but Chi didn't want to hear that shit. They were old, and he was too tired to be doing role-play just to keep her faithful. He didn't believe in switching roles and personalities to keep the fire hot in the bedroom. Chi wasn't about to be the mailman, the pool boy or none of that shit. He was Malachi Morgan and if that wasn't enough for her, then they needed to get a divorce.

"You don't get it...never mind, grand daddy." She had no problem sleeping on the couch tonight.

"Help me," he asked her in all seriousness.

She shook her head, refusing to even waste her time. "What's the point? You're stuck in your ways."

Chi was boring, and Jade had to *finally* accept that.

η

"I knew it!" Lauren stuck a fist in the air. She and Simon had just returned to his house with the ultrasounds in hand. She was going on eight months and was carrying a healthy baby *boy*. Every time they tried to find out the gender, her child's legs would be closed, but today they got lucky, and his little pecker was on full display on the screen. Lauren was elated to be carrying a little man.

She was eager to become a soccer, football and basketball mom. Her son would be involved in everything.

Simon was relieved, being that her mood changes had been all over the place. After her first meltdown because there was no more butter pecan ice cream, he quickly changed his mind and told her that he didn't want a daughter any more. Lauren was a diva, and he didn't think he could handle two of them. So, being a father to a son sounded more peaceful.

Simon was already on his phone looking at cribs and other things the baby would need. "I rather wait to see what we get from the baby shower before I waste any money." He was such a frugal man.

Lauren had tons of money put up. She wasn't sparing a dollar when it came to her son. He would have all the cute clothes and toys. Lauren couldn't wait to tear the malls up tomorrow morning all by her lonesome.

She had kept an extremely low profile over the past few months. She didn't want anyone in her business, not even the ones "closest" to her, such as Mary Jane. Lauren hadn't shared this blessing with anyone other than the man she went half on the baby with.

"Baby shower?" She didn't want to have one, but he came from a big family, and she did too, she just no longer talked to hers. And Simon was aware of that.

"Oh come on, baby. My mom is going to kill me if I don't let them throw a baby shower," he complained.

Lauren knew that, but she honestly didn't care. It wasn't fair to his family though, so she had to put her big girl panties on and play her part.

"I know, so I'll call her tomorrow and tell them the theme, and they can do everything else. It's just very important I pick the theme, Simon."

Being that in her past life she was a bomb-ass party planner, Lauren could have easily decorated her own baby shower, but Simon's family was very happy and wanted to be super hands-on with the baby, and she wouldn't take that away from them.

Lauren only wished she still had that connection with her folks, but ever since her dad revealed his "other life" to her, she hadn't spoken to them. They were hypocrites, and it took Lauren years to repair her soul and trust God again.

She prayed for forgiveness, and that softened her hardened heart because she was bitter in the area of family and having a solid support system. Some days she felt alone, wondering what would happen if Simon ever found out the truth....And then her baby would kick, and she would cry tears of joy knowing that now she had her child, and never had to experience life by herself ever again.

"What are you thinking about?" He could tell her mind was elsewhere.

Lauren shook her head. "Nothing other than what we're about to eat cus I'm starving." She leaned back on the couch and rubbed her soccer ball stomach.

"What's new?" All she did was eat and work from home now. Lauren was still doing consultations for non-profits and writing grants and such for private sectors of the government. It was something to do to keep herself busy throughout the day while her man worked diligently.

"I have to run into work for an hour or maybe two, and then we can go to dinner when I get back. So, how about you order a pizza to hold you over?" he suggested.

"Can we have sex before you leave? I'm so horny, baby," she whined with her lips pouted out.

Simon laughed, "Wait, so are you hungry or horny?"

She thought about it before saying, *"Both!"*

Lauren was always wanting her pussy ate or wanting him to fuck her from the back. Sex made her sleepy, and she was either sleeping or eating whenever she wasn't up and working.

Simon checked his watch. He hadn't planned on being gone from the office so long today, but the doctor was late for their appointment, so it threw his day off.

"Come here, big mama," he said and helped her up from the couch.

Lauren was now giddy in anticipation of whatever he was about to do to her. Whether it was by use of his amazing tongue or his lethal dick, she was guaranteed to be satisfied, and that's all that mattered.

Later on that night, work was done and Lauren had eaten enough to last her until tomorrow morning. The couple was in bed butt naked planning out their future. She could never find good enough words to describe how she felt about Simon. The one thing she would quickly tell anyone if they ever asked was to never say never. Lauren was all for the *black love is beautiful.* All throughout high school she proudly proclaimed that she would marry a black man and have brown skinned babies. And Lord knows she thought Nasir King was heaven sent, but look at her now, wrapped up in vanilla flavor. The swirl love was real, and she was head over heels for her man. His smile, his laugh, his touch, even the way he slept made her heart skip a beat. He was the most understanding man she had ever met.

Simon was a provider, he was strong and courageous. He was trustworthy and hardworking, and he was sharp as a tack. Simon was smart and wise beyond his years.

Lauren could watch him for hours and listen to him forever as he spoke about his dreams and goals with so much passion. He was a lover of the law and genuinely had a heart for promoting the well-being of others.

It was on perfect nights like this when they planned out their dream home and vacations when she wanted to stop the imaginary classical music from playing in the background and take the bow out of Cupid's hand and tell him the truth. He deserved to know.

In less than a few weeks, their child would be brought into the world, and Simon had a right to know everything.

"Babe," she interrupted him, ready to get it all off her chest right now.

"Huh?" He looked up from the baby magazine he was flipping through. Those beautiful ice blue eyes melted her heart. "Oh, before I forget..." Simon rolled over and grabbed a bag from the floor. Lauren wasn't surprised because he was always coming home with something thoughtful. "Check these out, be right back." He hopped out of bed and left the rom.

Lauren had quickly forgotten about telling him everything. She opened the white bag and flipped it over, and tons of little boxes fell on the comforter.

"My God!" Each box held a different type of ring. From two carat to four, circular, square, rectangle, birth stone...princess cut. Lauren's eyes filled up with tears, and they fell down her face.

"You're crying? Gosh, do they look bad?" he asked her from the door post.

She shook her head. "I love them all." She picked up one of the rings and tried it on. The ring fit perfectly.

"I'm not proposing today or tomorrow, but soon...just wanna make sure you love the ring before I buy it." He was so careful with how he spent his money.

Lauren knew she had to tell him the truth. This man wanted to spend the rest of her life with her...There would never be the perfect time, so she needed to just blurt it out, but she was so fucking scared.

"Come here," she cried.

Simon came over and wrapped his hands around her. "I love you," he told her with the biggest and goofiest smile plastered on his face.

She smiled back at him. "I'm crazy and moody and I'm spoiled..."

"You're not telling me nothing I don't know." He reminded her that he had been with her for a while now. Simon wasn't going anywhere. "Which one?" he asked her as he combed her hair back with his fingers and wiped her face.

Lauren took a deep breath and looked at them all again. "This is the one...just not now." She wanted him to know she wasn't ready yet.

"Oh trust me, it's not now, I gotta get on a payment plan. Of course your stuck up ass picked up the most expensive one."

Lauren told him, "You can tie plastic around my finger, and I would still marry you." The size of the ring, cut, or clarity...none of that shit meant anything to her anymore. Foolishly, she used to value love by materialistic things.

Lauren remembered back in the day when she would stand in the mirror and practice arguments with Jordyn. The first thing she would start off with was everything he had bought her. Now that she was older and had experienced life a little more, she now understood that love couldn't be bought. Love, her love, had no price tag.

Lauren didn't need all that superficial shit to be loyal to someone. That's where Simon and Nasir differentiated. Simon used words and actions to show Lauren how he felt. Nasir used his dick and diamonds. With much confidence, Lauren knew she had chosen the better man. A man who was after two hearts, hers and God.

He worshipped no idols, not Benjamin Franklin, Andrew Jackson, none of those. Simon honored and respected Lauren. He never raised his voice, cursed at her or even laid a hand to her precious body. He didn't lie or demean her for his own personal satisfaction. In so many ways, Simon was better. Life with him wouldn't come with pain and regret because he wasn't fighting demons from his past. Nasir needed a hug, and he needed God and therapy.

Lauren didn't want a man she had to train and fix. Simon didn't come with instructions. He was easy to love, and his guard was down. She didn't have to beg or plead with him to be with her. It came without hesitation. She now realized the blessing in Jordyn, and she was grateful she was stuck with him and not her.

Little did Lauren know, Mr. King was sitting outside, wondering should he kill Simon now or later.

η

Their house was finally complete, and Jackie, who wasn't technically a social butterfly, wanted to have a housewarming. She had been in New York for a while now and hadn't properly invited the wives of The Underworld over, especially when they've always been so nice to her and welcoming.

She vowed to make changes in herself and was starting with being more open and outgoing. Years of not trusting women in her house had a strong effect on her, but she had to realize that the man was to blame as well.

Luckily, Sean didn't make her feel that way. Jackie was comfortable enough to leave a room where gorgeous women were around her man and know he wouldn't be trying to fuck them.

So tonight, over fifteen guests ate and drank to celebrate their new home. No one could believe she didn't hire an interior designer. Jackie had done each room herself, even sewing the curtains and pillows on the couch in the main living room.

The menu consisted of what she thought were light appetizers, but everyone was full and told her they couldn't wait to see what she cooked for Thanksgiving. Jackie only made collard green egg rolls, salmon and turkey burger sliders, macaroni and cheese bites and a salad, but the food was delicious.

Sean made sure there was plenty of liquor and weed to satisfy everyone's cravings. Jackie also made mini sweet potato pies and Hennessy cupcakes for dessert. As a thank you gift for attending the housewarming party, each guest was leaving with a soy candle she made herself. All of that free time on her hands had turned her into a black Martha Stewart.

Sean was always boasting her head up and telling her that she was a woman of many talents and could do anything she put her mind to, but Jackie preferred to be a nurse and come home and cook.

The bowling alley he purchased was only collecting more dust and rats and once a week she drove past it, vividly picturing people there...and the parking lot full.

One day real soon, she would get it together. Seriously.

"Do y'all need anything in here?" Jackie peeked her head into the dining room where the majority of the women had gathered engaged in girl talk.

Demi shook her head. "No, I think we're good. If I eat another one of those egg rolls things, Papa will have to carry me to the car," she giggled.

Jackie looked at her to be a child, but when Sean told her a while ago how old she was, she couldn't believe him. Demi didn't look a day over eighteen and had a house full of damn kids. Jackie needed to know whatever her tricks were and gym regimen.

She told her, "It's plenty more, so take them home with you."

Jordyn praised her cooking skills. "You really should open up a cute little eatery, from the hours of nine to two, four days a week. Keep it exclusive."

Jordyn was a mastermind of putting shit together. Jackie actually liked that idea; something small and intimate and not demanding so much of her time.

She leaned against the wall and crossed her arms. "Jordyn, that's a good idea," she admitted.

Jordyn smiled and took another sip of the homemade sweet tea that Jackie raved about, and it was actually good as hell. For an extra touch of juiciness, she added grilled peaches and pineapple juice to the tea, and it was a hit.

"Let me know if you're serious about it, I can get my realtor on it this week."

Of course, Jackie had to talk it over with Sean, but she knew he would be all for it. Her husband was very supportive, as were all the men of The Underworld.

"I'll be a weekly customer," Nia told her, enjoying the food as well.

"I thought you were on a diet," Jordyn reminded her.

She rolled her eyes and flashed a middle finger. "Starting back tomorrow." Nia couldn't resist the good food, it smelled absolutely amazing. As soon as she crossed over the threshold, she went to the kitchen.

"Hey, that's what accountability partners are for!" Jordyn blew her an air kiss.

Jackie smiled and told them she was coming right back. She continued to make her rounds through the house before checking on the boys who were playing the game.

"Y'all good in here?" she asked.

They nodded their heads, never saying a word.

Teenagers these days...

Jade was in the middle of presenting her argument to the other women when Jackie doubled back into the dining room.

"I'm not on social media, but I don't even have the time, and my baby plays games on my phone anyway," Demi told the ladies.

Jackie asked, "What y'all talking about?"

"Social media."

Nia, of course, was a heavy influencer via social media and had made a killing in the fashion industry. She credited a lot of her success to her followers on social media, mainly Instagram.

"I'm on there for business, but now and then I do post pictures of my kids, but never of East."

"Why though?" Jade didn't understand the reason to be so private.

"Well, it's obvious. I don't want anyone tracing his past to what we are working so hard on now, and that's our future," she explained.

"I'm not even posting the kids, I'm just scrolling, and he still gets mad," she told them.

Jordyn wasn't on social media either and neither was Jackie.

"What's the number one rule in marriage..." Demi wagged her ring finger as if she had written a guide for wives.

"Suck his dick every day!"

"A nut a day keeps the problems away!"

"Pray as a couple!"

"What goes on in y'all bedroom stays in y'all bedroom!"

All the women threw out their ideas of what the golden rule of marriage was, but Demi shook her head at each one.

"Come on now. None of us at this table are newlyweds except Jackie, and she's been married before. Samira, what do you think the number one rule is?"

She tapped her chin before answering, "Compromise." At least in her marriage that's what was most important and the hardest to do.

Demi was now tipsy as she banged her hand on the table. "Bingo!" She then followed up with that by telling Jade directly, "If he's constantly talking about it then that means he really feels some type of way...get off of there, you're already rich and famous anyway." She gave her a soft smile for reassurance.

Jade held on to her comments, not wanting to fuck the night up but what she really wanted to say was, "Demi, your husband doesn't even view you as his equal. You're another one of them damn rug rats." But she didn't. She lied and told them she would compromise for the sake of love.

Jackie was about to break out a new bottle of wine when she heard commotion coming from Sean's man cave.

"Oh shit...sounds like my husband," Samira said and hopped up. She knew firsthand how Boo's temper was and didn't want him to tear up Sean's brand new house. She thought it was so sweet that he invited them to come up for the weekend and stay in the house with them. The past four days had been full of adventure and fun, and she wanted to end things on a good note.

Jackie followed Samira down the hallway and was shocked to see her man in the middle of Boo and Papa.

"What's going on?"

Chi stood up, always trying to be the peacemaker in every situation. "Nothing, this was a beautiful night, let's end this on a good note."

Papa was seething and shooting daggers at Boo's chest. "I shoot niggas like you for breakfast," he threatened.

Boo laughed him off. "Man, please, I ain't my cousin."

But of course, Sean twisted his neck and asked his fam, "What the fuck is that supposed to mean?"

Samira reached in and grabbed Boo's arm before things escalated way too quickly.

"These niggas don't get to lil bow wow me," he spat.

Sean wanted to know who the fuck was lil bow wowing him cus he handled his all day, every mother fucking day.

"Boo, put a name on it," he begged him to do so.

Papa reached for his gun, but Samira had never taken her eyes off him.

"You pull that pistol you better shoot it cus I'm about mines, you won't leave up out of here." And she was not playing.

"Sean, what the hell?" Jackie finally opened her mouth to speak.

And now the boys were walking up behind her with a gun. "Sean, you good?"

Jackie was in disbelief. "Who gave y'all a gun?" Were they fucking serious right now? This shit had gone left way too fast.

"Man, how about everybody put the pistols down, and we all go home and start this shit over next week," Chi tried to diffuse the situation.

Nasir told Jordyn that he had a headache and had opted out of coming over.

"Sean, pillow talking is for hoes, bra. You can tell your cousin all your mother fucking business, but keep my name out of your mouth, and that's on my kids," Papa let him know.

"Look, man, it wasn't like that," he tried to explain.

"It is what it is, man. Why is you going back and forth with these lame ass niggas?" Boo clapped his hands with every word he spoke.

"We family, I'm not 'bout to be beefin' with him over a misunderstanding!" he shouted.

The word *family* crushed Boo in a million different ways. Even Samira took a step back. "Wow."

Boo didn't need to hear nothing else. "Take care," he told Sean and then told his wife, "Get our shit so we can go."

Jackie knew that Sean was caught in the middle of this.

Papa could give two fucks, and Chi was just thankful that no one got to shooting.

One by one, everyone sort of filed out the house, telling Jackie thank you and not bothering to take a to-go plate.

An hour later, Sean still hadn't come out of his man cave, so she started breaking everything down and cleaning up, getting the house back together.

He couldn't believe that Boo and Papa got into it, and so damn fast. He replayed the conversation over in his head, trying to see when it went from joking to death threats, but in all honesty, they were two of the same types of personalities and had clashed heads.

Boo wasn't fucking with him right now, and some of the shit his cousin said had rubbed him the wrong way, so he needed to give himself some space anyway.

Jackie knocked on the door before entering with a hot plate, knowing he hadn't eaten yet. Sean moved everything off the couch so she could take a seat beside him. After she got comfortable, she exhaled loudly.

"What are you going to do?" she asked her husband.

Sean refused to dwell on this shit for too much longer. "Stay, pray and stay out of the way, baby."

η

Toxic is defined as of, pertaining to, affected with, or caused by a toxin or poison. Acting as or having the effect of a poison; poisonous. It's also defined as causing unpleasant feelings; harmful or malicious. Pertaining to or nothing debt that will probably not be repaid. A toxic chemical or other substance.

Nasir was toxic. He wasn't good for the soul, hell, for the heart either. He was something so infectious that once he touched you, kissed you, felt you or stroked you, he could hurt you. He will hurt you. He did hurt you. It wasn't easy to shake yourself of him either.

Lauren had tried. It was as if every time she took off running, he snatched her back. The more she despised him, the more he lusted after her. The more she cursed his name and begged him to please leave her alone, the more he stalked her and begged for only an hour of her time.

He had learned everything about her...he knew her so well, to the point where he knew when she was getting weak, giving up on being strong. He knew when his advances were working.

Simon was out of town on a work assignment, and Lauren was home alone. The setting was perfect. Lauren answered the door in a collegiate t-shirt and fuzzy socks. The school girl look was always a turn-on for him.

"Whatttt in the fuck do you want?" She rolled her eyes as she stared at him on her doorstep looking pitiful as hell.

He smiled at her, sheepishly. "Do you remember when I used to ignore you for days and then pop up unannounced and man...you would jump on my dick so fast." That's how he greeted her. Lauren was waiting for the romantic part of whatever he was trying to say. "That's the you I miss," he told her.

She shook her head, disappointed in herself for dealing with him for so long. Stupidly, she had been by his side for too many years to count, and the nigga never ever deserved her.

Nas wasn't shit. He was filthy rich, handsome, intelligent, a lover of all things book-related and witty and charming, but that wasn't all. And those qualities weren't enough to keep her head over heels and stupid either.

"Nas, what can I help you with?" She was tired and sleepy and missing her man. Lauren was damn near thirty seconds away from going into labor, or at least that's what her uterus felt like. It's as if Noah had begun to A-Town stomp all in her womb because with every move she made, her body was in cramps. Her child was coming.

Simon promised he would be back in two days and to hold him in the oven until then. She didn't know if Noah would wait that long.

"I brought you a gift," he said, holding up a bag.

Lauren could only imagine what this deranged lunatic had in that bag. "Is it a bomb?" she asked him seriously. Lauren stopped putting shit past him a long time ago.

He laughed as he made his way into her haven without an invitation. "Silly you, I'm basically the kid's step-father, so I had to get him something that I know you would love."

Step-father? "Boy, please."

He followed her into the living room of her place. "Open it." He handed her the gift bag and then took a seat on the couch.

Lauren paused the television and removed the light blue tissue wrap and stuck her hand into the bag. "A book?" she questioned.

He tilted his head. "Your favorite one."

She wondered how in the hell did he know her favorite book when she really didn't think she had one. And then she pulled out a Holy Bible. Out of all the gifts she received from co-workers, business associates and Simon's family being she invited no one who personally knew her, the gifts were sort of generic. Lauren didn't register at Target or Babies R' Us, so she was given typical gifts that most expecting mothers received; a million boxes of pampers, wipes, outfits, bibs and cute gadgets that she didn't know existed. But this...this right here...*this* came from the heart.

Lauren was speechless as she held the small bible in her hand and fingered the gold engraving. *"A Child Of God."*

"I don't know the child's name," he explained for the reasoning of the engraving.

She looked at him with tears in her eyes. "Noah, I'm having a boy," she finally shared with someone she knew loved her.

Nasir was broken on the inside. If things had played out how they were supposed to, they would have a daughter and a son by now.

"A boy? How do you feel?" He kept his feelings at bay and focused on her.

Finally, she was able to exhale and vent to someone other than God and her prayer journal.

"I'm nervous…you know everything I've been through, Nas. I just want one good thing to happen for me. Just one." She held up her finger.

Lauren had been going through bullshit her whole life. Nothing good ever lasted forever, and she always wondered where would she be if she obeyed her parents and went to Seminary school. *Or if she wouldn't have chased after Nasir, or if Ben was still alive, or if she would have remained in London all those years ago.* Her life was full of so many "what if's".

Lauren was tired of guessing and second guessing and thinking about the possibilities of happy endings and fairy tales. She desired real love and now she had it. And through that love, a child had been conceived when she was told she would never carry again. God had done the ultimate in her life, and she was so very grateful.

"You're going to make a great mom, Lo," he told her truthfully.

Lauren broke down crying into her own hands, dropping the gift on the floor. "I wish my mother was around or my sisters, or hell, even Miko and MJ." She was living a secret life right now, ducking and dodging corners not wanting to be seen.

Nasir wanted to console her, but in the midst of her emotional state, he couldn't help but to be turned on by her. She was so fucking sexy, and the protruding belly only made his dick harder. She cried and cried and for every tear she dropped, he swore his penis grew an inch. It was some fucked up shit, but he couldn't control his hormones.

Nas finally stood up and went to rub her back. "It'll be okay," he told her. His hands didn't just stop at the middle of her back, they went down to her butt and under her shirt to palm her ass. Boy, it had been so long since he felt her booty.

"Nas, are you for real right now?" she asked, looking up to him while tears of sorrow fell down her face. He was such a nigga.

"Let me make you feel better." He had a weak ass approach as he tried to get some pussy. Nas no longer had game, he was getting older and couldn't care less about bagging bitches.

"I don't need you to make me feel better. Look, thanks for the gift. I really appreciate it, but it's getting late so you need to go home." She turned around so she could lead him up and out of her house, but he stopped her.

"One last time...please."

She shook her head. "One, it's never the last time with you and you know that, and two, I'm pregnant. You don't see this big ass belly?" Lauren wouldn't dare disrespect herself, Simon or their baby. Plus, she was due any day now.

"Let me feel home...give me three good strokes, Lo." He was now sounding quite pitiful at this point.

"Your wife is *home*...so go there," she reminded him. She was so turned off by him it didn't make any sense. "Come on, Nas," she tried again to head to the front door, but this time he wasn't going to be Mr. Nice Guy.

He grabbed her and bent her over the couch and pulled her shirt up.

"What, you gon' rape me now?" She was heated.

Through clenched teeth as he pulled her panties to the side, "I said give me three good strokes...damn," he said as if nothing was wrong with what he was about to do.

Lauren couldn't believe this man. "Nas, you are losing your mind!" She wouldn't allow him to do this to her.

"Shut up." He dropped his pants and pushed himself into inside of her with little force. Pregnant pussy felt better than cashing a million dollar check. He was in heaven right now. Nas loved him some Lauren.

She wished she could control her body but she couldn't. After a few minutes, she felt something in her soul erupt, and it was an orgasm, followed by another.

"Damn, cum all over this dick, baby," he sang into her ear using his native tongue.

Lauren was so embarrassed by her actions. She didn't bother moaning, groaning, throwing her ass back or even encouraging him to fuck her harder. Lauren refused to stroke his ego and participate in this horrible act. She knew that Simon had never cheated on her, and it made her feel so fucking guilty.

But Nas was hitting that spot and damn, it felt good. Her eyes rolled to the back of her head as he went balls deep over and over again. Sex was a sin, and it was even more horrid that she had allowed the devil himself to enter her without much of an argument.

Lauren knew that if she really wanted him off of her and out of her she could have used more will, but it was always something poetic about Nasir. For goodness sake, he was her first, her first in many arenas. He knew her when she didn't know herself, loved her when she didn't love herself. He had been the only man that cared for her when her father didn't, and that's what he always used to his advantage.

Nas pulled her hair, bringing her neck towards him. "Kiss me," he demanded.

"You got me fucked up." She wouldn't dare. Now that was one thing she wasn't doing. Her lips on his....no sir. Her body didn't belong to him anymore. Nas loved when she cursed at him, and he ended up nutting all in her pussy.

"Shittttt, Laurennn, damn," he groaned as he emptied all of him inside of her.

She fell over the couch, out of breath and purely satisfied. "Get out...please," she begged him, unable to look at him. Lauren was disgusted with herself.

"I love you, don't you ever forget that," he reminded her as he pulled his boxers up and buttoned his jeans. She didn't respond.

Lauren got up minutes later and locked the door, and then set the alarm. She scrubbed her body for two hours while crying and beating herself up with her own words. Nasir was toxic, Lauren had finally figured it out. He wasn't good. She wished he would have met another girl that day so someone else's life he could have been ruined. Even the way he said I love you scared her. Those three words no longer made her smile, they made her cringe. Why could she never stand her ground in his presence? What was it about him that she still allowed herself to fall weak? Lauren prayed so hard, she prayed without ceasing until she fell asleep.

The next morning, she woke up thinking she had to pee, but it was her mucus plug.

"Oh My God!" It was time. Why did Noah have to come right after what she had done? How could she look her son in his eyes and promise to be a good mother when she couldn't even be a strong woman?

Lauren cried again on the floor of her bathroom. What was she going to do? Nasir was guaranteed to make her life a living hell as long as he was alive.

A strong cramp damn near knocked her out, and she knew these were contractions. Oh, how she wished her man was home with her right now. She refused to have this baby without him holding her hand. Lauren finally found strength to get up and go grab her cell phone.

Simon answered on the third ring, "Yes, my love." He was headed to the gym in the hotel before a scheduled meeting.

"Noah is coming!"

Their lives were about to change...forever. Lauren never had a chance to tell him the truth...but as the old saying goes, *"What goes on in the dark will soon come to light."*

Chapter 12

"Underworld. Underground. Underline." – 2Chainz

One Year Later

Simon Schwartz, District Attorney of New York City, was headed out. He had been at work since early this morning and looking forward to going home and curling up with his lover and their son. Simon needed a vacation but knew he would never take one. He loved his career entirely too much.

The phone on his desk rang and rang, but he didn't break his stride as he gathered his brown satchel, laptop bag and stack of folders that he probably wouldn't open when he got home.

His receptionist barged in without knocking. "Frank is on line two, says it's urgent."

Frank thought, *everything* was urgent. Simon growled as he sat his stuff down and picked up the phone and pressed two.

"Yeah?" He was tired and ready to go home.

"Guess whose pretty lil wife I just picked up, and she's singing like a bird?"

Besides making love to Lauren Howard, securing a confession was as good as sex. He instantly grew a hard-on and what that meant for this case. This case right here had been building for so fucking long. Simon honestly had given up on it, but apparently, the team that had been put together hadn't.

"Where are y'all?" he questioned while checking his watch again for the time. He was no longer interested in going home but wanted to know which wife it was and what all she had to say. And for goodness sake, why was she out at that late hour? Did she not know who her man was? Regardless of which member of The Underworld it was, they all were dangerous men in Simon's book.

"Precinct," he told him and then hung the phone up.

Simon texted Lauren and told her that he would be late, work had him tied up.

Her quick response back was, "Me too."

Their decision to hire a nanny wasn't an easy one, but the woman was needed. Lauren had jumped right back into work a few months after their son was born. She refused to stay home, getting fat and obsessing over her beautiful baby. His chubby cheeks, fat thighs and light colored eyes that resembled his father's had her smitten, but she preferred to be a working mom versus a stay-at-home man, and Simon had to respect that.

When he first met her, he learned a few things about her that he had grown to love. She was a spiritual woman, going to God about any and everything. Lauren was focused and very ambitious, they often pushed each other to do better and aim higher. She loved hard and cared about the people close to her. He had seen her get out of the bed, breastfeeding Noah while consulting a client who couldn't sleep the night before a big meeting or speech. Her voice was so soft and nurturing.

Sometimes, Simon would lie in bed and watch her sleep, thanking God for the many blessings he had sent to him. Lauren and Noah were the light of his life. And then there was work, and this fire ass case that was sure to excel his career.

Simon hurriedly grabbed his things and headed to the precinct.
He parked his Mercedes in the nearest space he could find. From the parking lot he could tell that everyone on the case had come to see which wife it was since no names were being spoken over the phone.

Simon checked in, showing his credentials and such before being brought back into a room full of FEDS.

"Well, who do we have here?" He shook a few hands that he was familiar with.

"I can say that she wasn't as dumb as I thought she was," Frank told him.

"We showed her a few pictures and she identified a few people, so that gave us something."

Russell handed the folder to Simon. "I'm about to get on this now, let's meet tomorrow." Simon should have gotten here faster.

"Let her go home before he starts calling," Monica told Frank.

"Damn, I came up here for nothing," he mumbled under his breath as he got back in his car.

Simon started the engine and curiosity got the best of him, so he locked his doors and began going through the folder. Black and white photographs of various members of The Underworldwere captured, pictures he had seen before in one version or the other. But only a good eye, an eye that knew someone very well would catch the beauty leaving out of a building with a pair of shades on, shades that he knew without a doubt because he had purchased the four-hundred dollar pair for her.

What in the fuck? He hopped out of his car and ran back into the building. "I need to ask her something!" he told Monica.

She shook her head. "She's had enough tonight, Simon."

"One question, I'll owe you on this I swear."

Monica looked at her partner before sighing. "Two minutes," she told him before leaving the room.

The wife of The Underworld member looked at him as the door closed.

"Please help me," she begged him.

"What's her name?" He slapped the photo on the table and pointed to the woman.

She asked him with hopeful and fearful eyes, "Are you going to help me?"

He nodded his head, willing to tell her whatever to get the confirmation he desperately needed.

"Lo?"

Lo?

"That's Lauren, she works with them."

η

Simon hadn't cried in years, not since his father died when he was fourteen. Even when he finished law school after being stressed out every day not knowing where his next meal would come from as he put himself through school, he didn't cry. He didn't shed a tear when he received the position as District Attorney. He didn't cry when he was able to retire his mother and tell her that she never had to work again. Simon didn't cry when his son was born, although he was a spitting image of him. He wasn't an overly emotional man, but for someone to lay beside you every night and live a lie...when someone who you trusted with your entire being...How could she? His career was on the line now. He had a child with a criminal.

Simon was damn near perfect, and that wasn't an exaggeration. He rarely drank, and nothing more than wine with her during a night out on the streets or a beer after he won a case. He didn't smoke, and he had never had a ticket in his life, not even a speeding ticket. He lived his life on God's good side.

She was a fake. A hypocrite. A fraud. He was angry, and Simon didn't even get angry.

Noah was sleeping, and he told the nanny she could go home for a few days. He had a lot to think about and process. When he heard her keys jiggling to open the front door, his heartbeat increased. She had a key to his home, access to his accounts, he shared his bed with her...they were building a life together. He had even thought about marrying her lying ass.

Simon stood, pushing the folder of photos under the couch cushion and rushing up the steps. He didn't want to talk to her or see her right now. He didn't know what to do. He wiped his face free of those tears that he never thought would fall from his face again and got into bed.

Lauren stayed downstairs for a while, and he wondered what she was down there doing. *Living a double life all these years, how did she manage to do that?* His stomach was hurting so bad, and it wasn't because of the Mexican food he had for lunch either. Betrayal never felt good.

When she made her way into their bedroom, he heard her moving around the room most likely gathering her things for a shower. She was so peaceful, lime a swan. Simon had openly admired everything about her all the time and wondered was it a façade. Was she really as sweet as can be? Oh God, Noah...what about their child?

Lauren was about to go to jail. Simon was sure of that, but would he tell his son about his mother who he would never see again? He closed his eyes again, wishing this was all a bad dream.

Lauren came to bed thirty minutes later. She didn't snuggle against him or anything. That wasn't normal. She got out of bed and went downstairs.

The Underworld wasn't a group of petty ass hustlers, they were professionals. The reason they hadn't busted them yet was because the case needed to stick. Everyone was aware that they would try to get the charges to be dropped in any way they could, and that's why they had been pulling up any and everything that they could find on them bitches.

Simon wasn't as hands-on with the case because he had other obligations and duties as the district attorney, but now he wanted to know everything. He was anxious for the meeting tomorrow.

Simon got out of bed, wanting to know what she was doing downstairs, so he went to find her. She was praying on her knees, calling out God's name and speaking in a heavenly language.

"Are you asking God for forgiveness?" he interrupted her time with God.

Lauren slowly pulled her head up and looked behind her to find Simon staring at her.

"Huh?" Her eyes were filled with tears, he had caught her off guard. When you are deep in the Spirit, it isn't easy to be pulled out.

"For your sins, are you asking God to forgive you?"

She didn't know where that came from, but she told him, "Uh, I guess so."

Simon slowly nodded his head. "Cool, I'm going to bed. Goodnight, *Lo.*"

η

Lauren pulled up on Nasir first thing the next morning. He was at MJ's house preparing for a run.

MJ hadn't seen Lauren in a while or even spoken to her, so when she knocked on her door without speaking to her directly, she was bothered.

"Where is Nas? Cus I know it's the first of the month." She would never forget his schedule.

Nas swore he was so discreet and oh so private, but on the low-low he was a boring ass man who had been living life by a strict routine to keep him sane. Even if Jordyn moved the toothpaste from the left side of the counter to the right, Lauren was sure the shit would fuck his day up.

"Good morning to you too, stranger." She took notice of Lauren's weight gain; fuller breasts and thicker thighs. "You've been eating well," she commented.

Lauren wanted to tell her, *No, I just had a baby,* but instead she pulled her in for a hug. "Please don't take it personal, I been going through some shit."

They were more than friends, M J treated and viewed Lauren like a sister. She had held her hand and wiped her tears while she mourned Donovan's death, so whatever Lo had been going through, she could have come to her.

"I'm going to take it personal because I love you. Are you okay?" she asked her with her hands now on her shoulders and forehead pressed to hers.

Lauren nodded her head. "I want to be okay," she told her the honest truth.

"Simon?" MJ questioned.

She damn near blinked back tears. "Nas won't let me go...is he here?"

MJ hated the control he had on everyone, and she swore to God she was about to just run off on that nigga's ass. They could have her house. As long as her brother and grandmother lived in her spirit, she would be quite all right. Her daughter had been on her mind heavy lately, and she wanted to be a mom now. MJ was ready.

"Downstairs," she said and nodded her head towards the door of destruction.

Lo headed down there to talk to him, it was important and couldn't wait.

Nas was on top of a barstool counting money and shit. The man was a boss, a good one at that, but she couldn't care less about how good he looked or any other day. She was over him.

They had sort of kept in touch over the past year, her giving him broken promises of trying to get into in Simon's files at work. Nas would text her every blue moon reminding her who she belonged to, and every time the message came through she felt sick to her stomach.

The day her son was born he sent roses, and she instantly knew who they were from while Simon thought her family had them delivered.

"He knows," she told him as soon as she got in his face.

Nas didn't look up from the money counter. "Know what, man?" He wasn't in the mood for her today. He had been focused lately.

"Last night Simon called me *Lo*. He never ever calls me that," she told him.

"Everyone calls you that, you're tripping."

Lauren saw the look in his eyes. She was far from a dummy. He knew. Simon had found out her darkness.

"Nas, he never calls me that, he said it in this condescending tone," she tried to explain him. Lauren's arms were flapping up and down, and she was sweating.

"No the fuck he don't. You said shit been good, so why would he know? We not on their radar, Lauren."

"So what was the point in you even hooking me up with him?"

He stopped fingering through the hundreds and gave her his full attention for a few minutes. "Just in case shit gets sticky."

Lauren had a funny feeling in her stomach, and those gut instincts never told her lies. "He knows," she told him again.

He really had to get back to work. "Keep me posted," Nasir sort of dismissed her without saying so. She rolled her eyes and headed for the steps "Don't come over here no more. If you think he knows then that means he got somebody following you." He had been doing this for years, and if Simon was as smart as Lo claimed he was, he would definitely have her trailed.

Lauren said nothing in return. Her nerves were shot, so she smoked for the first time since she had her son with MJ before leaving.

And he was correct. An unmarked car was definitely parked across the street from MJ's house. Her only question was, were they following her or them? *Them was The Underworld.* Lauren hadn't associated with them folks in years and prayed that if everything came to light, Simon would believe her and the government as well. She had a child to fight for. So, Lauren wasn't going to jail.

MJ was washing dishes when Nas emerged from the stairs many hours later.

"I would stay and eat, but I got something to handle," he told her as if she had actually extended an invitation to have lunch with her.

She gave him an, "Oh, okay" look but remained silent.

"Pick-ups are on time today."

Nasir needed a friend because MJ was not it. He was always telling her shit that she didn't give a fuck about nothing. Ever since the death of Donovan, she had been numb, moving through life with grace but suffering mentally. This was no way her for to live.

"I need you to let me go, without me having to run," she blurted out.

He put his phone into his pocket and folded his arms. "Run for what?" he asked her.

She turned the water off and faced him. "Nas, I have been doing this for years. Same shit every day," she reminded him of her ongoing dedication and loyalty to the organization. She had put her time in. MJ wanted to retire without having a price on her head. And that should be possible.

"We all have," he shot back. Nas was sick of everyone acting like they hadn't eaten good.

"I want to travel."

He chuckled. "You got your passport and we have several planes, baby. Long as you back before the next shipment comes in, I'm cool," he let her know that getting out wasn't an option. MJ was the one person he actually needed.

"Please," she begged him with tears forming in her eyes.

"No." He was firm on that decision. He had to go. "I'll be back through here later. MJ, I don't wanna have to kill you, man, so suck them tears up and stay focused."

Nas was close to the door when he heard her say, "I know you killed Ben, and I know you had something to do with Lauren losing that baby all those years ago. I also know you're the reason behind a lot of other fucked up shit that's happened." She had been holding that in for years.

"What are you saying so I can follow you?" He knew how to keep his cool in any situation.

"Lauren is dating the DA, I will have your ass locked up." She was aware of everything going on around her, even if she never said anything.

She was funny as fuck. "I know you think you and her are oh-so-cool, but do you really think she will turn on me?" Nasir spoke to her as if she were a child, a child who had disobeyed her father.

MJ wondered would she? She had gone back to him so many times...*"He won't let me go."* She heard Lo's words again and knew she wanted to get rid of him.

"I can have her tell Simon about a few murders."

"Don't worry about it, I'm sure they already know." He had paid plenty of folks off at the DA's office over the years. Nasir wasn't too worried. Simon was a rookie. He didn't know shit. "Yeah, baby girl, pick your face up," he smiled at her, almost daring her to try another approach so he could shoot it down.

MJ went back to washing dishes as if she had never said anything. She was scrubbing the hell out of those dishes too. She really had to figure something out and soon...

η

In the streets, you learned how to pay attention to the signs that were there, and the signs that weren't. In the streets, you learned how to roll with the punches. In the streets, you always had to have an exit plan.

Sean was smarter than most niggas expected him to be, and although he couldn't put his finger on shit, something wasn't right.

There was a scheduled meeting with The Underworld today since it was the first of the month, and Nas didn't show up. Now, to the other members this wasn't a big deal being that Ramone, Nasir's son, was extremely good in basketball, and they were all aware of the boy possibly being the next Michael Jordan, but to miss a meeting...nah, that wasn't Nasir.

Sean sat in his car, observing his surroundings, debating on if he was getting out or not. Something didn't feel right, and it wasn't sitting well with him. He saw Papa walk in the side door of the church followed by a now pregnant Miko, and then Chi hopped out the back seat of a Suburban truck. But no Nas.

Sean shook his head. "Catch me next time," he mumbled and pulled off from the block, not knowing that he had passed a FED who had been trailing Papa all day.

He went home and sat in his man cave with a few grams crumbled up on a magazine. His phone had been ringing, and it was various members of The Underworld wondering where the fuck he was, probably not wanting to start the meeting without him. *Fuck that meeting.*

For the next two days, Sean didn't sleep or eat. Something was off. He finally pulled himself together and made a phone call.

"I'm sending a plane to get you this afternoon, you'll be home before dinner," he promised.

The person on the line didn't ask any questions, although they hadn't spoken to him in quite awhile.

"Okay."

After he handled that, he went to shower and put something on his stomach before taking a nap.

Jackie knew when he was one of his moods, so she picked up an extra shift at the hospital and stayed out of his way. The house was quiet now that both of the boys had moved out. He missed them and sometimes regretted not granting his wife's decision of adopting, but then that uneasy feeling of things not panning out how he imagined it would came back on his mental, and he remembered why he didn't want children. This street shit didn't come with a promise. It was either death or jail for most niggas, but not for Sean.

A text message came to his phone exactly at 5:00 p.m. *"Arrived."*

Jackie was home preparing dinner early.

"Be back later," he told her in a dry tone.

"Hey..." She had so much she wanted to say to him.

Sean shook his head, he had enough going on. "Not now, baby," he begged her with his eyes.

Jackie sighed and held back tears. She needed to tell him what was going on with her. She got that he was busy and most likely dealing with some Underworld shit, but she had problems too. She was going through some shit and needed her husband's support.

Sean was so wrapped up in his thoughts that he didn't see his tough wife breaking right before his eyes. He didn't see that one tear of worry fall down her face. With a gun in hand, he walked past her, out of the kitchen and into the garage to go handle this thing.

When he pulled up to the building where he still had his loft, he nodded to the concierge.

"Long time no see, Mr. Carter."

He ignored her greeting. "Is my guest here?" He had shit to handle and had no time for casual conversation.

The woman nodded her head. "Yes, sir."

Sean told her thank you and headed toward the elevator. The door to his crib was unlocked.

"Doc," he called out as he closed the door behind him.

"This view is amazing, Sean," Dr. Robinson told him.

She still was beautiful in a crème top with a nude bra that she probably thought no one could see with black wide-legged pants and Gucci ballerina flats.

"You cut your hair?" He noticed everything about people.

She smiled and nodded her head. She had done a few things differently since she last counseled him.

Dr. Robinson came closer and wagged her ring finger. "Love found me...again."

He smiled, genuinely happy for her. Over the past few years, he had sort of developed a relationship with his therapist. He trusted her with his life and his freedom more than anything.

"You deserve it." Sean motioned for her to take a seat in the living room. "I won't hold you long," he promised her.

She told him, "I must admit I'm very interested as to why I'm here, thank you for the ride. I've never been on private jet before," she chuckled lightly. "How have you been?"

Sean didn't have time to go into all that. "Good, yeah this conversation couldn't be held over a phone."

She watched him with intent as he spoke. He appeared to be relaxed, but as a therapist she saw the hidden lines of worry and frustration on his face, and it was in the way he sat as well.

"Okay, well I'm listening," she encouraged him to begin.

Never in a million years did he think he would have to repeat this to anyone. The only person that knew was his cousin...or so he thought.

"I killed my wife's husband," he admitted. Dr. Robinson smiled. Sean was taken aback by that, so he asked, "What are you smiling about?" She was a good person, so her smiling at murder threw him off.

"If only you could see a few of my notepads, I have something written down that says you're haunted by something. It's either murder or tragedy." So, she was smiling because she had been right on.

"Wow!" He was appalled.

"Continue please, Sean." She wanted to know more, and then she was ready to know why he was suddenly telling her all of this.

"Jackie's husband was a very slimy nigga, but he was how I ate. We were partners you know, I loved him a lot. I fucked with him the long way." He took a deep breath. "There was nothing I wouldn't do for him, and he took that shit for granted one too many times."

Dr. Robinson understood how that could be. "So, you killed him?"

He shook his head. "No, that's not why."

"Quick question, were you and your wife messing around while he was still alive?"

He told her, "Hell no, I would have never done that." And that was the truth.

"But after he died, you found it acceptable?" She didn't agree if that was the case.

"Shit is complicated, let me finish," he told her.

Dr. Robinson crossed her legs and went back to listening to his revelation.

"So, you kept prodding about me and my mom, and I would never just come out and tell you everything." He hated to even to admit to this shit, and his heart broke as he thought back to that day.

"My mama set me up, and my cousin was the one that told me."

"How did she set you up?"

Sean shook his head. "She was going to help my partner...which was my wife's husband at the time and my very best friend, take me out. She was going to rob me for him. It was then that I found out my mama had been fucking him for years." He went on to break it all the way down. "My mom and him weren't too far apart in age, you know my wife is older than me. So anyway, man, shit was fucked up. My cousin stopped by my crib thinking I was there and when he saw my ma leaving my street with him, he said shit didn't add up, so he followed them for about two days before he came to me with it."

Dr. Robinson couldn't understand how someone's mother could do that to their son. "Why?" was her only question.

"Money hungry, she was always about her money. My mama gambles like crazyyy," he explained. "I was so hurt after I killed him. She loved me more, but then I realized it was because she had nobody else."

His mother was selfish. He still loved her though, that was the fucked up part about it.

"When was the last time you talked to her?"

He was disgusted with her. "Few days ago. She wanted a new car." And he sent the money for it too.

"Does she know you killed him?"

Sean shrugged his shoulders. "There were so many rumors circulating it probably crossed her mind, but she knew better than to ask me."

"And does your wife know?" was her next question.

"Nah." He could never tell her the truth. Even though that nigga was grimy, Jackie loved his dirty draws.

"Why are you telling me this?"

He held his hands together, this was the real difficult part. "In the case of anything happening to me, I need you to testify so that I can plead insanity."

Dr. Robinson stood to her feet. "Sean, you are one of my favorite patients but I don't do stuff-" She was about to leave and would find her own way home back to Atlanta.

"I will pay you ten-million dollars," he offered.

"It's not about the money, nothing is wrong with you!" she yelled. "For years I've told you that you were just a man dealing with life. Sean, nothing is wrong with you!"

"They don't know that though," he pleaded.

Dr. Robinson couldn't do it. "I'm sorry, but I am a very ethical person. I worked hard to build my reputation." And she was correct. She was very credited and respected in her field.

"Forty-million, Doc," he tried again, this time offering more money.

Now who the hell passes up that much money to get on the stand and lie? She bit her bottom lip and then put her hand on her back. "Even...if I wanted to do this, it's not that simple. I'll have to show proof of medication, admitting into a center, notes that show I was worried about you, voice recordings."

"Make it happen, I'll pay whatever."

Dr. Robinson sighed, "I cannot believe I am doing this."

"It may not be needed. I just need to have a plan in motion in case I do get knocked." Sean was such a smart man.

"Okay," she told him disappointed in herself, but that money would help her build a group home, open up a new office all on her own and pay her loans off on top of building her dream home. "I need the money to be wired to an account immediately in case they freeze your accounts...since we're speaking hypothetically." She was about her business.

Sean smiled. "Damn, Doc, I like that shit." He couldn't do nothing but respect it.

She fumbled through her purse for a recorder. "Before I go, I need to get a few tapings of you sounding deranged. Speak in different tones as if you have multiple personalities," she explained as she sat back down.

Sean never thought about acting before, but a nigga would do whatever to stay out of jail.

When he made it home hours later, he was hungry and tired as fuck. Doc didn't make it in time for dinner, but she would be a wealthy woman when she opened her eyes tomorrow morning.

η

Another long day of making people's lives better had Lauren extremely exhausted. Tonight, she was hoping that Simon would finally talk to her. Lord knows it had been days since he touched her or even mumbled a word to her.

He told her on Monday that he would be working late all week and in so many words, to stay at her own house. Rejection was an understatement, but she took it like a champ. However, she was missing home...his home...and his bed...and her man.

After toting Noah in the house, she went back to the car to grab groceries so she could hurry and cook dinner before he made it home. Lauren played the sounds of Sade while moving around the kitchen fixing spaghetti, corn, a salad and garlic bread while Noah bounced around the house in his walker.

Simon didn't come home until after midnight, but she was still up typing a report for a client. When he saw her car in his driveway, he cringed. He was the District Attorney, it wasn't okay for her to be at his house anymore.

"I left your plate in the microwave."

He ignored her, hating the sight of her and headed up the steps to shower.

Her heart dropped as he walked past her without even greeting her with a hug or a kiss. This was not how they normally operated, and it hurt. Nineteen long seconds later, and he appeared in the living room.

"I've tried all week to put this shit together, but I can't." He ran his hands through his hair.

She now noticed how dysfunctional he appeared to be. There were dark circles under his eye, and his suit wasn't fresh out of the cleaners. Had she stressed him out? Was she the cause of his anxiety? Lauren removed her glasses and gave him all of her attention.

"Simon."

"Don't fuckin' say my name!" he yelled.

She jumped in her seat. He had never cursed at her before. Oh God, he knew.

"How could you?" Simon felt so betrayed. She went to speak, but he shook his head. "Don't lie to me."

Lauren promised him, "I swear to God-"

"What? You swear to God what? That you didn't know who I was? That you didn't trap me with a baby? Huh? You swear to God what?"

This week he had put so much shit together. Yeah, Simon had big dreams, but it was Lauren who pushed him harder than ever. It was Lauren who stayed up at night helping with papers and funding out extra dollars for his balance the final semester of law school. It was Lauren who planned out the campaign parties and secured donors as he made his way up the government ladder. It was Lauren who wrote his speeches as he ran for council man and this and that. It was Lauren who helped him decorate his office. It was all her.

"Did y'all plan this? You knew I wanted to be district attorney..." He was now talking to himself.

She bent over, dropped her head, sulked and cried. She had never in life felt so attacked, and it was guilt that made her feel this way because he was right on with everything he said.

"Were you...*paid* to fall in love with me?" his voice broke. Tears sprang from his eyes. Simon didn't need her to say anything back. He felt it. "Damn." For twenty-nine minutes, he sat across from her with his hands in his lap, crying and thinking, plotting and crying.

She stared back at him, face now swollen. Noah hadn't woken up due to all the yelling, thankfully.

"I don't want to know anything about that...*organization*," he finally opened his mouth to address her. "You are nothing to me."

Lauren got up quickly. *"No, no, no! Simon!"*

"I can't even take you to court for custody because then I may get thrown off the case." He was mentally exhausted.

"You cannot take my baby away from me."

"Do you even love him, Lauren? Was having Noah part of the plan as well?"

She hated that he was now judging her. "You knew I couldn't have children!" she cried as she pointed her long fingers at him.

He reached forward and spat, "I don't believe shit you say anymore. It's all a lie!" he yelled as he banged his hand on the coffee table so hard it cracked and now his palm bled.

"I love you!" she reminded him. Lauren loved him. She would choose him over all of this bullshit.

He chuckled at her foolery. "Love will not save you from this...and me either."

She stayed downstairs on the couch all night for hours crying and blaming Nas for all of this madness. Lauren texted and told him, "*It's confirmed*" knowing he would get what she was saying and hopefully figure out a way to save them all.

Simon came downstairs with Noah in his hands to drop him off at daycare before work. She got up and ran to the two loves of her life. Lauren reached out to hold Noah, but he pulled her away.

"I'm going to try to help you," he said. She knew he would tell her to turn state, but that was not an option.

Simon offered her a way out. "I want you to understand that I am utterly disgusted right now, and I hate you," his voice broke as he held back his emotions. "But I don't want to hate you forever, Lauren. For the sake of our child, please do the right thing."

"Do you forgive me? Will you forgive me?" That was all she needed to really know. Simon and Noah was all Lauren had in this world.

η

Sean had one more thing on his to-do list before getting back to business. It had been awhile since he seen or heard from his cousin, Boo. Ever since that altercation at his housewarming, Boo felt as if he had chosen sides, whereas Sean didn't appreciate how his cousin came at him. Shit hadn't been the same. He knew exactly where Boo would be around this time, and that was at their Gammy's house.

He and Jackie had planned to be in and out of Atlanta. She wanted her hair done the right way since she was forever complaining that girls up top couldn't curl short hair for shit in the world, and Sean had to sit down with his family and make things right.

He pulled his truck into the yard and watched Boo look up from rolling a blunt on the front porch. His mouth full of golds lit up like a Christmas tree.

Sean saw that he was sort of relieved and maybe happy to see him, which put him at ease.

Boo was his nigga, and he didn't want to have to bring his strap with him but he did...just in case. He turned the truck off and hopped out, pulling his pants up as he walked.

"Look what the cat dragged in," Boo greeted him.

Sean dapped him up and took a seat. "I got something rolled already," he told his cousin.

"Well light that shit up," Boo said back. His voice was deep and raspy, and when he was younger they used to pick on him all the time, but a nigga wouldn't dare to do it now.

Sean sparked the blunt and took a few tokes before passing it to him. "How the kids and Sammy doing?" Sean asked.

"Good, we all living and shit, you know how we do," he laughed. In return, he asked about Jackie.

Sean hadn't done his part these past few days, and he promised he would make it up to her as soon as his mind and conscious was clear.

"We all right."

"Keep home happy," Boo reminded him.

Sean knew how to do that. "So look, man, about that shit..."

His cousin didn't need an apology, they were better than that. Time was the best thing that could havehappened at the time. "I know you love a nigga, and a nigga love you, we good," he told him.

Sean reached over and kissed his forehead. "My niggaaa!" And just like that, things were wavy.

But Boo being Boo and a street nigga, he knew that Sean came down to Atlanta for a reason. "What's going on?"

Sean knew he couldn't play him, so he told him honestly, "I really don't know. I think this shit coming to an end."

All his cousin had to say back was, "Well, if it is then cool. You had a good run. But-" He added extra emphasis on his next few words and made sure he and Sean had direct eye contact. "Do not let them niggas count you out or turn on you. *"You are the plug!"*

When Nas came to Samira about being a new connect for the organization, she made it clear that Sean was the supplier. For the past few years he received 54% of profit, making him the head of The Underworld, but Nas and his fucking pride, he never saw it that way.

And because Sean was more so about his money, he didn't need the extra attention or title, especially when the title didn't mean shit if you wasn't putting in the work.

Boo's words rang in his ear again. *"You are the plug!"*

And he was mother fucking right.

The ARRAIGNMENT 3 COMING SOON (FINALE OF THE UNDERWORLD)

If you enjoyed the story, please leave a **review**!

Authors love REVIEWS!

For more updates and sneak peeks into **upcoming** releases written by NAKO

Text NAKOEXPO to 22828

www.facebook.com/NAKO

Twitter: nakoexpo

Instagram:nakoexpo

Snapchat: penprissy

Join **NAKO'S READING GROUP** on Facebook…we're more than a reading group, join today and find out!

Join **NAKO'S READING GROUP** on Instagram…we're more than a reading group, join today and find out.

Join **@ALLTHINGSNAKO** on Twitter, we're more than a reading group, join today and find out.

Join **NAKOEXPO** on Facebook to unite with single women who are enjoying life and living it up to the fullest.

Text **SINGLEANDOK to 22828** for more information.

Text NAKOEXPO **to 22828** to join NAKO'S MAILING LIST and exclusive samples on **#samplesunday**

SUBSCRIBE TO NAKO'S YOUTUBE CHANNEL: NAKOEXPO

BEHIND THE PEN IS A BTS LOOK INTO BOOKS WRITTEN BY NAKO!

ALSO, IF YOU'RE INTERESTED IN PURCHASING THE UNDERWORLD, VISIT NAKOEXPO.COM OR EMAIL NAKOEXPO@GMAIL.COM TO PURCHASE YOUR COPIES TODAY.

THE FOLLOWING SHIRTS ARE FOR SALE:

"READ PRAY SLAY"

"BOOKS OVER BOYS"

"TRUE LIFE: I'M A BLACK GIRL WITH MAGIC"

"PROUD MEMBER OF NRG"

– VISIT NAKOEXPO.COM OR EMAIL NAKOEXPO@GMAIL.COM TO ORDER TODAY.

NAKOEXPO PRESENTS IS NOW ACCEPTING SUBMISSIONS. EMAIL NAKOEXPO@GMAIL.COM FOR MORE INFORMATION OR SEND THE FIRST THREE CHAPTERS OF YOUR MANUSCRIPT FOR CONSIDERATION.

Visit www.nakoexpo.com for **The Passport**, personal stamps written by women for women.

Nako's Catalog

The Connect's Wife 1-7

The Chanel Cavette Story

If We Ruled the World 1 & 2

Love in The Ghetto 1 & 2

The Connect 1 & 2

In Love With A Brooklyn Thug 1-3

The King and Queen of New York 1 & 2

No Fairytales: The Love Story in collaboration with Jessica N. Watkins

The Underworld Series

Please Catch My Soul

Pointe of No Return

From His Rib

The Christ Family

Stranger In My Eyes

The Arraignment

Resentment

The Arraignment II

Redemption

Orange Moon

Made in the USA
Columbia, SC
09 September 2021